THE BOOK SMUGGLERS

AWAKENINGS

AWAKENINGS

This first edition published 2018 by Book Smugglers Publishing
Astoria (USA) & Cambridge (UK)
www.booksmugglerspub.com

Edited by Ana Grilo & Thea James

978-1-942302-99-5 (Ebook)
978-1-942302-98-8 (Paperback)

Book Design and Ebook Conversion by Thea James

Awaken

Table of Contents

When The Letter Comes

SARA FOX

WHEN THE LETTER COMES HENRY is thirteen, a real teenager, and she's been reading about magical doors and portals and schools since forever. Middle school may have already started. Puberty may have wrecked her life with hair growing patchily in weird places and vocal cords stretching her voice into a warbling bass—but it's a waiting game. Henry believes that everything will turn out all right in the end and that everything will include *magic.*

Something will change because there are hundreds of thousands of books that tell her so. Maybe she'll fall through a puddle one day on her way to or from the bus stop and into a world that's both too big and too little at the same time. Perhaps magic school starts at fourteen instead of ten (Henry has a multitude of reasons why it would and they begin and end with *boys are gross* and, no, she says she's not included and *yes,* she says she is). Perhaps it's something else altogether and the bats who swoop among church steeples on warm fall nights will glide just a little closer and echo in her ear, *there you are, this is how things will change, this is what you were made for.*

Henry wishes it had happened before the bar mitzvah. If it had, she might have been brave enough to refuse to have a party for her nonexistent manhood. But since it didn't, since Henry can't change the fact she had one, she is determined to not be so concerned over the *hows* and *whys* and *whens* (except soon, she hopes; she would promise any sacrifice she could think of to anyone who offered if they could only make it *now*). Henry's more interested in the fact that when the letter comes, when the puddle gets too deep and sucks her under, when the bats or birds settle on lamp posts and tell her of destiny it will be different, *she* will be different, and all she has to do is wait.

Henry spares no thoughts for her sister.

And then, one day, there's a letter in the mailbox with Gabriele's name emblazoned on the front. Henry barely glances at it as she pulls it from the pile of envelopes and junk advertisements and hands it over.

"You want apples or oranges?" she asks in the kitchen and Gabriele huffs under her breath like every wronged ten-year-old little sister in the history of the world and then demands, "Fruit rollups!"

Like that's even on the list of "appropriate after school snacks" taped to the fridge. "What's that, you want me to give you celery?" Henry counters, expecting a shriek of disgust. She's never understood how Gabriele can claim that celery is *spicy*. Henry's made it the same way ever since she was Gabriele's age: watery green with peanut butter and, sometimes, raisins.

But there isn't a shriek. There isn't a grunt of disgust or sticky ten-year-old fingers jabbing into her side to push her out of the way for a pudding cup or illicit frozen fruit bar.

Instead Gabriele is sitting at the kitchen table staring at the letter. She worries her bottom lip, her too-big teeth making her appear rabbit like, and then she mutters, "Magic School?"

It's barely anything at all, two nearly inaudible words, but Henry's heart soars as she turns to look, her eyes catching the sight of parchment (real parchment!) and shimmering violet ink. It's a letter and it's real and everything is about to change... until, in between heartbeats, everything else about the letter starts to fall into place.

There's a name at the top of the letter and it doesn't say Henry. It doesn't even say Ms. Witkins, which might very well have meant Henry as Henry knows that a magic school would have immediately known that Mr. Witkins or Master Witkins had always been wrong. The letter says, Ms. Gabriele Witkins.

Gabriele hasn't even graduated elementary school yet. Her teeth dwarf her mouth and she keeps cutting off her hair to spite Henry—it has to be that, has to. She likes science and spaceships and alien adventures. On summer nights after chasing lightening bugs and each other around the yard, Gabriele searches the sky for UFOs while Henry stares at the ground looking for faerie circles.

But the aliens don't come to take her into intergalactic battle and Henry, as it turns out, isn't allowed to go to magic school.

After the letter came, they asked. Both of them on their own. Gabriele writing in her very best handwriting, Henry typing up a letter to explain that it would be best if Henry came with Gabriele, too, as Gabriele had never walked to school alone before. Gabriele might not have anyone to talk about aliens with. It's magic—*please.*

"Wendy had to grow up and leave Neverland too, you know. That doesn't mean growing up here is horrible." Their mother strokes Henry's back as she cries.

"Where do you think they could even hide a boarding school back there?" Their father wonders, staring out the window.

Their mother moves through buying Gabriele's school supplies like a hundred crickets, a broom made of all wood and no plastic, or a cast iron frying pan are normal things to buy. Their father doesn't ask questions. Sometimes at night Henry can hear them whispering, debating between certainty that this is a cruel prank and stilted wonder at a hundred previously unknown possibilities. She covers her ears and wills their words away.

That fall Gabriele waves goodbye to their parents and walks into the woods behind their house with a backpack that almost drags along the ground it's so heavy. She doesn't come back until winter break and Henry is glad for it. It takes her at least that long to stop crying over being left behind.

Henry stops promising to give up her favorite pens with pink and lime ink for the chance to go. She stops swearing to cut her hair short without complaint. She stops believing that if only she gives up enough something otherworldly will see her value and whisk her away.

If she puts her mind to it she can believe that she grew out of her dreams about magical schools and fantasy lands instead of being passed by.

It took Henry nearly a year and a half to realize that magic wasn't the only way to change. The first-year Gabriele was away Henry bowed into herself, half-bitter and grieving. She wore Batman t-shirts and plain hoodies two sizes too big.

As much as Gabriele caused Henry's despair, her return home on the first day of June was still a welcome relief. Gabriele had dirt on her cheek and a burn in her skirts and three different types of leather bracelets lining her wrist. She gave one to Henry the night before the sisters' annual summer clothes shopping trip and tied it to Henry's wrist with her teeth.

"Don't take it off," she warned, far too seriously for a girl of not-quite-twelve. "It's for luck."

There's no reason for Henry to think Gabriele is lying, especially since the next day Henry sees a pair of glittery purple shoes and *wants them*. Henry hasn't wanted anything for almost a year so she takes up mowing yards and dusting until she has just enough. No shoes, Henry decides once she tries them on, have ever been so perfect on her feet. They even have a hidden bit of heel to them. Henry wears them and the way her dad's lip tightens at the sight is unimportant. Henry wears them and feels *magical.*

Gabriele doesn't seem to notice the mounting tension within the family, even though she doesn't leave until August and that lands her squarely in the middle of Henry and their mother's clothing siege. Henry wants peplum shirts and leggings, fake earrings and concealer because why shouldn't Henry be able to hide pimples?

No, their mother says each time. *Absolutely not*, she adds as the clothing Henry brings to her becomes more and more outlandish. No makeup, no glitter, no shirts with a knot already twisted near the hem.

Henry mourns each clearance rack choice as she's sent to the other side of the store. "Be reasonable," her mother says. "I'm just trying to protect you."

Henry tries not to hate her. Nothing Henry's asked for will change high school but it could have changed Henry.

Later that night Gabriele piles clothes on Henry's bed, "These are too big," she says in a voice that's far too smart for twelve. "You can have them." Gabriele pulls one pair of leggings and a shirt from the pile of clothes, draping them over the footboard with finality before slumping backwards and into Henry's pillows.

It's nothing. Two pieces of clothes Gabrielle won't miss and their mother won't notice. The leggings are too small anyway and they don't match the shirt, but Henry hangs them in her closet nonetheless and pretends they go so well together.

"I'm not allowed make up either," Gabriele sighs dramatically.

Henry snorts and nudges her over so she can sit next to her. "Like you even care." It's easier not to talk about things. Henry isn't certain yet what words she'd even start with.

Fall whisks Gabriele away again, back across the field and through the woods. Henry watches her leave with their parents this time, and then even settles on the porch on December first to wait for her return. It's an unfairly long holiday for Gabriele, however, and it isn't long before Henry's newfound equanimity evaporates. She deploys one of the only magics known to all sisters: willing their younger siblings into invisibility.

They're both in her room on the first day of Henry's winter break, but Henry stares hard into her mirror, refusing to look past the reflection of her own eyes to acknowledge the girl sitting behind her on the bed. Henry has more important things to think about than Gabriele, anyway. Two weeks before the end of the quarter one of the girls in chemistry—so obtuse when it came to acids and bases but not, apparently, to other things—gave Henry her half-used eyeliner pencil. Since then, Henry's sharpened and practiced and sharpened again. Now the pencil barely exists anymore but it's all Henry has and she's determined to practice until it's gone.

"So I boiled it over," Gabriele is saying, like Henry hasn't avoided or ignored or shoved her out the door every time she talks about the school that Henry wasn't invited to attend or even see. "But it didn't even do anything cool so I think the class is pretty useless."

"Most classes are useless," Henry agrees, lining her left lid carefully with the pencil. Gabriele groans, flopping backwards into the pillows.

"I just want science!"

Henry curses as the tip breaks one more time and leaves a squiggly smudge above her lash line. "Damn, I'm never going to get this right."

"Sure you will. You actually care about makeup."

Henry watches Gabriele push herself up on her elbows in the mirror. She's starting to look kind of like a teenager, but still a bit straggly along the elbows and knees. "Do you want to learn?" she asks. She's trying to be nice, to be a proper big sister, even if Henry has always loved neons and glitter and Gabriele mostly loves cargo pants and navy blues.

"Nah." Henry tries not to take the dismissal personally. Gabriele is thinking about something; it's easy enough to tell since every time she gets this way she worries her bottom lip, gnawing and then popping it out, fish-like. "Hey, Henry?"

"Yeah?"

"I've been calling you my brother," Gabriele starts. She stares at Henry through the mirror for a long moment, then looks away. It's shyer than Henry ever remembers Gabriele being with her. "Do you want me to call you something else?"

"Something else? Like what?"

There's a roaring in her ears so loud that Henry swears she almost can't hear Gabriele mumble, "*Sister*."

Henry turns, on her feet and dragging Gabriele up with her in an instant. Her bedroom door opens with a *bang!* And her hands are on her sisters shoulders *shoving hard*. It's an unthinking thing, driven by the panic vibrating in her chest. "I—I'm..." Henry tries, stops, stutters.

Gabriele falls backwards, almost into her own bedroom door across from Henry's room. There's no surprise on her face, or fear. Gabriele just settles her forearms against her own door and stares, impassively measuring-out her sister's face by inches. Henry's cheeks burn. "Stay out of my business!"

The shout feels more revealing than anything else she's done so far, a plea instead of a demand. Henry slams her bedroom door behind her but the pit in her stomach continues to ache. Sister—a word tied to so many wants like a world and a life she doesn't yet have and may never have.

Henry buys Gabriele alien-shaped erasers, or pencils, or terrible extraterrestrial sci-fi books every Hanukkah and every birthday. Gabriele isn't too old for them yet, even if she stares at the sky differently now. None of the alien doodads are likely school appropriate anyway, but Gabriele grins and catches Henry's eye every time she unwraps a suspect package. This winter, she hugs the newest one to her chest and stares out at the sky on the back porch until Henry finally joins her.

"Do you see the bear?" she asks. She doesn't look at Henry. "Do you know the story of the sisters?"

Henry has heard the story before and she can find that cluster of stars by herself most of the time. She shakes her head and lets Gabriele take her hand to show her.

One day after school, there's a *crack* and then a *thunk* on the stairs and Henry goes from hanging her backpack on the hook by the door to whirling around to see what broke. Nothing, apparently, but Henry catches a glimpse of a red jumper disappearing around the corner upstairs and that's arguably more important than anything on the floor *because* Henry's the only one who gets home before six and Gabriele isn't due for another seven weeks, so Henry drops everything and shouts, "Hey! Get back here!"

The smart thing to do would be to call the cops but Henry's been angry since fourth period when Owen made fun of her purple notebook (thank everything he didn't see what's inside!) and she's reasonably sure whoever is in the house is smaller than her. She takes the stairs two at a time in great leaping bounds even though the second story has no exits for the intruder to escape through.

The mystery jumper had been moving in the direction of the bathroom and Gabriele's bedroom. Since the bathroom door is open and empty, Henry kicks the bedroom door open, tensed for a shout or a fight, she's not sure which. There's a buzzing in her arms and cheeks, anxious or angry or maybe a bit of both. She scans the room, shoulders drawn-in an uncomfortable play at being threatening while feeling threatened.

No one's there.

No one's there but the window is closed tight and so is the closet. Henry reaches for Gabriele's Celestial Star Globe resting on the bookcase, and brandishes it like a weapon.

"There's nowhere to go, you might as well come out." Three feet away the slats on the closet door part slightly.

"Or, what, you're gonna globe me?"

Henry refuses to feel ridiculous. It's taken years for her to feel somewhat comfortable in her skin. She learned eyeliner, skinny jeans, and that converses could be both pretty and functional. She learned butterfly clips and nail polish and how to hold her chin up and square her shoulders. She never learned how to fight off burglars, but she cocks her chin anyway and pretends to know what she's doing. Attitude, she's found, can make up for a lot of faults and failings while teasing out a place for herself in this world.

Sometimes their mom looks at Henry softly and, when they aren't shouting up and down the stairs, she allows Henry to press her cheek into her shoulder for comfort. Her dad's started watching reality tv and he parrots words he thinks are supportive. Henry tells herself to be happy that he's making an attempt, but it's awkward around the edges like when he tried to play catch with her at five and she kept trying to turn it into soccer. They've all been tiptoeing around the truth and she's mastered the art of not rushing things.

So she takes a deep breath and waits. She waits for nearly five minutes until the closet door is wrenched open and out spills a boy. Or, Henry thinks they're a boy. They're stuck at that babyfaced stage with too many spots and ill-fitted clothes worn a little too high or too low. As they stand they puff their chest out, trying to gain some inches on Henry who is at least a head taller than them.

"Who are you and what are you doing in my house?"

They sniff, an unrepentant smartass: "It's *Gabriele's* house."

"Yeah, but," Henry exaggerates, gesturing to the room that is little more than bed, bookcase, dresser, and a thousand sticker stars set on dark blue paint, "You see her here?"

The kid clicks their tongue to the roof of their mouth, looking mulish and slouching. "I'm Caden." Caden hesitates then starts, "You're H—He.... Hel?" It sounds like they are about to say *Hellen* so Henry beats them to it before they can continue to cobble a name out of thin air.

"Henry." Henry might choose a new name eventually but it certainly won't be *Hellen*.

Caden nods a little, not questioning the name as they worry their bottom lip. "Yeah—Gabriele's sister."

The word feels strange, like a coat in a style she always wanted but only just recently managed to put on properly. Henry told Gabriele not to say it and isn't sure how to feel knowing she did anyway, even to people other than Henry. She does know how it feels to have someone else identify her that way, though—and that is *good*.

"Yeah, yeah, Gabriele's sister," Henry says, putting as much cool disinterest in it as she can when she wants to preen instead. "Why are you here?" And then because the whole conversation begs the question, "Where *is*Gabriele?"

That's a squirm, Henry thinks. She's been an older sister long enough to spot that squint and evasive look a mile away—Gabriele's used it every time the topic of school came up for the past year. She doesn't think their parents noticed—or maybe they just didn't want to pick up a second fight when they were already in the trenches of Henry's femininity.

Henry drops the Celestial Globe and snatches Caden by their unzipped lapels. "Listen to me, you—" Perhaps she shook Caden a little too much or maybe it was just the proximity. Whatever causes it, something crackles between them and the next thing Henry knows she's hitting the bedroom wall.

She grunts, stunned, and scrambles back on her feet. She braces herself against the wall in pure disbelief. "What the hell was that?" Henry might be properly afraid of what appears to be a twelve-year-old but she's doing her best to hide it behind outrage. "Was that magic?"

"Charm bracelets," Caden offers, looking completely unfazed as they roll up their sleeve to display three different braided bracelets sets in pink, green, and gold. "I mean, they won't really help with all the serious magic but..."

Henry pushes herself off the wall and stalks carefully over, one foot in front of the other, and then stops short of touching Caden again. Two feet away feels like a safe distance. Henry knows she should be cautious but she can feel her temper boiling over. "What are you talking about?" she yells.

Yelling, at least, doesn't seem to activate whatever Caden is talking about and Henry makes a resolution to yell about everything.

"The war." Caden answers so simply it takes Henry a moment to realize how disconcerting the statement is. If there is a war, Henry knows nothing about it. Caden adds a moment later, "And Gabriele."

Henry's heart sinks. She's read enough books to suspect what Caden is going to tell her next. "Caden, where's my sister?"

Caden's happy to report that Gabriele is safe enough to bark out orders. It does little to soften Henry's resolve.

"You'll just be dead weight," Caden tells her over and over as they gather what they came here for. Henry just rolls her eyes and shoulders her backpack which is now filled to the top with strange stick-and-string traps. Apparently, Gabriele had been experimenting over break and had left passive magical weapons buried in her closet. Caden claims they're safe, claims that Gabriele was the best at building in safety-triggers for the potential snoops in her family, but Henry isn't wholly convinced. After all, Caden also used that as an excuse for why Henry had to carry the nearly five pounds of magical nonsense out of the house and into the woods.

"And you're, what? So good you're sent on retrieval far away from..." Henry waves a stick vaguely towards the rest of the forest which is quiet and undisturbed. "Whatever?"

Caden grumbles a little and, for a while, there's only the sound of their footsteps on freshly fallen leaves and the titter of birds and bats as the sun sinks into the tree line. Henry doesn't notice when the birds stop singing at first but once the wind begins to pick up and rustle she stops short. "Have you—" She licks her lips, reaching out a hand to stop Caden before they get too far away. "Have you heard any animals lately?"

"I—"

Night descends without warning, bursting around them with a blast of cold air. Beside her, Caden grabs her hand and jerks her close, whispering, "Oh no, no, no."

Caden's magic wand comes out glowing, the only point of warmth and light left in the world. When she looks at the wand, however, Henry can barely choke down a panicked giggle. It looks like nothing more than a stick plucked from the ground and Henry wonders, slightly hysterically, if her sister has just been running off into the woods to play make-believe this whole time.

Caden hisses, "Shhhh!"

There's a warm puff of air on the back of Henry's neck and a new voice says, "Boo!"

Henry's been taking self-defense lessons for three months. Gabriele started years ago but Henry's dad signed her up himself just before school started. *I want you safe*, he said, even though the kids at school have always been generally all right. His dawning realization that the world isn't universally safe has scared him more than it has Henry so far, but the new tension around his eyes when he looks at people around her worries Henry more than she likes to admit so she made only a token protest over the lessons. Henry wants to think that her dad would be proud of her right now, because even as she screams in fright and jerks away from the new voice, she also manages to land a solid punch to the speaker's nose.

"Ow!" the voice shouts, and there's the sound of feet stumbling backwards over the underbrush and then a crunch of branches. "Are we punching like heathens now?" The voice that rises from the foliage sounds far too polished, especially for someone who just had her knuckles in their face, and perhaps that is why Henry immediately decides whoever it is must be evil.

Before she can investigate further, Caden jerks free of their terrified paralysis and grabs her hand. "Hurry, hurry, hurry!" they cry, and she breaks into a run alongside them because the only other choice is to let Caden yank her arm right out of its socket.

They burst through the darkness and out into a sunset still bright with pink and purple.

"Who was *that*? Where are we?!" Henry asks but Caden must hear an entirely different question.

"Sorry, I'm sorry, I've only ever been good at healing and, like, sewing." Caden is clinging to a tree as they speak and then starts slumping downwards, red with huffing and puffing.

Henry isn't sure what to say to that. It doesn't even answer any of her questions. But she decides if Caden has stopped running, they must be out of danger. Henry settles beside them and leans her head against Caden's so her dark brown hair crushes part of their blue faux hawk. "Well, you any good with muscle cramps?" she asks.

"You that out of shape?" Caden doesn't move but they're a little less tense as they laugh. "'Cause I totally am, yeah."

Gabriele spies them the moment they stumble from the underbrush. She goes from mid-conversation with a tall blonde girl to rushing straight over, face white with worry that slowly reddens with heat as she clocks that Henry's damage is superficial. There's mud on her jeans, twigs in her hair, and sweat but there's no blood.

"Caden was supposed to bring back my traps, not *you*." Gabriele scowls, hands on hips. Then she says, louder, and tipping her head backwards so that Caden and the rest of camp can hear, "They never listen to instructions!"

"What's that supposed to mean? *You* were supposed to tell me everything!" Henry yells back, flushed and angry, as though she were the one being chastised and as though her statement has ever been true.

Gabriele pulls out a crooked-looking stick wrapped in colorful string and flicks it three times like she's batting away something invisible. Suddenly a dozen leaves streak from Henry's head. "Yeah right, when have you *ever* told me anything?"

Henry glares, shaking her head against something that feels like fingers dragging across her scalp. She wants to rewrite a long mental history in which *of course* the two of them always told each other every secret thought and revelation. But, at the same time, Henry finally realizes that she's with Gabriele and *surrounded by magic.*

Unfortunately, that realization has to timeshare with the fact that *here* is apparently a campsite with tents and a bonfire (not a Victorian-style house or gorgeously refitted medieval castle). Henry's never been able to attend scout camp but she is pretty certain this is the equivalent and all that's missing is a singalong and watered-down fruit juice.

"I'm the eldest." Henry tries to counter Gabriele's truth, but she's distracted and it comes out wavering. "You know, dad always said I'm the one that's supposed to deal with—"

"Deal with *what*, Henry?" Gabriele interrupts. "What could you do about *any* of this?" She raises her voice to a mocking sing-song. "I can't do magic but I aced my last AP Bio exam—whoop dee fucking doo, Henry!" She waves a hand as though brushing the conversation away in disgust. "This isn't a playground bully. Frog livers are for potions, not a perfect score on a science quiz. They won't listen to *us*; they certainly won't listen to you!"

Henry's mouth snaps closed and Gabriele pushes gamely onward, although her voice dips low and tired. "They're trying to get enough backing to build barriers, Henry. Barriers between us and you to protect magic."

"What do you mean? Who are *they*?" Henry feels her throat dry with the words. For the first time since she started trudging through the woods with Caden, Henry realizes she *doesn't* understand. Some sort of battle, okay, that sounded like a story. But like a story, it wasn't *real*, was it?

"Look, it's complicated." Gabriele winces, looking ever more like their father when he burns Sunday pancakes. "But the short version is…" She sighs, glancing to the trees past Henry's shoulder like it'll help her explain. "Some people think that cellphones and internet are burning up magic. Like fuel."

When Henry frowns at her, Gabriele quickly adds, "It *doesn't*."

A part of Henry wants to grab onto the idea that technology took away her magic. Thirteen-year-old Henry would have latched onto the idea like a safety blanket and thought: *it's not my fault*. But Gabriele doesn't believe it and neither does Caden. Maybe that means Henry can't blame her phone for the lack of wand in her pocket, either.

"I'm supposed to protect you," she says at last and it makes her feel small, inconsequential. It has nothing to do with what Gabriele has told her, but it feels like a truth, even if it's hollow.

"You can't protect yourself," Gabriele says and it's so serious, so no-nonsense, that it almost makes Henry smile. Her next words wipe away all chance of that: "I don't even know what you could do to help."

It stings to hear her say that but Henry shrugs, pretending indifference. "Well, I already punched someone in the face."

Gabriele's mouth makes a perfect 'o' of surprise. "You... what?"

"Right in the kisser, I think," Henry adds, and Gabriele cracks a shaky laugh.

"Good!"

Gabriele doesn't say who it might have been or what would have happened if Henry and Caden hadn't been able to run away. Henry decides not to ask.

It turns out Henry can help, after all, by cooking and patching people up. Not every magical person seems to have the same skill set: there's always someone who needs a bandage, and someone else who burns the toast because they don't understand the concept of low sustained heat. Henry can even set magical traps—so long as someone else builds them and adds a bit of Henry's hair or blood in the process to make her *an exception.* Henry screamed the first time she caught Annabel picking hair out of her hairbrush but it's become so commonplace that now she simply drops it off once a week with a "Don't put any charms on it! Spelling my hair blue is only funny once!"

The weather turns and before Henry knows it, Caden is sharing mittens and charmed scarves with her when they go to lay the traps.

"You ever miss it?" they ask, picking their way along the newest layer of leaves. The traps they lay are supposed to painlessly detain their targets but they both know there are accidents and more than accidents.

"What's that?" she returns, catching sight of a faerie circle and tugging Caden around it. "Miss what?"

"School. Real life." Caden, Henry's found out, is from a blended family, a fact that makes Caden laugh.

I'm just all blended you see, they said when they told her. *Can't be all nonmagical, can't be all one gender.*

Henry doesn't really understand the second part, but she's learning. She's learning about the other kids who change and build and become whoever they always were. Almost everything is a shade of gray: gender, magic, belief. Sometimes she even catches herself understanding too much, with all the learning she's doing. There's a boy, the one Caden thinks Henry punched, who is like her sister—from a nonmagical family. If his side won, he'd be cut off from his parents or grandparents and everything. Yet there he is, on the other side, desperate to try and save magic for fear that a cellphone might blow it up and burn yet another faerie ring out of existence. Henry tries not to sympathize.

He was always a dick, Caden says when asked about him, but they say it in such a way that it feels like hero worship gone sour.

"School'll keep," Henry says. "Nothing lasts forever."

Though, in some ways, Henry wishes this would. It's a war, a conflict, but only a few have ended up truly injured. One girl lost an eye and a boy blew off two of his fingers once, but that was temporary and they were reattached with a song. It almost doesn't feel real sometimes because Henry's never been happier than these moments between and around the fights: dancing among the campfires or putting a princess band aid on a burn mark until someone magically trained can get to the wound. She's useful here and it's a glorious feeling when someone comes up and graces her with their own personal charm bracelet. Henry has enough now that they trail almost to her elbows on each arm. Even still, most gift them while saying something like, *You need all the help you can get.*

It'd be insulting if Henry couldn't see that they cared.

There is no chosen one.

Henry doesn't see battle and although Gabriele fights, she makes the most impact with pen and paper. Gabriele drafts essays about the skirmishes, Caden with their theories on how magic and technology could strengthen each other, and both send them to magazines that masquerade as tabloids. It's a six-month stint in the woods while the adults play politics and squabble over the theories teenagers half their age have broadcasted all across the magical community. By summer there are compromises and the units of students and adults doing tactical fighting are rounded up or disbanded.

No side wins all aspects but no side loses either. Technology is banned from a few schools; there are technology-free sanctuary towns for those who wish for it. But there are also magic-heavy towns which dismiss the idea of anti-technology as luddite fear mongering. They keep their wands and their internet connections, setting up extra cell phone towers out of stubbornness or maybe just spite. Between the two extremes the magical community should find out if cellphones really do impact magical quality or quantity in a decade or two. Maybe there will be war again then depending on which hypothesis comes out on top—but at least it will be war based on facts, not fancy. Maybe that will make it better.

There is no fanfare when Henry is sent home. Two adults she doesn't know walk her to the edge of the woods and plop her back into her ordinary life, not even staying long enough to explain things to her mom and dad.

Her parents thought she ran away and they split time between shouting and crying over her. Henry lets them, because she feels guilty for not even leaving a note. Gabriele had never bothered to let their parents know she was playing truant in order to fight a war, so they never knew to worry about her; there was no such ready-made excuse for Henry's disappearance. Somehow it had never occurred to her to send word back.

In the ensuing weeks, she constantly stares out over the field that leads to the woods and waits for someone to come out and collect her again. There's no way for a nonmagical person to find the magical towns and schools on their own; the paths twist and turn and disappear whenever mundane eyes seek them out. She needs a guide to go back.

But no one comes.

Six weeks later, in the middle of the deepest heat wave Henry can ever remember, her sister and Caden finally turn up.

Henry runs to hug them, relieved.

"What did you think they were going to do? Erase your memories of war and Caden's of you?" Gabriele laughs and there's a scar Henry never noticed crossing deep into her left cheek.

"Maybe," Henry says.

"Like anyone could do that to me!" Caden says indignantly. Henry tries not to fuss although all she wants to do is ask over and over, *You're okay? You're okay? You're okay?*

"So I'm trying to think of majors for school," Henry says instead. "I can't major in frogspawn like you two. Do you have any *other* ideas?"

Henry's sixteen and she still wears twenty-seven friendship and leather charm bracelets. Some of them jingle when she moves and some of the bells have become so mangled they can no longer sound off. Henry refuses to feel ridiculous. It's taken years to finally be comfortable in her own skin. She's learned how to be someone she likes now and it's going to take more than a few snide comments about her bracelets to undermine that. She's mastered leggings and cuticle care, learned the difference between hair products, and discovered the glory of black moto booties that go with everything in every season.

She comes home from school and sorts through the mail. It's junk, mostly. Advertisements and bills for her parents. There's one college pamphlet for Henry and, at the very bottom of the pile, there is a letter in a cream-colored envelope with her name on it. When she opens it, it starts, *Ms. Henry Witkins* in bright purple ink.

Henry is too old for magic now. She's deep into applying for early admissions to college and everyone knows it's Gabriele, not Henry, who can wiggle her toes and change a toadstool into a rabbit. If Henry has anything like magic, and Gabriele insists she does, it's in choice and learning and sheer damned stubbornness.

But the letter came anyway with forty-seven signatures breathing out a belated *welcome home* and a *thank you for your service.* Across the field her sister turns up in-between a pair of old oak trees which are black with soot and green with fresh growth.

Henry folds the letter into the pocket of her skirt and stands to wave Gabriele towards the house. Welcome home indeed.

Inspirations and Influences

SARA FOX

I NEVER RECEIVED MY LETTER and I'm willing to bet I'm not alone. Oh, sure, I received regular letters. My grandmothers sent me cards with crisp one dollar bills and I had a pen pal or two while the internet was young and I hadn't ventured much past AOL. But I never received *the* letter. I also never stepped through a wardrobe or found an alien in a construction site, although I would have welcomed both. I have always been an equal-opportunist adventurer.

Like most people, I grew up wanting even as I also learned our world's structures, categories, and expectations. Metaphoric slamming doors were all over the place—here you are too loud, there you are too quiet, you only half fit this box. There were instructions, too: stand up straight, sit down, smile. And expectations for the expectations! So many of them tied together with gender presentation and only a handful made sense.

I wanted the magical fix where I would step into a world and belong—wholly as my messy, unexpected self. But I didn't get it. I made space for myself here instead and, eventually, I realized many of my childhood favorites didn't really have space for me either. First, bits of me were seen only in characters vaguely mentioned (and some didn't even get that) and second, the characters who were not invited to magical school always seemed to get a more negative arc, if they got one at all.

You are either magical or you aren't. You're either a part of a world or you are left behind to bloom bitter and often villainous. But how strange is that when here we are, all the readers and most of the writers: the children and adults who wished, who wanted, but were left behind without fairy rings or aliens or invitations.

I have been thinking about those left behind since 2011. I thought about Petunia Dursley and her childhood letter to Dumbledore, or Peter Parker and Harry Osborn in some Spider-Man renditions. That jealousy and vengefulness that often culminates in victim or villain and sometimes in both.

I saw them and wanted to put those characters back where they could be—fierce friends and family; naive, maybe, but loving in the complicated push-pull of all long relationships with decaying jealousy. They didn't have to be nice to join the story, they didn't have to be more to be the story.

And so, one day, I saw Why Millennials Yearn for Magical School by Sarah Gailey appear on my twitter timeline. I read two seconds, turned, and went to put Henry back into the story she›d always belonged to but that I had never been able to sit down with before. Sometimes all that's needed is a push—and that lovely essay was just that.

When The Letter Comes touches on the experience of not being invited into a world (this one, a different one, something else altogether) and finding a way to make space for yourself anyway. I hope that even if you don't see yourself in this story, you continue to write your own invitations to make space for yourself and those who come after.

A Chat With Sara Fox

***When the Letter Comes* came as a submission to our Awakenings call for short stories. Why did you choose to submit this particular story and how do you think it fits the theme?**

The first draft of *When the Letter Comes* was written a few months before I found the Awakenings call for short stories. I honestly wasn›t sure what to do at first—I thought it fit but I am not always the best judge so I sat on it. I read and reread more of Book Smuggler›s stories. I tried to feel more settled about it. Sure, Henry goes through several moments of personal awakening, I mulled, but maybe a story with something more overt would be a better fit?

I am trying to avoid detailing the whole plot here but for me it was not the first letter that made me decide the story fit. Sure, that is an awakening for Henry: a bitter disappointment. Rather, I decided to submit it because of the ending where letters are lovely but may not matter as much anymore.

When you sent your submission, you mentioned that it was inspired by an article about Millenials yearning for Magical School. Could you expand a bit on this source of inspiration and how it spoke to you?

A story like Henry's has been bubbling in my head for several years. I've thought about writing it but decided not yet. Not yet, I'm too busy. Not yet, I am not quite at the level I want to be to write it. Not yet, what's the flavor of this story, anyway?

When I read Why Millennials Yearn for Magical School what struck me was the wanting. It was like cutting my teeth on that awful, wonderful, growing-up feeling of want—which still exists today but less sharp somehow. It›s expectation, it›s hope, it›s learning how to work around defeat and disappointment and all the could be, should be, pleases that have touched every person I have ever known in a multitude of ways.

Sometimes things don't happen as we want or we think we deserve, but that doesn't mean we can't all keep moving to cultivate some of those same things. I also thought: so what if that world doesn't want us? We can still have a place in it.

What are some of the books, films, TV shows, or other influences you drew from when writing *When the Letter Comes***?**

The most obvious is probably Harry Potter which is a world I feel drawn to and also removed from due to representation or lack thereof. I'm also a big fan of Seanan McGuire's Wayward Children series, although I don't recall thinking specifically of it while writing, and without Tamora Pierce's books I'm not sure I'd be writing today. Above all, however, my biggest influences are my friends who indulge my chatter on magical philosophy (or what I think it might be) and challenge me to think about things in new ways.

Tell us a bit about your experience writing short stories: what would you say are the advantages and potential pitfalls of writing short fiction?

As of right now, I really *only* write short stories. I›m trying to build myself up to longer works but, for now, the short story is where I feel most comfortable. With a short story, I find, you can kind of assess: *have I hit all the major points?* a little more easily than with a longer work. The longer I go the more worried I become. Of course that doesn›t mean short fiction doesn›t need edits (or that I avoid blind spots—I have loads of those!) but that there is a sort of comfort in being able to sit down and mostly see the whole.

But… there are a lot of downsides to short fiction as well. I sometimes describe them in the way of homes. A short story is a studio or one bedroom apartment (or just one or two rooms in a house). You can give a really great study of those spaces… but there's always a world outside the window (or in the next hall over) which has to be left out.

Looking specifically at *When the Letter Comes*, I know several of the hallways I left on the cutting room floor. The most interesting ones, to me, are the enemies-to-lovers subplot and extended world building around the tension between technology and magic. Will I ever write those stories? I would like to! For now, however, this story is an introduction in 5,000 words verses the longer reader friendship of 50,000 or more.

Finally, a question we ask all of our interviewees: We Book Smugglers have faced condemnation because of the sheer volume of books that we carry back home on a daily basis. As such, we have on occasion resorted to "smuggling books" home to escape judgmental, scrutinizing eyes. Have you ever had to smuggle books?

While I love books, I have very little shame regarding how many I have or how many I am reading/listening to (even when moving and stuffing them into nearly a hundred alcohol boxes pilfered from ABC/Package stores). Therefore, I have to admit my biggest delight, most titillating book smuggling thrill, has always been smuggling books to others. This could be because a given book was 'banned' by parents (when I was younger) or just taking a wild guess at a guilty pleasure for a new acquaintance who might not want to admit to a large group why, yes, that is my poison right there. Come to think of it, isn't writing a way of smuggling stories? So let's add that way as well.

Nussia

MICHELE TRACY BERGER

Nussia. I said her name like a wish.

I was elated that our family was chosen to host Nussia, an alien child. My family was this regular black family that owned a house in Parkchester, in the northern section of the Bronx. Nussia, well, Nussia was Fike (pronounced Fīkē).

The Fike landed on Earth in 1975. In 1976 the President announced a contest to build good relations between humans and Fike. The winner of the contest would get to host Nussia (pronounced Nōōsēä). Sixth graders had to write why their families should be chosen. The Fike and the President chose the host family. Nussia came to live with us toward the end of spring in 1978. I was thirteen. It was at a time when "firsts" for black folks still mattered.

When my family found out that we'd won, my sister and I ran around the house shrieking. My Dad put on some George Benson, and my Mom opened the 1972 Burgundy. That night my family toasted me, Lindsay Fields, and my sixteen-year-old sister, Virginia. We were each allowed to have a glass of wine. Mom wound up drinking several glasses that night.

It's strange how things work out: Even though Virginia helped me write the essay that won the contest, it was all my idea to enter it. We said sophomoric things like the Bronx is a fun place, and that we would take Nussia roller-skating at Skate Key, and to the Botanical Gardens where she would be astounded by the variety of flowers. I also said that Mom made the best baked pork chops and potato salad. It was the kind of potato salad that's real sweet 'cause Mom used Miracle Whip, and put sliced green apples in it. I put in that our grandmother had been a "hoofer"—a dancer at the Cotton Club in Harlem in the 1930s (as she would say, "When Harlem was *Harlem*")—and was one of the adventurous black expatriates who still lived in France.

I argued we were a family of pioneers, so hosting Nussia would fit right in. Maybe we were the best family chosen out of those that applied. Maybe not. I was, however, a sincere child when I wrote the essay. I wanted to have a best friend very badly.

My sister and I sat up all night preparing and rearranging our dolls, games, and toys. We did everything over again as if to familiarize ourselves with who we were. I couldn't wait for Nussia to experience the newest craze, video games. We made lists of things our parents would just *have* to buy us in order to host Nussia properly. I wanted to play *The Game of Life* with Nussia, though I figured it'd have to be adapted for the Fike way of doing things.

I proudly hung up the acceptance letter in the midst of an ever growing collage of photos, articles, and pinups of Michael Jackson, Rod Stewart, and Shaun Cassidy that cluttered my room. I wanted to look at the acceptance letter every morning and evening.

Later that night, I sat in the foyer next to the phone anxiously waiting my turn to call my favorite person in the whole world—my grandmother. I waited for what seemed like an eternity while my parents broke the news over the phone while it was also being broadcast on TV by the White House. First, they called the pastor of our church. After that, they called Dad's lawyer, a reporter from the *Amsterdam News*, our doctor, and then all their white friends. Dad talked the longest; he paced back and forth with his hands wrapped around the snaky, yellow telephone cord. He said, "My daughter, this family, an alien… can you believe it? Uh-huh, Lindsay's going to be able to write her own ticket. Maybe I'll even stop going to the race track," he said with a chuckle.

When I finally got through to Grandma it was very late. For at least five minutes, I didn't give her a chance to speak. She finally broke in with, "I'm so excited for you, baby. This is a big first for the family… for America… for America," she said. Her deep voice crackled and several words echoed. The connection to France wasn't so great.

"I know, Grandma. I'm going to try to make Nussia real happy."

"I bet some white folks are eating their hearts out," she said, giving a real hearty laugh. Grandma was an "uplift the race" type of woman.

"But… you don't worry about that, you hear?" she said.

"Okay," I said.

"Those Fike are a good-looking group. Even the French are saying that. God knows we got enough ugly people in the world. We don't need anyone or anything else that hurts the eyes."

"Oh, Grandma."

Nussia. I said her name until it became a song.

Soon after the decision, the exchange committee sent us pictures and information about Nussia and her people. I had read a lot about the Fike already, so I skipped most of the background on them being humanoid aliens. But I studied Nussia's picture. She was beautiful.

In the picture they sent of her, Nussia stood against the backdrop of the Black River Ridge, majestic mountains in the background and the sky dusted with yellow clouds, on the southern tip of her planet. Her blue tunic played off the deep amber color of her skin. Flipping to customs and traditions, I found more about their surricille, or head covering in English. The most striking characteristic of the Fike was the contrast between the iridescence of their surricilles and the darkness of their eyes. The surricille was made of thick cartilage, which covered the top of her head and came down to just above her eyes—the place where we humans have eyebrows. When I looked at her surricille, a peacock eye shimmered back at me.

Fike surricilles fall off in adulthood, and is replaced by less luminous skin. This phase was called the Time of Awakening because Fike went out unprotected into their world. Their physical self was biologically and literally changed; they took on a different identity within their community.

Although our ages didn't correspond directly, Nussia was considered an adolescent by Fike standards; that is, an age when she was to practice under guidance from elders for the Awakening. She was making a great sacrifice by coming to Earth. I should have thought more about this fact, this price. At the time, I had no idea what she was giving up.

Most Fike had some telekinetic powers. I was hoping that when Nussia came she would be able to make me levitate like I had seen other Fike do on television. They also could manipulate matter on a small scale. In the packet sent to us there was a letter attached from Nussia that I spent time reading over and over, especially the lines that said, "When I come to you, it will be as if Fike and humans had always known of each other. We will create a lasting friendship for us and our peoples."

The letter went on to talk about how much fun she was going to have on Earth, and how she was looking forward to meeting me and my family.

Mom helped me put together a care package to send back to Nussia with jacks, *Betty and Veronica* comics, and *Tiger Beat* magazine. I hoped she would love all the items in the package and know that I was taking care of everything on my end. My new friend was going to be great! Her coming to stay with us was going to erase how invisible I felt. Yes, I had one or two friends at school, but I never was first on their (or anyone else's) list for parties or teams. I faded into the background easily. And, lately, Virginia and I weren't getting along so well. Teenagers can be mean.

We only had two months to prepare! So much to do, including setting up Nussia's special sleeping chambers (a domed tank elevated on a platform, called a floatbed), get training in the eating habits of the Fike, and meet the Secret Service team that would be working with us. My mother put the calendar on the fridge and I marked off every day and task, closing in on Nussia's visit with big red 'X's.

No one told us how tiring it was going to feel being the first family, the only family, a black family, hosting an alien. Photographers camped out at the house. Soon my family appeared on every magazine cover in America. Within a matter of weeks our hopeful faces were splashed across the world.

There was Dad at his job as Bronx Lebanon's hospital administrator. *Click. People.* There was me at school answering a question. *Click. Time.* There was my sister helping Mom in the kitchen cutting up green peppers. *Click. Good Housekeeping.* There was my mom with her telephone headset on, plugging into the switchboard. *Click. Life.* The *Click.* buzzed in our ears, and the flashes blinded us for days, stealing our lives away from us slowly. We lived through the negatives they left us.

I saw so many photographs of myself that I never had to look in a mirror. From every magazine cover, every newspaper article and news program, a short flat-chested girl with a crooked smile and sleepy eyes always stared back at me. My mom would fix my wiry hair the same way—a part down the middle and two buns on either side of my head. I use to think of them as idiot dials. It was a different story when I looked at Virginia's picture. A tall, shapely sixteen-year-old with a small well-groomed Afro, perfect teeth, and high cheekbones smiled back at me. Every picture made her look like a model.

If it wasn't the press people that we tripped over, then surely it was the nest of Secret Service men who were stationed in our house and around our neighborhood. Their head of operations was a large man with the complexion of spit up grits, ears smaller than most rodents and mean shovel gray-colored eyes. I always thought of him as "Mean Grits." Whenever he said my name, he drew the "Lind" out for an unbearably long time. *Liiiindsay.* I immediately disliked him and avoided him as much as possible.

The press picked up and promoted every scrap of information about us. We moved like shadows in our own house. My sister said she wanted to be a doctor, but I knew the thought hadn't occurred to her until some pinched-faced reporter asked. Reporters portrayed us as an all-American wholesome family—a good old fashioned popsicle that had been surreptitiously dipped in dark chocolate. We were so much more than that, both good and bad.

Mom played right into their hands. First, we needed a better vase for the living room, then a new recliner, then better china. Next, Virginia needed to go to the hairdresser more often to get her Afro shaped. I kept to myself while waiting for Nussia, not sure of what we were becoming. Were we just hosts for Nussia, or something else?

The editorials started showing up just a few days after the announcement. These were pieces in *The New York Times, Washington Post*, and *The Wall Street Journal*, mostly tirades about how the Bronx wasn't a fit place for an alien child to visit. Even beyond the OpEds, the phrases "Affirmative action" and "charity case" were heard everywhere on the news and in radio shows.

My parents told Virginia and me not to open the piles of mail that greeted us after school, but I was *into* mail. Mom should have known that. I'd been mailing myself letters since I was six years old.

I only remember one letter. A manila envelope arrived with cheerful animal stickers of giraffes, monkeys, and lions on its outside. The envelope was addressed to me. I pulled out a poster board collage from the envelope. On the poster board there were ripped out pictures of monkeys from *National Geographic* magazines. The makers hadn't been very concerned with accuracy. They had different types of monkeys, gorillas, chimpanzees, marmosets, and baboons cavorting together who would never live together in real life. Even I knew that. The primates had enlarged lips and genitals drawn over their bodies in red ink. The primates' penises jutted upward, and the scrotums were intensely swirled red circles.

Each of the monkeys in the middle was named after someone in my family. These monkeys were placed around a picture of Nussia being boiled up in a big black pot. The forks in some of the monkey's hands were so big that the tines reached the top of the page. The speech bubble over Nussia's head read, "Help! Get me away from the niggers!"

A bubble over one of the other monkeys read, "You suuuuure gonna taste gooood."

I pulled the picture of Nussia up from the crude monkey collage and put her on my collage in the room. I threw the rest of it away, and I didn't tell anyone about what I saw. I stopped wanting to go to the mailbox after that.

Nussia. I said her name like a prayer.

I asked God to please keep us all safe so we could welcome Nussia.

When she came back to the States, Grandma became the spokesperson for the family. She took a hiatus from her traveling, finding that it was great to be back in the limelight. No matter what my Mom did, she could not drag Grandma away from the reporters. Her height and commanding presence made people pay attention. Grandma was the calm in the midst of our storm. She'd never change. I took great pleasure in spending every moment I could get with her. And, although she never said it, I always felt like I was her favorite grandchild.

That day, she took me out to a restaurant. Grandma wore sharp black trousers, a man's crisp white shirt, and a blue and white scarf tied around her neck. The colors of her clothes accentuated her powdered ginger-like complexion.

After we ordered, she sat erect and very still, focused on my current observations and questions about life.

"Grandma, when am I going to get… y'know?" I ran my hand over my chest, hovering over two significant places.

"Oh those? Don't be ashamed, Lindsay. You'll get them when it's time. All in due time. Just like you got Nussia." She winked at me.

Grandma was good at answering questions so I asked her what I should say to reporters because I often sat tongue-tied and close to tears. I usually wound up repeating what I had written in my essay.

"Well, you know what kind of ice cream you like, right?" she said, bunching up a napkin.

"Yep, butter pecan. Chocolate is also right up there, too."

"You can think of a question as asking you what kind of ice cream you like," she said. "Go ahead now and close your eyes." Her face turned serious. "Get comfortable with the question. Take it apart in that mind of yours. Think about how much you like butter pecan. You know how to describe the taste of the ice cream, right? That's how you can approach any question, really—break it down into something manageable. That's not so hard now, is it?"

I opened my eyes and, smiling, shook my head. I never have quite figured out what ice cream and questions have in common, or how thinking about butter pecan would help me, but I got better at talking to reporters anyway.

With all the talk of questions, ice cream and breasts, I forgot to ask Grandma the question that scared me the most: *What if Nussia doesn't like me?*

That night I wandered into my mother's bedroom. My mother and father had kept separate bedrooms since I was six. Hers was the cushy and comfortable one. She once told me they had separate bedrooms because she worked all the time, being a telephone operator and all. Most often her shifts were from twelve at night until nine in the morning, and Dad didn't like to be woken up in the middle of the night.

The vanity table where she sat held all of the magic she used to get her through the evening: a bottle of wine, bath oils, Lindt chocolates, and a variety of perfumes including Enjoli, Charlie, and Chanel No.5. Her eyes looked tired.

"Do you think she'll like me?" I asked. I sat down on the edge of her bed.

"Lindsay, now don't go worrying about that." She pulled a few bobby pins that held her hairpiece, styled like a large French roll, in place.

She added, "You know she won't know any better. You're going to be her first real human contact."

"Mom!"

Giving me a quick glance over her shoulder she said, "Oh, I'm kidding of course. If you like her, she'll like you. You are going to make a big impression on her." She came over and squeezed the top of my shoulder twice. Her squeezes always came in twos—never more, never less—and were always very tight.

I watched her walk back to the vanity table in her slip and stockings; the stockings were too light for her complexion. Silently and deliberately she pulled the hairpiece off; bobby pins falling everywhere. It was a spider's nest of blackness tumbling to the floor. She winced slightly. Her nightly ritual nearly complete, she poured herself a glass of wine, put her robe on and shooed me off her bed.

"Can I sleep with you tonight?"

"You're too big to be sleeping with me, Lindsay."

She was probably right, but it would be nice to be next to her. I could close my eyes, and the apple-y smell of Enjoli, baby powder, and sweat would carry me off to sleep.

I moped back to the room I shared with Virginia. My sister was on her back staring off into space. Virginia's enthusiasm over Nussia's visit had ground down to nothing. She preferred experimenting with pot and hanging with some of her rowdier friends who lived in the neighborhood, rather than generating excitement for our visitor. Pot had made her moodier than usual.

"Virginia, do you think we should take Nussia to the movies?"

"I don't know," she said.

"Well, what about the Botanical Gardens?"

She rolled on her side. "Whatever."

"Come on. We need to have things planned," I said, whining a bit. "Wouldn't it be cool if we could take her to France to see Grandma's place? We haven't been since we were little."

Virginia sat up and shook her head. "Little sister, did you ever think that she might not want to do any of the stuff we've planned? She's an *alien*." Her lips pressed into a red slash.

"Forget you. I'll plan things on my own," I said, cutting off the light. I lay there thinking about how things will be different when Nussia arrived. Like Christmas every day.

I woke up to the sound of hammering, drilling and a loud beeping sound.

Virginia lifted her head, "What's that?"

I jumped out of bed and opened our door. My grandmother popped her head out of the guest bedroom and looked at me. "What's all this commotion? On a Sunday no less?"

"I don't know." But I did know it was only one month to go and I was eager to check off another 'X'.

As I came downstairs, I saw two large men, carrying a big green box, walking through the living room toward the kitchen. A quick peek out the window revealed the source of the beeping. A large white truck was parked out front.

In the kitchen Mom stood talking to Mean Grits. She didn't look awake, her hair had been thrown together in a hasty French braid and wisps of stray hairs framed her face. The clock on the wall said 7 A.M. Too early for breakfast. Sundays weren't guaranteed family time because often both my parents worked during the weekend, but recently they were making an effort to be at home.

"What's going on, Mom?" She ignored me, continuing her rant at the large Secret Serviceman in our kitchen.

"I don't appreciate you smoking in the house. I've told you that before," she said pointing her finger at Mean Grits.

"Sorry, Ma'am." The apology didn't change the coldness of his eyes, though. "We've acquired a house down the block and will be there around the clock for the next several months."

"Great," she said flatly.

With a shake of her head, she finally looked at me and smiled wearily "Nussia's floatbed is being put together downstairs, hon."

Floatbed! I zoomed down the stairs toward the basement.

The basement was crowded. Boxes leaned against the wall. Mechanical looking parts like dials and levers covered the floor. Three men were moving furniture around.

My father stood in the middle of the chaos. "Christ, this is going to take all day."

"The engineer's late, Mr. Fields. I've already called him twice," one of the Secret Service men said.

"Hi, Dad," I said.

He gave me a curt nod and then moved to open another box.

The main table against the wall was covered in instructions for assembling the floatbed. I looked at the Polaroids that accompanied the written materials. The floatbed was a domed tank, elevated on a short platform. Notes next to the pictures said, "Ideal construction—five feet wide and eight feet long."

"What I don't understand is why this couldn't have been done any other day," my mother said as she walked down the steps. She stood on the last step, arms crossed and her jaw clenched. "You couldn't have asked us about our schedule?" my mother said, locking eyes on the nearest Secret Service agent.

No one said anything.

"We cleared it with your husband," someone in the room said. I swear, the temperature in the already-cool basement dropped another ten degrees as my mother turned and glared at my dad.

"You neglected to mention that detail, Rodger," she said. I shivered. That was my mom's *you're in BIG trouble young lady* voice and I wanted absolutely no part of it.

"Not the right moment, Jesse," my father said in a carefully controlled tone, every syllable clearly pronounced. This was his familiar *I-don't-want-to-fight-in-front-of-company* voice.

I practiced staring at the ground and making myself as inconspicuous as possible.

"I suppose I should just be glad you're gracing us with your presence. You'll have to make the racetrack wait today, huh?"

Ouch! I didn't know much about Dad's gambling, except that he liked to do it. Maybe he was doing it more now?

My head snapped up. I saw my father's nostrils flare and how the veins in his neck bulged though he said nothing. Instead, he inspected the box he held and said, "This is what I was looking for earlier."

My petite, easygoing mother sniffed and fixed all of the men downstairs with her stare, "For the record, gentlemen, my husband didn't clear it with me. And since I run this house, in the future, I'll thank you all to clear this kind of information with *me*."

I just stood there stuck in place like a barnacle.

As my mother turned, red-faced she pointed at me, "Lindsay, get upstairs and get dressed like a proper person!"

My mother's anger was rare but powerful and unpredictable, coming and going like a tropical storm. I slunk off, but still secretly excited that Nussia's bed had arrived.

With just two weeks to go and still much to do, none of us were in a good mood by the time the xenobotanist, Alton Cruse, arrived. He was a young white scholar from MIT, and the most knowledgeable man in the world about Fike eating habits. Parading around wearing light blue rubber gloves on, he inspected our kitchen while he spoke in terms which included the gastrointestinal rise and fall of the dorba, aka the Fike's stomach. He was here to teach us how to cook for Nussia.

It was mandatory that our entire family attend the session with Mr. Cruse. We stood side by side, crammed against the back wall of the kitchen, as he lectured us and paced back and forth. His red hair stuck out in puffs on his head.

He listened and took notes as Mom proudly spoke about the meals she most often fixed for our family.

"Mrs. Fields, this all looks good. Not too much pork—I was worried about the possible pork intake. You haven't mentioned any southern dishes like salt pork, chitterlings, pigtails, and that kind of thing," he intoned gravely.

My grandmother made a grimace. "Mr. Cruse, first of all, our family is not from the South. And, second of all, what are you trying to imply? My daughter is an excellent cook."

"*Dr.* Cruse," he corrected her, then shrugged, arms opening wide, "I had no idea what I was going to find in your diet."

"It's fine, Ma. Let the man do his job," my mother snapped.

I bit the inside of my cheek. I didn't like it when they fought.

"If he's going to teach us something new and help us prepare for Nussia then that's fine, but if he is going to insinuate and speculate about what *we* eat then forget it."

My father, who had been impatiently tapping his fingertips against his leg while *Dr.* Cruse was talking, cleared his throat and moved toward the door. "Look here, it may be the weekend and time off for everyone else in this house, but *I* have to go into the office today."

"Yes, Rodger, we all know that," Mom said. Then, aside, in a low voice, "It's not like *you* ever help out around the house anyway."

Dad swung back around on his heel, his face contorted with anger. "And what is that supposed to mean, Jesse?"

"Nothing."

I noticed a throbbing vein on the left side of my mother's neck.

"I can call all of this off anytime! Right now if I want to!" he said, bits of salvia spraying my mother's face.

Call it off? It felt like a crater opened in my kitchen and was going to swallow us. Why was he always so upset lately?

"Dad?" I said.

"Now, Rodger... that's a bit dramatic. Don't you think?" Grandma said, moving between them.

Dr. Cruse was watching us as though observing animals in the wild, then cleared his voice and said, "I haven't even got to the part about how the Fike eat."

Dad was still standing close to the door. I looked at him, my eyes pleading with him to stay. He sighed and then waved his hand at the scientist.

"Well, get on with it, man. This is *all* for my Lindsay's future."

Virginia sucked in a deep inhale through her teeth. I elbowed her to be quiet.

Dr. Cruse continued, "The most interesting part of the eating processes is the way in which Fike digest their food. They cover what they eat with a substance, which is similar to what oysters in the mollusk family do with bacteria and dirt—"

"I haven't had good oysters since we all went to the Cape," Grandma interrupted.

"Ma, will you let him finish?" my mother said.

"For oysters, the result is a pearl. For Fike... Well, Mr. Fields, about a third of their digested food particles then take on special importance. Hardened food debris is then regurgitated, and are called monunis. Fike feel the monunis are part of them, extensions of their Fike spirit if you will. Fike like to have their monunis where they can see them. They often build community shrines."

He paused and then chuckled. "Now, the young tend not to be quite so reverent, so we'll have to wait and see what Nussia does with her monunis. I'm not an anthropologist, but monuni worshipping is very culturally significant." He pulled out a Polaroid picture and passed it around.

"This picture gives you an idea of what monunis look like," he said.

"My God, Mr. Cruse, you're telling me and my family that they revere their excretions?" Mom said.

"It's not excretions to them. The monunis are still part of them—they just take on a different form."

"Why didn't anyone say anything about this before? Is there anything contagious about these monnis?" Mom shifted her weight and pulled at the back of her bun.

Virginia and I studied the picture of an adult Fike with slender hands holding up monunis, which looked like hard purplish balls. Cruse didn't mention that each monuni had a stringy curlicue tail of gray matter attached at the end of it. "Ewwww," Virginia said. "That's nasty."

"That is monunis, Mrs. Fields, and no, it is not contagious or harmful to humans. I personally have been studying the Fike and their monunis at MIT for the past three years and there has been no discernible dangerous effect on the researchers."

"Mrs. Fields, there is no need to worry about these aliens. There's no possible harm that can come to your family," Mean

Grits said with his hands clasped behind his back. He had been so quiet in the kitchen that I had forgotten about him. "Our government wouldn't let anything in your home that wasn't safe." He gave a stern look to Cruse.

"Are we done here? Jesse, you can fill me in tonight," Dad said, rushing out the kitchen door.

Mom rolled her eyes.

"It's vomit. Vomit balls are going to be rolling all around our house!" Virginia shrieked.

"Hush, girl," Grandma said.

I hadn't bargained for monunis either, but I figured I could get used to it—we all could get used to it.

The big day finally arrived. Our whole family turned out, and many people from the neighborhood crammed themselves into our house. Mr. Alvarez, the Puerto Rican baker, was there, with a big T-shirt that said, *Welcome Nussia!* The Willacys, our Jamaican next-door neighbors, were present, looking regal in their Caribbean colored clothes of reds, greens and yellows. Mrs. Willacy's hair was done up in a high bun. Kids from school and their parents were there and flashed smiles for the news crew and waved at loved ones watching at home. I thought people only waved and said, "Hi Mom," on television shows, but people were doing that everywhere.

I wanted to be on our doorstep for the greeting, but Mean Grits said no. For security reasons, Nussia would be escorted to the front door.

And, before I knew it, Nussia stood in the middle of my living room.

She looked different from the pictures, and from what I had imagined her to be like. Her eyes took up an enormous amount of space on her face, and they possessed the calm, inky darkness of a dream. She didn't have any eyebrows, but had deep groves right where her surricille ended. She was bald and golden all over, except for her palms which were a leathery bell pepper green.

Nussia wore a loose orange and white tunic. Her shoulders were exposed and her family markings, or acraeturas as the Fike called them, were visible. The markings told of her family's history for the last three generations. She was large, too, about two of me across—definitely someone Mrs. Willacy would call a "wide gal." Her surricille was even more luminous in person. I felt transfixed by it, and I imagined that it called out to me. I wanted to touch it, but restrained myself.

She came toward me with me, like a glowing amber wall of energy and swept me into a hug.

I forgot everything. All the anxiety, the nasty letters, the fights between mom and dad. My new friend was here!

Her hug was full and made me feel like everything was going to be all right. She was taller than me, so I fell a little to one side in her grip. She smelled of apples—I wondered if she really smelled that way or if she got that smell while staying at her top secret location.

When the hug finally broke, I bounced back on the balls of my feet, exploding with energy and ideas of things for us to do. Then she spoke.

"Lindsay, I greet you with the highest welcome from me and the Fike." I wasn't prepared for the sizzle-sound in her voice. It reminded me of when it was like when a hot comb is left too long on a stove and then pulled through hair. An overheated hot comb touching fresh hair almost ignites it—that's how her voice made me feel. I could taste the burn in her voice and for the very first time, I was a little scared of the alien girl in front of me.

But then I remembered that this was important, and that she was just as nervous as I was and I shouldn't be scared of my new best friend. "Nussia," I said remembering my rehearsed words. "We are so proud to have you here with us."

As I started speaking, Nussia's large tubular shaped retractable mouth, kind of like an elephant's trunk, puckered outwards. She leaned down slightly and I felt the briefest kiss land above my eyebrows.

My heart almost froze for a moment and then pounded. An undignified squeal escaped my lips. The room swam around me. I pressed my hands to my cheeks. I felt so light for a moment like I would float away. That was one distracting kiss! I sucked in my breath and calmed myself down enough so that I could speak.

"I have so much to show you. You will get to know us."

"We will make both Fike and humans proud," she said.

I hugged her again, feeling the warmth of her skin. The apple smell reminded me of Christmas. I smiled up at her and nodded.

But that moment shattered as all the adults crowded in with their cameras and their questions and swept Nussia away from me.

Mom brought out a large bowl of candies to set on the dining table. She tripped over a TV camera cord that had snaked its way into the dining room. The bowl flew out of her hands with candies scattering everywhere. Press people eagerly caught the misstep.

"Damn it, Jesse," my father muttered. He bristled, then bent down quickly, grabbing fistfuls of candy.

"I'm sorry. I'm just a little nervous, I guess," Mom whispered to no one in particular.

Nussia noticed this commotion. She walked into the dining room. She looked at my father on his knees. With her eyes closed she brought her two hands out in front of her. The candies came up from the floor swirling in the air. They made a colored tornado over to the now floating bowl. The press moved in closer. *Click.*

"We might need you around all the time with Jesse being so clumsy," my father said. He came over and patted Nussia on the back.

"Isn't that sweet?" someone cooed.

"Thank you, Mr. Fields… Dad," Nussia said with only a little bit of hesitation, returning his gesture by patting him on the back.

Nussia nodded as if she confirmed something she had been thinking about.

People clapped. Everyone was laughing again, and animated conversation burst out across the rooms. The crush of bodies descended around Nussia again. This was getting me nowhere.

Grandma had yet another reporter cornered between the grandfather clock and wall.

"What do you think it says about America in this century that your family, a black family, was chosen to host Nussia?" the reporter asked.

Grandma took a deep breath. "Everyone's harping on the fact that we're black, from news folk like yourself and others that have been obsessed by this one detail about us—and not in good ways. And to be honest, I am pretty tired of hearing about it."

The reporter's face tightened and puckered like he had sucked on a lemon. He was about to respond but my grandmother continued.

"It is a fact we're black, but the aliens don't really care now, do they? Why shouldn't we be the first family to host Nussia."

I had lost Mom in the crowd. I squeezed my way past Mrs. Willacy, who was telling Dr. Cruse that goat meat was just as natural to eat as any other kind of meat.

I went into our kitchen, where Mom stood looking out the window with what looked and smelled like a rum and coke in her hand.

She turned to look at me. "So much going on, baby," she said absentmindedly.

"Yes, Mom. It's okay." I put my hand around her waist. She patted it and then smoothed away a tear from her face.

I was tired by the time everyone left, and where tiredness left off, my frustration caught hold. I couldn't find Nussia anywhere. I hadn't had a chance to spend more than two minutes alone with her.

I went upstairs. There was giggling coming from our bedroom. Nussia's giggle was like a slap—quick, loud, and sharp.

I pushed opened the closed door to find Virginia and Nussia sitting side-by-side. "Hey, you guys disappeared," I said, a little hurt that they were becoming friends without me. Virginia picked nervously at her bracelet.

"We have to get up early, Lindsay. Mom told me she wants you to take your shower," Virginia said quickly.

"Oh."

They were both quiet and sat looking at me.

"Nussia, do you want to sit on the porch for a little while? There's nobody around. You're probably sick of all the fuss," I said.

"No, Lindsay. Virginia and I are talking fine."

"*You're* probably tired. Little sisters do need their sleep," Virginia said, rising. "Nussia, why don't we go outside and let Lindsay get ready for bed? There's a big day tomorrow, too, with the block party and all."

"Every day will be a big day. Big day," Nussia said.

Before I could object, they were making their way out of the room.

As she closed the door, Nussia flicked her tongue out. I remembered reading that the gesture was the equivalent of a human waving good-bye.

I told myself I had the rest of my time with Nussia. What was the first night? Before getting undressed, I fingered the collage on the wall. I wondered if Nussia had noticed her picture there.

Later in the night I awoke and I crept downstairs. The whole house was quiet, dark, and asleep. I could hear the stray, sad sounds of Roberta Flack on someone's stereo floating in from our neighbor's house next door. The door to the basement was unlocked when I pushed on it, and padded down the wooden stairs.

I hadn't spent much time in the basement since the workmen were there. It was still the same place—though a bit brighter and cleaner than usual. It had been repainted in coats of specially formulated gold paint that was considered soothing to Fike. My mother's homemade curtains of bright red stars against a black background hung in the windows.

The floatbed under the stairwell we had set up for Nussia to sleep looked sturdy; Dad and the Secret Service men had done a good job installing it. Nussia floated vertically in the little chamber. She slept soundly with her arms folded on her chest. This time I was able to gaze at her undisturbed. I was so happy that she was here. Now I would have something that I never had before—a best friend.

I woke up the next morning feeling excited all over again. It felt like Christmas. Nussia was in my house! Downstairs, Mom was getting ready to make a batch of eggs.

"I bet you couldn't sleep last night," she smiled at me, seeming more like her usual self without all of the reporters and Secret Service men in the house.

"I may never sleep again with Nussia here, I'm so pumped up!"

"Go set the table. Use the special dishes." My mother shooed me on.

I did as she wished, running around to get the dishes and silverware in place. I then went and got the special things I wanted to show Nussia.

Then I waited and waited for everyone to get up and join us. It took forever!

Nussia arrived last.

"How'd you sleep, Nussia?" My mother asked.

She paused before speaking, looking to the left and right and then nodding, "Quite comfortably. Is that how you say it?"

I pulled out a chair for her and she walked over and sat down.

"Yes, very good, Nussia. I'm glad—" my mother began, but I was done waiting on pleasantries.

"Nussia," I interrupted, "I want to show you some things." All around the table, I had assembled small and large boxes covered in gold wrapping paper.

"Presents!" I said.

"Presents?" she looked at me, her dark eyes searching my face.

"Yes, presents!"

I felt time speeding up, just like during Christmas. I pushed one of the bigger boxes next to her.

Her hands touched the outside of the box.

I opened it and pulled out the item.

"I got you a pair of roller skates."

"Let her open them," my mother said. "Lindsay's a bit excited. Nussia, would you like orange juice or cranberry juice?"

"No juice."

"I didn't quite know what size your feet are, so if they don't fit, we can take them back," I babbled.

"Take back?" she looked at my mother and me.

"We can get you another pair," my mother said.

I pushed another box toward her.

"She hasn't eaten yet," Virginia cautioned. I looked at her as if she were crazy.

Mother laid a hand on my shoulder and whispered, "Your sister is right. Nussia might need a bit of time."

I shook my head in disbelief. Who wouldn't have time for *presents*?

Then Grandmother walked in the back door. "Good morning, everyone! Good morning, Miss Nussia. I was just putting the finishing touches out back. Did they tell you that's where your shrine will be?"

"Yes," Nussia nodded.

"Ma, sit down. We're getting ready to eat."

My mother set down a platter of eggs, bacon, sausage, grapefruit (a Fike favorite), pineapple slices, and blueberry muffins.

"And you know besides roller skating, we want to take you to the zoo. Do you have zoos? I think I read that you do, but on Fike, you can spend the night in them or something like that. We have a big zoo. The Bronx Zoo." Now that she was here in front of me, I couldn't stop myself from talking.

"It's time to say grace," my mother said holding up her hands.

We held hands while my father said a rather long-winded grace. Instead of keeping her eyes closed like everyone else, Nussia looked around the table, taking each of us in. When she came to me, she shut them quickly.

I kept staring. I wanted her to look at me. Virginia opened her eyes for a moment and winked. I smiled.

"Nussia, hand me your plate," my father said.

She did and gave him the first smile of the morning.

I stopped talking, took a breath, and buttered a muffin.

Nussia took a little bit of everything, then began eating.

Now that I had stopped talking, Grandma kept the conversation going. I tried not to stare at Nussia, but I couldn't help being fascinated by her retractable mouth as it extended and nibbled the pineapple slice on her fork.

Although we were all smiling, eating, and Grandma was still talking, I could feel the tension in the room. We really had an alien at our table. I was pretty sure all of the humans were wondering when the monunis were going to start.

After a few bites of food, Nussia rose. "I can't eat here," she said. "I have been told it is impolite to create monunis at the eating table. I will go."

The wait was over! I felt a fluttery feeling in my stomach, like the moment you are on a roller coaster ride and are climbing up the first hill.

"We understand about the monunis," my mother said holding her hand out. "It won't bother us."

"No, I will go outside."

Virginia wrinkled her nose, but no one else saw.

"You do whatever you need to," my father said.

Nussia nodded her golden head, and walked out to the garden.

"That went well. At least she's not going to make those things at the table," Grandma said as soon as Nussia was out of earshot. "A relief, if you ask me."

"No one asked you," my father said.

Nussia joined us about fifteen minutes later. My mother had brought out her much loved French toast casserole and we were digging in.

"Excuse me, family ones. I am tired and will go to rest," Nussia said.

"Of course," Grandma said. "It's been a lot to take in, hasn't it?"

She nodded.

"Going back to bed? Don't you want to open up presents?" I asked.

"No," she said walking to the basement door. She closed it and I heard the new lock clicking into place. For privacy, Nussia could lock the door from the inside. The key hung on a little hook next to the door.

I looked at the unopened presents and ate the rest of my meal in silence.

The neighborhood had planned a massive block party that day to celebrate Nussia's arrival. Folks wanted to show off and show out. On this perfect June day people milled about. My sister was still upstairs getting ready.

I took Nussia by the arm and tried to talk with her. She sure wasn't acting friendly, even for an alien. Maybe she was shy.

We walked along the length of the cordoned off blocks. I pointed out the street gallery of the block party. Over here were the Dominican and black men sitting like brown griffins playing dominoes; there in another corner were girls jumping fast in the crisscross ropes. Baby oil glistened on their quick legs. Some lanky teenagers were playing Steal the Old Man's Bacon. There were long tables of food, each platter and main dish sectioned off by pitchers of city champagne—Kool-Aid with ginger ale. I wanted her to see it all. I talked too fast, my words coming out like bullets.

At the other end of the corner a new rap group called the Sugar Hill Gang was setting up speakers and deejay equipment. I was looking forward to hearing them later. Yep, Nussia was going to get a real Bronx welcome.

I pointed out cool people like Peter Newport, my friend from school, who always smelled like cocoa butter and had freckles and legendary dimples. He was there with his sixteen-year-old brother Jake. People in school joked about how good-looking they were, calling them the "L&L" brothers, long and light-skinned.

"Peter's going to be my boyfriend one day, I hope."

Nussia barely said a word, politely nodding and declining to eat anything. Not even one nibble from the table.

"So, did you like the comic books?"

She stared back at me.

"I sent them to you along with the jacks and..."

"I didn't have time to be instructed on human games," she said, interrupting me.

"Oh."

"What about the letter you sent?" I asked.

"Do you know what I have left back at home?" she burst out. "This is the most beautiful time of year. It's the time when Fike my age get to walk in the forests of Per and practice for when we will be Awakened. And instead, I have this. And you." Nussia flung her arms wide. She rocked her head from side to side.

"I'm sorry. I guess I thought... I didn't know how important the Awakening was. I mean I *do* know how important that is." I rushed, trying not to seem like a complete idiot. My head was beginning to hurt.

She muttered in her native language; angry sizzling sounds escaped.

I fought back tears. This was going all wrong. She was angry with me, and I didn't know how I could fix it.

"You remind me of my sister, the minnos a minnos," she spat out. She pointed to a small spot on her shoulder that had dense words and symbols on it. The dye surrounding the spot was a deep maroon.

"You have a sister?" I said. What was she talking about? I didn't remember reading anything about a sister!

Virginia came outside and Nussia bolted toward her.

I stood shaking, wanting to chase after her. To call her name.

Nussia. I said her name like a spell that I could use to bring her back to me. A spell that didn't work.

Later that night while we were getting ready for bed, I told Virginia about Nussia's revelation.

"That's strange," she said.

"Shouldn't we tell Mom and Dad?" I said pulling my pajama top over my head.

"If it was that important, they would already know, right?" Virginia said. "Let her keep her secret," she shrugged. "Sometimes older sisters need their secrets."

I looked at her and felt my whole body tense up. I turned away because I didn't want to cry in front of her.

She came over, sat on my bed and gave me a hug, "Stop worrying like it's your hobby."

I leaned on her shoulder. "What do you think of her?" I whispered.

"She's cool. Mysterious."

More like you than me, I thought while soaking up the warmth of her body. She gave me a quick peck on the cheek as I snuggled under the covers. I felt sneaky, competitive with Virginia. Ick! It was wrong, I know, to feel jealous of her. But this didn't stop me from happily fantasizing Virginia being shipped off to a camp for the summer and being unable to hang out with Nussia as I drifted off to sleep.

A few weeks after Nussia arrived, my mother threw a surprise birthday party. It wasn't a total surprise. I overheard Mom talking about it on the phone the week before. My mother talked loudly when she drank. On the day of the party I thought about how different my life was with Nussia around. She came the first few days to school as was planned and then after that, she was whisked away by the Secret Service men to various places that we didn't know about to get more instruction on human culture. She spent most of her free time with Virginia. They called me Elkouri. It was a name that Nussia made up for me. It sounded like a curse, though I never found out what it meant.

She wasn't even trying to be my friend, let alone a best friend.

I didn't feel like seeing people from school. They all just wanted to see Nussia anyway. Most had made that clear just days after her arrival. They crowded around her when they could, asking her about Fike, questions they could have easily asked me. Often they begged to touch her surricille, and she usually consented.

I walked into the house and smiled as people with colorful party hats on shouted, "Surprise!"

Fourteen. Would it be special, I wondered? I tried to get into the party spirit. The house was packed. Most of the furniture in the living room was moved to create a dance floor. There was even a deejay setting up his equipment. Peter was talking to Virginia. He was looking cute as ever, in his black warm up suit and red sneakers with big fat laces. My attention turned to Mom as she walked out with a huge five-layer ice cream cake, from Carvel's famous store, with little blue roller skates on the top layer. She set it on a long table with my gifts. I went over to admire it.

"Dad sends his love. He's sorry he couldn't make it but promises he'll take you and Nussia both to do something together. Okay, baby?" Mom asked.

I nodded. Typical for my dad. He'd already missed two of my birthdays in a row.

Virginia, looking great in a tight white peasant shirt and her hip designer jeans, pulled out an envelope from the stack of presents and handed it to me. She had gotten me subscriptions to *Tiger Beat* and *Teen*. More photos of Michael Jackson and Shaun Cassidy for my wall. She could be so fucking cool! I gave her a big hug.

My friends clamored for records and the DJ started spinning. This was my cue to retreat to the dining room—I hated dancing. I have two left feet. My sister, of course, didn't—she requested the most popular song of the year, "Le Freak" by Chic and started grooving on the dancefloor with the rest of the party.

I sulked quietly in a chair off to the side so that I could watch Peter. Everybody, Peter included, was doing the freak: bending their knees and swaying back and forth.

Peter caught my glance from across the room and ran over to me. "Come on, Lindsay. Didn't Virginia teach you the freak?" Peter said, breathless and all dimples.

He caught me off guard. He had *never* asked me to dance before. "I can't do it," I mumbled, stuffing potato chips in my mouth. My palms were sweaty and greasy—I tried to wipe them off on my jeans.

He leaned over and said in my ear, "I don't want to dance with no one else."

I broke out in goosebumps. Well, how could I refuse that?

I peeked at the dance floor. Everyone *did* look like they were having a great time. Even my mom was showing off in one of the groups. She was doing the Mom thing, staying planted in one place with her arms raised in the air, every once in a while snapping her fingers and shouting, "Woo woo!"

"Come on," he said, pulling me out of my seat.

A crowd cleared out a space for us. This was exactly what I was afraid of—too much attention. I tried to follow Peter and Virginia's lead. I felt sweat sliding down my back, but I think I was blending in OK. I hoped.

Toward the end of the song, Peter danced in front of me. He then improvised on the freak with different arm movements, and it was just… cool. I couldn't believe I was dancing with Peter Newport! I didn't want this moment to end.

"Uh, yeah. Go 'head," Virginia said, from another corner.

Nussia moved over to us. I didn't want Nussia to see me with Peter. Something inside me clenched. My scalp prickled. I shouldn't have told her anything about him. I should have kept him a secret. But, why would I want to keep this from my best friend?

Nussia put her hand on the small of Peter's back. Peter turned, and in an instant the two of them rose at least seven feet off the ground.

"Wow! Mrs. Fields, do you see that?" exclaimed Lila, a Jamaican girl from around the block.

I couldn't believe it. I stared open mouthed. We had seen Fike levitate themselves and humans on television. We'd seen Nussia levitate the candy on that first day. I mean, that's what the Fike did, and I had come to accept it but not like this. Not now, at my party, with Peter.

We stood under them in a circle. Peter looked a little unsteady as he kept kicking his left foot out like that would balance him. Nussia was above him, and she held him by his forearms. Nussia then let him go, and he bounced on the air. She dipped, and bobbed, almost to the beat of the music. Peter, getting more confident by the moment, strutted in the air.

Everyone was laughing and pointing. Within a few minutes, she had half of my friends off the ground; she didn't need to touch them. I waved to Nussia and kept my hand up. Nussia looked down at me and then away quickly. My arm just stood up in the air, waiting, like a little brown flag with no wind. I pulled it down and lowered my eyes. Maybe no one had noticed.

"You kids are so crazy," Mom said from the dining room. "Nussia, please, please be careful. You be careful with them."

Nussia nodded, still not coming down. The deejay put on another popular record, and soon half of the party was in the air with Nussia.

"Oh, Nussia, this feels so good. You are so cool," Virginia yelled above the music.

As I watched people, I could see that their excitement was about more than the thrill of being up in the air. Something that I had never seen before was happening up there. Some of them had their eyes rolled back in their heads and their bodies alternated between a joyous limpness and then a powerful surge of energy. My airborne classmates had a kind of feverish look about them. It looked like scenes from a documentary on revivals I'd seen on TV. Sometimes, Nussia floated over to them and held their arms, patted their faces and wiped their sweat onto her face. They looked as if they felt safe and protected with her tending to them. Peter freely stroked her surricille, back and forth, it shimmered. Virginia's eyes were now redder than if she was smoking that stuff she wasn't supposed to smoke. It hit me—they were *high*. She was getting them high!

They sure didn't need me. I looked up at Peter, and motioned for him to come down. Peter shrugged his shoulders. I guess that he couldn't get down unless Nussia allowed it.

Although the Secret Service guys were not in the air, they too were mesmerized and caught up in the drug-like atmosphere. I couldn't stand it any longer. I moved through the crowd, mostly adults that were left on the ground and went to my room. No one stopped me.

Virginia found me later as I finished wiping my tears away.

"Mom asked me to find you. People are still here, you know."

Her eyes were still glassy and her face looked softer. She pulled the chair out from our desk and plopped down on it.

"It wasn't any fun watching everyone else have a good time," I said, my throat raw.

Virginia sighed, leaned back in the chair and looked at her fingernails.

"I can't believe you're in here feeling sorry for yourself," she scolded.

"Nussia just ignored me. You did see it, didn't you?"

Virginia tutted and shook her head. "You're being such a spoiled brat. Nussia was doing all that for you! Don't you see that? She made your party! Your party was the best."

I felt slapped. She sure didn't see things the way I did. What was Nussia doing to my sister to make her act this way?

My fists clenched. "I'm not going back out there," I said, hitting the bed.

"Suit yourself! Stay in here and rot for all I care. You're acting like you're ten instead of fourteen anyway!" she said, getting up and slamming the door.

After the birthday party, I called Grandma and she came and got me for the weekend. (When she wasn't staying with us, she visited with old friends in the city.) She assured me that everything would be fine with Nussia, that maybe she was being a bit rebellious and that I should try to get to know her. Try to find common interests, she had said. I thought it good advice.

The day after I returned, while my parents slept, I went out to sit on the porch. Nussia joined me. A bowl full of peaches and nectarines sat in my lap. Nussia took a peach and moved it across her surricille, seeming to enjoy the soft fuzz. Her retractable mouth took small bites from the peach. I tried to ignore her. But I still found her eyes absorbing, and I still wanted her to like me.

"Nice feeling," she said.

I nodded. Our block was quiet. Bits of gray and red firecrackers, pre Memorial Day celebrations dappled the black tar.

After sitting in silence for a while I blurted out,

"Do Fike girls get a period?"

"We don't have vaginas like human females do," she replied without the barest trace of embarrassment.

I laughed nervously. "You should be thankful for that fact. Periods can be so nasty and sticky. They're a pain. Dad says that Mom gets evil when she has her 'friend.' I think *that's* why they have separate bedrooms."

It was Nussia's turn to laugh. Then she said, "During the Awakening we have what humans would call convulsions. We can wander around ill for days if someone is not there to guide us. The elders must give us our new name. They must help us remove the old surricille, and care for our newly exposed head. My father said that my mother suffered during her Awakening. But the Awakening only happens once in our lives and it's not, as you say, sticky."

"Nussia, what you said before, about your sister and the Awakening..."

"Let's not talk of it. There's a saying on my planet that when one speaks out of turn, the mountains frown." She put her hand over mine, her hand feeling of comforting worn leather.

"Tell me more about periods."

She stared at me so I blabbed on. "Susan, a girl in my class got her period when she wasn't expecting it. The stain got all over her dress. She tried to play it off like she sat in some Pepsi. My period is not real regular yet. I get bad cramps. Grandma says my body hasn't 'settled' yet."

"Does Peter know about your periods?"

"No." I squirmed a bit. "Boys and girls don't talk about stuff like that. Earth boys are always saying stupid stuff about periods."

"Oh." Casually examining another peach, she said, "Next time you are with your period and feel bad, I could bring you up in the air. It might make your time go better."

"Oh, really, Nussia? Really?" I got so excited I sprang up and did a little dance around the porch. "I'd be so happy if you would."

In that moment, she made me forget everything that came before. I thought maybe that we could be friends after all. She had just needed time to warm up to me.

Two Fike representatives visited to socialize with Nussia. Mom used it as an excuse to host a formal gathering for friends and local officials. Before they arrived, my mother frantically ran around the house asking if Virginia or I had seen her favorite scarf. "I've looked everywhere!" We hadn't. Then she turned, slapped her forehead and said, "Oh, I bet Ma borrowed it without telling me. She's always doing that." She shook her head and raced off to check on last minute details. After smiling and faking the answer that Nussia and were getting along great I excused myself to get a glass of juice and headed for the kitchen. The door leading to the basement was unlocked. I entered, sure I had slipped away unnoticed. Now that I was down here, I decided to do a little exploring. My curiosity and boredom lead me underneath the stairwell to the floatbed.

Hearing my mother's constant refrain in my head, "Don't mess anything up", I carefully opened the dome of the floatbed and with some effort climbed in. It was heated and made me immediately feel sleepy. I imagined what it would be like to sleep without pillows, slowly floating up and down the whole night. Fike go into a mini-hibernation each night; they sleep deeply.

I suddenly heard noises from upstairs and panicked. I would get in so much trouble if anyone found me in her bed.

They were already coming down the stairs. Who could it be? Mom looking for something from the freezer? No, the meal was catered. Dad? Mean Grits? No, I ruled him and the other Secret Service agents out as they rarely came inside the house anymore.

They stopped at the second set of stairs leading down to the basement.

I crouched, frozen, in the tank.

"Here, here… there are probably no wires here." I recognized Nussia's slightly grumpy voice. The other belonged to one of the visiting Fike, a high ranking diplomat.

"Practice English?" Nussia said.

"It is terrible in my ears," another voice, also Fike said.

"I have to hear it every day," Nussia said then paused. "Humans like levitation. Much."

"We know."

"Jerrgil, they like it more than anything else. It makes them feel like a drug… No, like they have been drugged. Better than you thought," Nussia said.

"What else?"

"My monunis gives me power here. Different. Not like on home."

There was a pause. "We have no other reports of this power. Continue to monitor. Your father does not need to know. Other Fike representatives do not need to know. Your sacrifice is so great akesshhhh-No more English. I part with practice."

Then all I heard were the sizzle sounds. No one had offered to teach me any of the Fike languages and I regretted that now. They talked for another five minutes and went back upstairs. I stayed perfectly still, wondering more and more about Nussia.

We were due to be interviewed on *Sixty Minutes* in less than an hour. This was our big exclusive TV debut.

Thank goodness, Mom had packed an additional shirt for me as the one I wore now smelled funky and you could see a ring of sweat stains. I could barely concentrate as I was so stressed about being interviewed on TV without anyone else there besides Nussia. I kept repeating the words ice cream and butter pecan to myself. They had refused to send the questions to my parents, so my father made us practice the kinds of questions the interviewers might ask us. I soaked my T-shirt on every round.

The makeup woman was dabbing foundation on Nussia and even dusted some powder across her bald head, which made Nussia frown.

The assistant producer, a young white man with strawberry blonde hair, walked in and reminded us that we were up in less than an hour. "You both look great!" he said and made the OK symbol with his fingers.

Nussia was more talkative today and I carried on our conversation that began on our ride over to the studio.

"Does Mean… I mean Mr. Johnson ask you questions?" I almost referred to the head Secret Service agent by my private nickname for him.

"No, he never says anything."

The staff had set up a snack table for us and I got up and grabbed a soda.

"Where do you go?"

"It's what your people call top secret," she said. She paused and smiled, "But it is nothing so fun, Lindsay. I would rather be at home. I am mostly meeting with core diplomats—many are considered elders on Fike."

Nussia made herself a plate of fruit and cheese.

"Do you tell them about us?"

She smiled, dipped her head. "They let me know what is going on back at Fike."

The alien girl struggled with eating strawberries. In a moment, three fell down her front and left stains on her white and gold tunic.

"Oh no," I said. She responded in kind with an angry sounding unpronounceable Fike word.

"You might be able to get it out quick, if you go to the bathroom and run it under water," I said. She nodded and headed for the bathroom.

"I'll get the wardrobe person," I said.

Before I went to get to find the wardrobe person, I thought I should check both of our duffle bags for other clothes that Nussia could wear. I ruffled through my bag reminding myself of what my mother packed. I hastily pulled out a peach ruffled shirt—probably too small for Nussia and also a blue cotton dress that might work. I looked in Nussia's bag, too, and discovered a white skirt and two pairs of sandals. A flash of color caught my eye from one half-zipped inner pockets of the bag. I pulled out my mother's scarf that she had been looking for a few weeks ago.

Nussia entered looking frazzled. The stain hadn't come out and her tunic was wet.

I held up the scarf, "Did Mom give you this to you?"

Nussia looked away and pushed past me, "I need help getting this stain out, Lindsay."

"This is her favorite scarf. What is it doing in your bag?" I could feel the color rising in my cheeks.

Just then, the assistant producer entered, a clip chart in his hand. "Ladies, fifteen minutes," he said. Then taking one glance at Nussia's outfit, he barked, "Christ, we've got to get you into some new clothes. Come with me."

"Yes, thank you," Nussia said.

She left me there holding my mother's scarf. I wasn't thinking about ice cream or the interview anymore.

Despite everything the interview went well for both of us. Nussia refused to talk about the scarf or anything except the interview during the ride home. When we got home, I caught Virginia, in our bathroom, while she was getting ready for a date. She asked about the interview and I told her about the scarf.

She shrugged. "If Mom didn't give it to her that's wrong. But, we don't know that, do we?"

"I don't think she did," I said.

"But, maybe taking things that don't belong to you is different for Fike. I don't remember reading much about their moral code."

I watched her apply several coats of mascara. She looked great. She wore a black blouse and black pants that were all the rage. The pants looked like exaggerated bell-bottoms and when Virginia stood with her legs close together, it looked like she was wearing a long skirt or dress.

"Will you talk to Mom about it?" I asked.

"Sure," she said. "We'll keep an eye out for anything else that goes missing."

"Yes. Glad you have my back."

"Always."

I noticed something was happening between my parents. Sure, they had always had separate bedrooms, ate their meals at different hours, and had different friends. And that *hadn't* changed. But Nussia had somehow inserted herself in the natural rhythms of my father's life: he now ate with her, and even talked with her in the monuni shrine. When she first came, Nussia asked my father to expand the shrine in the backyard, which he happily did. They spent much of their time there. Their laughing voices often carried all the way to the front porch. I'm sure he even asked her for gambling tips.

One evening I heard laughter coming from my father's bedroom. I opened the door. My mother sat in a chair holding an almost empty glass of red wine against her face. I looked up and saw Nussia and my father floating up at the very edge of the ceiling in the far right corner, to the left of the light fixture. They smiled and held on to each other's hands. They were higher in the air than people were at my party. Their positions were also more horizontal than what I had seen at the party; they really looked as if they rested on air.

"Hey, Nussia, take me up. I really want to go flying. I know what you said before, but I can't wait. Now seems like it would be so fun," I said.

"Forget it," Mom said. "She won't bring me up there either, Lindsay."

Her eyes stared straight past me. Nussia and my father ignored both of us.

The way that Nussia was playing with my father suddenly made me very angry. I wanted her to either stop this game, or bring my mother and me up into the air. Nussia and my father continued to ignore us. There was a sound coming out of his mouth; it was a sound that I hadn't heard from him in a long while. I realized that it was pure laughter.

My father pointed to a corner.

"Look, here's a big old spider web. It doesn't have a spider in it, though," he said to no one in particular. He laughed again.

"Curl up in a ball, Rodger," Nussia coaxed.

Immediately he pulled his body together tightly. Then just as quick he stretched out of it. He stretched his arms and legs as far out from his center as they would go.

"This… being up on the air. It's like being held by someone who loves you. It's magic."

No, it's a drug, I thought to myself. Nussia had a drug like no other.

My mother held her glass up to them in a mock toast, downed the rest of her wine, and walked out of the room. I followed her, slamming the door.

I went looking for Nussia the next day and I found her tending the shrine of monunis in the back yard. She went out every day after dinner and spent some time with them.

The shrine was decorated with stargazers and purple and pink zinnias. My grandmother had planted her favorite shrub, gardenias, around the borders of the shrine. On closer inspection the monunis were hard yellow and purplish spheres, about the size of kiwis, and they were arranged along the back of the lean to.

I stood away at a distance until I saw that she was finished.

"Hi," I said. "I wanted to, uh, talk with you. I haven't been able to see very much of you recently. You and Virginia have just been doing so many things together. Anyway, I'm still very happy that you're here. But," I continued with a nervous laugh, "I feel, Nussia, that something's not right with us."

"My sister wanted to come here, not me," Nussia said quickly.

"What do you mean? Will you please just tell me about your sister?" My anger spilled out so fast that I accidentally bit my tongue.

"You really don't *know* about me, Lindsay." She pressed her green palms against my chest, pushing me back forcefully, causing me to fall down flat on my behind.

"Owww! What's wrong with you? Why'd you do that?"

"My parents sent me to Earth. I was told to go. My sister, Lillandra was supposed to be here," she said, pointing to the house.

I got up and brushed the dirt off me. "No one told me anything about your sister, you have to believe me."

She looked away from me, her voice dropping to almost a whisper, "My sister is beautiful, by Fike standards, and is what humans call charming, and we call meenill. She became very ill and she could not come here. In her condition, Lillandra would not have survived the trip."

I was stunned by this revelation. No, not only stunned. I didn't want to hear it.

"But you're here now. You're here—that's what matters. We're friends. It will be all right," I said and reached for her hand.

She backed away from me. "You remind me of my sister. She talked endlessly about having a lulla, a human friend. But I'm not like her. I'm not like you, either. I've always been different."

"I'm different *too*, not everybody wanted an alien," I said. I could hear the whininess and the desperation in my voice. I felt my neck and ears flush red. I looked at the ground.

"'Humans are not hard to deal with,' my mother said." Nussia mocked. "My father, the diplomat, pushed and pushed to get me to come, though he could have sent many other Fike my age."

"So now I'm stuck here. Stuck, stuck, stuck. You brought me here, Lindsay! It was your *essay* and your *needs*. I will miss all the preparations and training for the Awakening. I might never be Awakened now, and my parents don't care."

"I don't believe that," I said, shaking my head. I couldn't imagine her parents doing this to her, making her give up everything. "Please, don't be mad at me, Nussia. I didn't know any of what was going on behind the scenes. I wouldn't have—"

"Tell me, what can I go back to?" Nussia said and stomped her foot. "I'm not one of you. I'm on my own here. Do you understand? I can't be fully Fike anymore. I'm a sacrifice. I don't care about the Awakening now! I hate my parents for sending me. This garden is the only thing I ever want to remind me of home. I have a new family. Virginia and Rodger are the best things about this place."

My brain felt fried trying to understand all that she was sharing with me.

She turned her back to me and walked toward the house. "You've seen how I can do things for them that no one, not even you, can do. My powers through my hands are strong here and I don't know why." She smiled and jutted her chin out, "Even the Elders can't explain it to me. My mother was right about humans being easy to direct, she just didn't go far enough." With a pause Nussia said, "Humans can be controlled."

She couldn't mean that. A numbness spread from the center of my belly outward. Deep inside, I felt a piece of myself falling away.

I grasped Nussia's hands, looking at her deeply, directly into those dark eyes. "Is there someone else on Fike that might take care of you? I have my Grandma and if anything happened to my parents, I'd stay with her. Do you have someone else besides your parents? Let me help you. Let's try to figure this out together?" I asked, my voice cracking some.

She twisted away from me. "No, and I don't want to see my family again."

"You're still special to me." Though I said the words out loud, they felt hollow inside of me.

"I don't need you to have myself," she said pushing past me.

After I had the argument with Nussia I decided to look over my essay. I was shaken and had forgotten why I had even wanted Nussia to stay in this home. My eyes caught this passage:

There is something in each of us that makes us special. It is not the obvious things. For my grandmother, it is her sense of adventure. For my mother, it is her cooking. For me, I have a burning desire to connect with something larger than humanity. "Alien" is a relative term. My neighbors are Jamaicans, and some people in my neighborhood think they are aliens. When we can see that what is alien is something that is also in us, then we can live without fear of the word. When the word "alien" can mean friend in all languages, even those yet to be discovered, we will have made something new.

After reading that I knew what I had to do.

"Absolutely not!" my father shouted. My parents were uncharacteristically enjoying a night together in Mom's bedroom. The television blared a chase scene from *Starsky and Hutch.*

"Send her home, Dad. She is unhappy and doesn't *belong* here. Can't any of you see that? Mom?"

"If Nussia was as unhappy as you think, she'd come to us."

"No, she wouldn't, Mom. She's told me some things."

"Speak up, Lindsay. Now, just what did she tell you?" Dad asked.

I didn't want to tell what an awful conversation I had with her. Maybe I wanted to protect her. I could see now that she hadn't come of her own free will. I hedged a little.

"Just that..."

"If she leaves now, what will people think of us?" my mother interrupted. "She's just a little homesick. And besides you and Nussia are scheduled to go to the White House, an event it has taken months to plan for. How would that look if she didn't show up?"

"Do you know what being Lindsay Fields *means* now?" my father asked, rising up out of his seat.

I shook my head. Right then I wasn't sure anymore what Lindsay Fields even thought.

He stood up shaking his finger at me. "It means that the whole world knows you, Lindsay! It means that the whole world is open to you! It means that someday you'll be able to go to any college or university you desire. That includes Virginia, too. *Anywhere.* Anywhere at all. It means a goddamn shortcut in a world that doesn't want to give us anything."

"But, Dad, I didn't write the essay for future plans." My parents always talked about college and my future at the most inconvenient times.

"Lindsay, *I* would know if she's unhappy." His words rang with finality.

"Would you, Rodger?" Mom's face hardened.

They excused me from the room. As I walked down the hall I could hear Mom crying, her voice indistinguishable sobs.

It was a broiling, humid August day. I had to go to the store because I had started my period, and I had only two maxi pads left. Mom sent Nussia with me.

"I need some paprika, butter, and some frozen spinach. It would be real sweet if you could pick those up for me while you're out. I've got to run to an early meeting at work soon," she said. "Come right back, you two."

"Yeah, Mom."

She called after us again when we got to the porch. Stuffing more money in my hands, she said, "Get some orange juice, too."

It was going to be a long fifteen minute walk each way. Nussia and I hadn't talked in days. We walked in silence, with the Secret Service men following in their car behind us. We could have taken a ride with them, but I didn't want to. When we reached the block of stores, I left Nussia outside next to the discount meat market while I went into the supermarket.

She stood, fascinated, by the legs of lamb, pig ears, and the fat burgundy cubes of goat meat displayed for sale in the window.

On the way out of the store I saw Peter and his older brother Jake sitting on the hood of Jake's car. Peter wore shorts showing off his freckled legs.

"Hey girl. We just came from playing ball. We saw Nussia and stopped," Peter said.

"Get in." Jake said. "I'll give you a lift home. Can't be walking in this heat."

"That'll be great," I said. My stomach was feeling queasy because of my cramps. I ran over to the Secret Service car and told them I was getting a ride from my friends. Over the last few months, they had worked through our list of family friends and acquaintances, clearing almost all of them. Mean Grits had sunglasses on and gave me a lazy nod.

I walked back over and clutched the grocery bag closer to my chest.

"What'd you get from the store?" Peter asked.

"Just stuff," I said.

"Oh yeah? What kind of stuff?" Peter playfully grabbed at the bag.

"Stuff," Nussia repeated from behind me. Before I knew it the bag flew out of my hands and rose over my head.

"Don't, Nussia!" I pleaded, but Nussia ignored me and kept them levitating in midair.

"Cool," Jake said. He sat on the hood of his car.

"How long can you keep things up in the air?" he asked.

"For a long time," Nussia replied.

I screamed, "Stop it!"

Most of the contents of the bags dropped to the ground in one heap. The white and blue maxi pad box, however, hovered and then opened. The contents flew out of the box. The maxi pads fluttered in the air. They twitched and flapped like white mythic birds.

Nussia, Jake and Peter laughed. Peter laughed so hard he held his stomach and slid off the car's hood.

I ran until I could not hear Nussia's laugh, like a slap across my face, anymore.

From my mother's room, I heard drawers close. I inched closer to the door, which was cracked open. I hadn't come out of my room for almost a day. Finally, my grandmother had arrived.

"Ma, Lindsay has always been a fanciful child. God knows she's the one that brought Nussia here."

"Fanciful my ass, Jesse. She called me up hysterical last night—while *you* were at work, of course. Something is just plain wrong about that *thing* living in this house."

How could Mom say that about me? I knew she had been under a lot of stress lately and very busy, but couldn't she see how wrong things were between me and Nussia?

"How would it look to everyone? She's just different. That's what aliens are."

"Everyone? Who the hell is everyone? Your daughter—my granddaughter—is very upset. I don't care if Walter Cronkite calls us a pack of raving backward ass niggers! That alien needs to go back where she came from. Look at you. You're a mess."

"What do you want me to do? Call it all off? Say that we can't deal with this—that *our* family can't deal? Nussia is not the problem. *Lindsay* is."

"Do you hear yourself, Jesse? When did keeping up appearances become more important than listening to your daughter?"

"You have no right to tell me how to deal with my children."

"Look, I can call a spade a spade. Maybe we were all a bit too hasty about this arrangement," Grandma said.

More drawers slammed.

"Jesse, I'm an old woman and I'm tired. If anything happens to my granddaughter... If I get one more hysterical phone call while I'm over at Maggie's house, I will personally ship that little tyrant back up to her planet my goddamn self."

"Ma, I've got to finish getting ready for work. I'm on an early shift!"

"You think about what I said. I'll take Lindsay with me to France if this mess keeps up. She needs to feel loved. Safe," Grandma said.

I moved stealthily down the hall and then back to my room. I heard the basement door close.

Good, I thought. I hoped Nussia heard every word. My grandmother was no one to mess around with—ever.

In my bedroom, I tried reading a book, but quickly put it down. I couldn't focus. I couldn't stop replaying Mom's words over and over again. Feeling her words pound in my head made me want to shrink away into nothingness.

After my mother left for work, Grandma called me downstairs for dinner. Virginia and Nussia were nowhere to be found. Virginia was probably out with friends. I tried Nussia's basement door but it was locked and the key was not on its hook.

"I'm going to talk with Nussia before I leave tomorrow morning."

"Good, Grandma," I said.

"If that doesn't help Nussia get her act together, we'll have to figure out another way. Don't you worry, sweetie."

She got up to get dinner from the kitchen.

Nussia walked into the dining room. I felt her dark eyes sweep over me, but I just looked down at the table. I didn't want to be alone with her. I didn't want *anything* to do with her.

"Now, this isn't my recipe for liver and onions, but it will have—" Grandma began as she came through the kitchen door.

"May I have some dinner?" Nussia interrupted. She sat in the chair next to me.

Grandma rolled her eyes. "Nussia, we called for you." She placed the two dishes on the table.

"I'm sorry. I was outside."

Grandma went into the kitchen and brought out another placemat and plate of food.

"I want to talk with you, now, tonight. We need to talk about you and Lindsay."

I watched out the corner of my eye as Nussia nodded.

"Nussia," she said and began coughing.

She wiped the back of her mouth.

"I want to talk about your conduct regarding my granddaughter. Do you understand me?"

"You want to send me home."

Grandma sat down at the table and shook her head. She took a bite of the liver. After a pause Grandma said, "Nussia, your actions have been unexpl-"

"Yes, unexplainable. Grandma." Nussia dragged the edge of the knife back and forth across the edge of the plate.

"Stop that!" Suddenly my grandmother stopped talking and started coughing hard. I was on the edge of my seat, warily looking back and forth at the two of them. Nussia just stared ahead calmly.

"Grandma?" I got up from the table. "Do you need some water?"

She waved her hand at me. "Not now child. I'm fine. I've just got some sort of tickle in my throat." Authoritatively she cleared her throat and resumed, "We've all been patient in waiting for you to adjust to this home—*Lindsay's* home."

Abruptly, Grandma started gagging and coughing. I'd never heard coughs like that before—it was like something was rattling around in her chest and throat. She started shaking, her face becoming blue-tinged and panicked.

"Grandma!"

I jumped from my seat and ran to the kitchen, frantically pouring tap water into a glass. I ran back almost spilling it.

But as soon as I crossed the threshold into the dining room, Nussia's power lifted me up into the air. I started screaming. I kicked and fought, tumbling in the air—all I could see was my Grandma collapsing on the dining room floor.

The air held me tight and pressed into my back, it burned against my body. Her hold on me gave me the feeling of being smothered in a hot bubble. With all my might, I threw the glass, aiming for Nussia. But, with another wave of her hand she averted it. The glass hit a spider plant on a nearby table before shattering against the wall.

"Stop fighting me, Lindsay," Nussia said, calmly.

Slowly, my limbs started tingling. It was as if all my limbs had gone to sleep at the same time, but then were being wakened quickly. All my fears were draining out of me, and being replaced with a sweet numbness centered at my core and spreading outward like a spiral of warmth and calm. I watched my grandmother as her tongue lolled out of her mouth a mottled brownish red. This sweet numbness located itself in my tongue. I could not resist. I sucked that sweetness even as I watched my grandmother's eyes bulge.

I screamed with all my heart, pushing against the numbness, kicking listlessly at the air, but it was no use. The overpowering sweetness moved across my neck and shoulders making my head loll from side to side. I couldn't resist any longer as the feeling invaded my newly forming breasts, underarms, torso, privates and legs. *Everywhere.* I was defeated.

Grandma coughed one last, horrible rattling breath. With one hand, she grabbed the back of the seat. The other hand pulled off her scarf. Her eyes rolled up in her head and then she stopped moving.

Nussia dropped me hard. I landed on my butt. The sweet numbness died away. My whole body trembled. Silence pervaded the house. Taking advantage of my slowness and fear, Nussia ran to the basement door and locked herself in.

I picked up my grandmother's hand. It felt rubbery and cool. Her ginger colored complexion was turning a subtle gray. I had to get help. Hysterical, I ran over to Mr. and Mrs. Willacy's house, sobbing, willing away the tingling that still resonated in my body.

"Mommy, you've got to believe me. Nussia did it!" I cried over and over to my parents. There was no real reason for them to understand. Everyone wanted this whole thing to work. I had wanted it to work more than anyone else. I thought that she would save my family and me.

"Girl, you've got to pull yourself together. Do you hear me, champ?" my father said, holding me. "Your grandmother choked on a piece of her food while having a stroke. What you saw was probably awful. However, there's no need to blame Nussia. You've got to be strong for the family."

My room was crowded. My parents were there, Mean Grits, Secret Service agents and a man named Dr. Richards that said he was called in to assist. I didn't know where Virginia was.

"Lindsay, now you know that what you are telling us is preposterous. Don't you?" Mean Grits stood over my bed with a tight face. "Do you really think we would let a violent, unruly alien child stay with you?" He turned to my parents and put his hand on my mother's shoulder. "I know that this is a time of trauma, but the Fike have never displayed any significantly violent behavior toward humans. Never."

"Where were you?" I screamed. "Why didn't you stop her?"

"She's in shock. Death is a difficult experience for anyone to undergo. Kids will look to other things to validate or understand what is happening," the government doctor said casually, preparing a syringe intended for me.

I caught him by surprise as I slapped the needle from his hand.

"You're not the family doctor, where's Mr. Connelly?" I hollered.

"Lindsay! Have you lost your mind?!" my father said.

Mom said through her tears, "Baby, this is a special doctor just for you."

"We are going to have to hold her down if this behavior keeps up," the doctor said.

"Is that what you want, Lindsay?" My father said.

I couldn't stop myself from crying long enough to get words out. My throat hurt and though there were no burns on my body, my skin felt hot to the touch and as if I had been rubbed with a giant loofah sponge.

"Grandma tried to tell you, Mom," I said clutching at her hand.

The doctor signaled to one of the other Secret Service men and before I knew what happened they pinned me, putting the needle in my arm.

Turning to my father, Mom said, "We've got to see what Nussia says. Rodger do you hear me? Suppose Lindsay..."

"Yes, in the morning, we'll talk to Nussia," the Secret Service man interrupted. "By then Lindsay will be able to remember what happened to her grandmother. She will see things clearly."

My mother rolled her eyes and looked away.

"Being in the air with her, it's not like being held by someone who loves you at all, Dad," I said as he was leaving the room. He did not turn around to answer.

I needed to get up and warn my family, protect them. Nussia's powers were much more developed than anyone knew. Would she kill us all in the middle of the night? I had to stop her! My stomach felt like a rock and I felt feverish. I shook in agony and frustration, but then everything went fuzzy and gray and blank. A different kind of numbness settled over me.

I woke up in the middle of the night, disoriented and scared. Then, I remembered what had happened to my family. My body was wobbly, but my heart was clear. I tried to run through everything that had happened on this horrible afternoon in my head. Where were the security people while that *thing* was killing Grandma? They must have been at their headquarters, or taking a food break. Maybe Nussia had done something to them and that's why they weren't around earlier, I thought soberly.

I knew what I had to do to make things right. Quietly, I slipped from my room and gathered the things that I needed for my task from around the house in the darkness. I crept downstairs and tried the doorknob to the basement, grateful when it opened without protest. I made as little sound as I could pulling the door open. I paused once on the other side and then gently locked the basement door behind me.

"All in due time" are the words that I heard when I stood next to Nussia's floatbed. Nussia was perfectly still, asleep. Her body levitated a few inches from the bottom of the floatbed. Every few seconds the top of her surricille gently bumped the top of the tank, and then she'd float down again. I quietly opened the top.

I waited until she floated back to the top of the tank. When she reached me, I carefully grabbed one her right hand and put one of my mother's gardening gloves on. Touching her made my stomach queasy. While I had her hand, I took the strips of masking tape that I had pulled off and left at the end of the tank and wound them around her gloved hand. I held her right shoulder and reached across to get the other glove on her hand and taped it, too. I released her and she floated to the bottom of the tank, thankful for the depth of her sleep. I knew she would hover for at least a minute before floating up again.

The next part was going to be much harder. My father had long ago stopped working out at home. He had abandoned the cast iron plates to the back of a closet in the living room. I couldn't lift his twenty-five pound plates, so I settled for carrying two ten pound plates. Breathing heavily, I put the first plate on her forearm. Her body tilted sideways. I got the other weight into place on her other side, pinning her how I wanted, so that when she woke up, she wouldn't be able to use her hands—at least for a few minutes. Next came the shears. I stabbed at her surricille, sloppily making two large gashes. Then I used my hands, tearing pieces of it back—it was soft under my fingers, and gave way easier than I expected. I had never touched or rubbed Nussia's surricille before. She didn't deserve to be Awakened. She didn't deserve my family. She didn't deserve to *live*. Nussia's eyes flew open and her tubular mouth stiffened. She was screaming now, writhing on the bottom of her float bed in pain. Her screams weren't at all like the sizzle of her normal voice—this was a jumble of ancient alien sounds merged into an overpowering eruption of emotion.

The sedative had made me weak—weaker than I should have been for a task like this. She twisted violently and when my hold was broken Nussia shot up through the floatbed with the force of three people and physically threw me back against the basement wall.

Dazed and hurting all over, I tried to get up but the room was spinning and all I managed to do was lay on my side. I touched the back of my head and my fingers can back slick with blood.

"I'm not going back! This family is mine! Not even the Elders can make me stop." Blood flowed down from the angry-looking wound, streaming down over her lips and chin. She stood upright in the now levitated tank.

"No! You'll never be a part of this family. You're a murderer!"

"They need me. Your father needs me. All humans need me, they *want* me." Her retractable mouth snapped open and closed over and over.

"You're drugging them or doing something. But soon they will figure it out or it will wear off or something," I shot back.

"Will they?" Nussia said, as her eyes crinkled and a hideous smile crept across her face. She bit at one of her restraints.

"You've done terrible things, Nussia." I wanted her to stay focused on me and not the bag that I needed to get to.

"No one knows what I want. The Elders think they can control me," she shook her head from side to side. "They can't. They want me to spy and report to them, but here I will do what I want. They wanted me to be an experiment—well, I will be one that no one ever forgets!"

In the distance I heard a ferocious banging on the door, and Dad and Virginia's voices.

Her dark eyes pierced me. The strips of blue tape floated down from one of the gloves.

With my breathing coming in shallow gulps and my back in pain I got up and used my last bit of strength to reach the bag laying on the float bed's platform. I dumped the monunis on the floor and stomped on them. Many of them cracked easily under my feet.

"No more ways to hurt us!"

Nussia was pulling off the gloves.

Nussia gaped at me in shock and horror, throwing her power at the monunis that weren't crushed, levitating them into the air. I snatched at them but they were already above my head.

"You stupid human child," she spat.

"I don't need you. Not now. Not ever," I said.

"I know."

These were the last words I remember before I started to choke, and entered darkness.

Nussia. I said her name like mine. It is a nightmare, which has come to pass.

The doctors say that I suffer from debilitating paranoia and extreme depression. The room I'm in is large with a TV and paintings of bright yellow flowers. It has a desk and a small couch. The door is always locked except when I get to go outside which is twice a day. Most days I don't want to walk, but stare out of the window. The doctors say I'm in a special kind of hospital, but as far as I can tell, I'm the only one on this part of the floor. When I recovered from the concussion, my father decided that I needed some time away from the family. He told me that even if everything that I claimed about Nussia were true, it was still not a good enough reason to hurt her. He said I should have come to them. On TV, I saw him telling the press that there had been an "adolescent disagreement" between Nussia and me. I haven't seen my family in a long time and have been given no way to contact them.

No one knows where Nussia is. The night that I attacked her, she ran out of the house before my father could restrain her. Mean Grits and his team slipped up on their job. From the TV I learn that The Fike are upset and the President believes that diplomatic relations are strained. The National Guard had been called in to New York City to try to find her. Lynne, my private nurse, updates me. She's a slender, red-headed black woman. She thinks I have set back civil rights by 100 years and tells me so daily.

Everyone thinks that I fucked up. That I'm the ugly, unpredictably violent American from the Bronx. *Click*. They don't know Nussia like I do. Anchormen say that I am a maladjusted and jealous young girl. When the camera zooms into the average person on the street and a news reporter asks for an opinion, they say things like, "What do you expect? That's the way they are. They can't control their own, let alone an alien. Choosing that family was a mistake."

When I try to sleep, I hear Nussia's sizzle sounding laugh and wake up screaming.

Lynne brings my breakfast in and says with a triumphant smile, "They've found her."

"Alive?" I ask, hoping for the opposite.

"Yes, and you're the luckier for it," she says.

She turns on the TV. She keeps the remote with her and when I don't take my medicine, she takes it away. Watching TV is the only way I have to keep track of the days.

"She's such a trooper. Twelve-hour surgery with intergalactic communication from the Fike. A miracle," Lynn chirps, handing me a cup of orange juice.

I drink my juice and say nothing as I watch Nussia on the screen.

The news clip shows Nussia looking peaceful with her head bandaged.

"... extensive surgery on her surricille. But the real question is whether Nussia, our brave visitor from another planet, will be allowed to return to the Fields' home," an anchorman declared.

The next news clip shows how in wake of all these problems three families are fighting to host Nussia. None of the children or the families had entered the original contest. The families describe themselves as "concerned citizens." One little white girl named Susan Raffety from New Hampshire says in a cultivated voice, "I've always wanted my own alien." Her father, a slim gray haired man adds, "Yes, Nussia could ride horses here, swim… they do swim, don't they?" he questions his daughter. She nods affirmatively. "Yes, Nussia could enjoy the fresh country air." Aiming right for the camera and America's heart, Mr. Raffety says, "Should we let this family have another chance given the unusual circumstances that have surrounded Nussia?"

Lynne boos at this.

Then it cuts to Dad. My throat tightens.

Standing erect and with lips tight, he stands on the front porch of our house pointing his finger declaring, "I will fight any family that tries to take Nussia away from this family. I will fight them all the way to the Supreme Court!" Men in black suits that the anchorperson identifies as Dad's legal team stand next to him. Mom and Virginia stand behind my father. Virginia looks tired, dark rings bordered her eyes. Her hair has lost its sheen and her face looks older. I wonder if she misses me, or if Nussia's effect on her (and my father) is still strong. Is it chemical? Does it work long distance? My mother is stiff with glazed-over eyes. Is she so deeply ashamed of the way things worked out that she drinks herself to sleep? I miss her the most. Sometimes I dream that I lie in bed next to her and that she smells of Charlie perfume and peaches.

"There is no reason why we can't provide a loving home for the rest of the time that Nussia remains on Earth," Dad drones on. "We need to keep Nussia with people that she knows, at least until she recovers. Anything else will be traumatic for her. Our daughter Lindsay has been under a lot of stress following the death of her grandmother. We've only recently learned how unstable and ill she actually is. She's being treated by the best doctors available and will return to us as soon as she has made a full recovery."

The news segment jumps quickly back to Nussia, who says she wants to stay with my family when she leaves the hospital.

I watch her carefully. Her dark eyes are alien and dangerous, yet familiar.

"This opportunity for myself and my people I will never let go," Nussia says.

When I wrote the essay I hadn't realized that my understanding about aliens should have worked both ways. Nussia made me see that I should have written, "When we can see that what is human is also sometimes what is alien, then we can begin to understand ourselves and them. All the good and the bad."

One never knows what they might desire, until they are here with you, breathing the same air, sharing your family, and your life. No one knows it about Nussia but me.

Lindsay. I say my own name for myself.

Inspirations and Influences

MICHELE TRACY BERGER

AN AFRICAN AMERICAN GIRL "WINS" an alien in the 1970s who comes to live with her family. What could possibly go wrong? I like to think of the tagline for this story as *E.T.* meets *Fatal Attraction*.

I didn't intentionally set out to write an anti-*E.T.* story. I was probably the same age as the main character, Lindsay when I saw *E.T.*, around twelve or thirteen. Like many, I enjoyed the movie despite its saccharine feel. And, like the speculative fiction media that shaped my early life (e.g. *Lost in Space*, *Bewitched*, *The Bionic Woman*, *Star Wars*, etc.), themes of race and gender as well diversity in casting were habitually absent. So while speculative media served as a fantastic conduit to imagine different realities, it didn't give me the conceptual tools or language to understand the inequities that I experienced as a young black girl that were a feature of my everyday life. On some level, I noted that absence.

At the same time I was absorbing fantasy and sci-fi end when I was young; I was also deeply into horror. My mother was a serious horror fan and I think my younger sister can quote most of Steven King's work. Typical of my generation, I watched and read material that was definitely age inappropriate. I credit my early horror interests in giving me an alternate way of looking at the world, one that is grittier and less idealistic. I've gravitated more toward horror tropes in my writing as they provide a powerful way to dig into the complexities and contradictions of race and gender.

The kernel of this story was inspired many moons ago by the biting, incisive comedy of Paul Mooney. He did a famous bit on racism, sci-fi movies and how some white people would rather embrace an alien living as a neighbor, next door to them, rather than an African American family. His routine challenged me to reflect on the absolute irrational nature of racism and explore that irrationality through storytelling. The structure of *Nussia*allows me to play with the external challenges that the Fields family faces as they host Nussia, and the way each family member responds to that pressure.

I am generally interested in themes of paranoia, obsession, conspiracy theories and the intricacies of race and gender. You'll find many of those themes in *Nussia*. It's also an intimate story in that much of the drama and conflict happens behind closed doors.

Voice and character usually come first for me when writing. Once I had the frame of the story, Lindsay's voice came to me pretty easily. I had a lot of fun remembering what it was like being a thirteen year-old girl and even though I didn't grow up where Lindsay did, I did grow up during that time in the Bronx.

I loved that I got a chance to do some sci-fi world-building in developing the Fike and the challenges Nussia faces as being a representative for her people at such a critical time in her life. The story also combines several interests that recur in my writing: rites of female adolescence, mother and daughter relationships, and female friendships.

Imagining and wrestling with this story helped me, and hopefully my readers, to see some uncommon angles by which we can all deal with the perceived alien differences in ourselves and others.

A Chat With Michele Tracy Berger

***Nussia* came as a submission to our Awakenings call for short stories. Why did you choose to submit this particular story and how do you think it fits the theme?**

Given my good fortune of being published with Book Smugglers last year, I was eager to work with your talented team again. When I saw the call for Awakenings, I immediately thought of my quirky 1980s tale about a young African American girl "winning" an extraterrestrial.

Because the story explores the rites of female adolescence, including first crushes and menstruation, and friendship between a young female alien and a human girl of thirteen I thought the story might work well in the series. Additionally, both Nussia and Lindsay "awaken" into different versions of themselves than what is expected of them at the beginning of the story.

In many ways this is an anti-*E.T.* short story—can you tell us a bit about what inspired you to write *Nussia*? What themes or elements in particular would you like people to keep in mind while reading?

I was interested in exploring the pressure that many people from marginalized communities experience with being "the first" when breaking any societal barrier. There is often an emotional, physical and spiritual cost to being the first in a society with a history of discrimination. I took that idea and wove it into a story where the stakes are very high—an African American family being chosen to host an alien (on a diplomatic mission) as part of diplomatic relations.

Setting the story in the 1980s allows the reader to consider similarities and differences in racial attitudes between then and now as events play out for the Fields family. Lindsay's family comes under a kind of racialized scrutiny that destabilizes family dynamics. In the story, the grandmother's perspective is important as she is able to recognize how the family has internalized the need to appear perfect (because they are "the first") in a way that Lindsay's mother and father can't.

Playing with an iconic *E.T.* model of a friendly alien encounter and turning that upside down was also a lot of fun. I wanted to interrogate the intimate aspects of an alien living with a family, aspects that include jealousy and desire. When Nussia decides she wants a lot more from the family than Lindsay bargains for it makes for a strong conflict. Elements from films *The Bad Seed* and *Single White Female* also shaped the feel of the story.

I also liked delving into the "be careful what you wish for" theme as it almost always often turns out differently than one imagines.

As with your novella *Reenu-You*, *Nussia* combines elements of science fiction, horror, and incisive social commentary—especially with regards to women of color and racism. Can you tell us a bit more about these elements and how they feature in your writing?

That nexus that you described above is the emotional territory that I tend to mine. I've only become aware recently, since the publication of *Reenu-You* that much of my work could be classified as psychological horror or "dark fiction." I am fascinated by how coping with "otherness" shapes the worldview of many of my characters. Lindsay is thirteen and she is beginning to recognize and understand how both race and gender have an impact on her life.

Tell us a bit about your experience writing short stories: what would you say are the advantages and potential pitfalls of writing short fiction versus a novel or novella?

My experience is mostly trying and failing! Short stories don't come easy for me. My tendency is to write long. For years, I didn't think I could write anything under 10,000 words. In the last several years, however, I have studied the craft of short fiction. One of my writing teachers said that writing a short story is like a hosting an exquisite dinner party. It has a well-planned beginning, middle and end. From that I realized that my short stories weren't working because instead of getting the characters out the door, they were sleeping over and having breakfast the next day! My structure didn't fit the format. Precision is everything when crafting a short story. How many lines will you provide a character, in introducing them and giving them lines to speak? Do you need three minor characters? How many subplots can the story hold? Longer form work allows you to entertain many more possibilities. When I started selling stories under 1,000 words, I knew I finally understood the nut and bolts of the short story form well enough to write a credible story.

Finally, a question we ask all of our interviewees: We Book Smugglers have faced condemnation because of the sheer volume of books that we carry back home on a daily basis. As such, we have on occasion resorted to "smuggling books" home to escape judgmental, scrutinizing eyes. Have you ever had to smuggle books?

Absolutely! Since I make my living as a professor, being surrounded by books is normal in my world. It is true, however, that when tote bags full of novels, become conspicuous in my house I will say that I'm reading them "because I might teach them." And since I'm not a literature professor, a new book pile may grow out of the floor as a part of an unspecified "research project." My partner pretends to be none the wiser as he dances around the piles to reach me. I'm afraid he might one day start naming those literary mounds after some of our favorite mountains we've climbed!

The Girl With The Frozen Heart

Y.M. PANG

SHE WAS DYING WHEN THE god of winter found her.

She stumbled through the snowdrift, one hand pressed to her chest. Blood dripped between her fingers, mingling with the heavy white snowflakes. She had snapped off the arrow's shaft, but its tip remained embedded in her heart.

She managed three more steps. Three steps into wind and emptiness. Three steps from the bodies, Vilocet and Casenna alike. Then her legs finally collapsed and she fell forward, one more body in the snow. Her blood pooled around her, marking her grave, if only for a few hours—soon, the snow would bury every trace of her.

Then she heard his voice. A voice like snapping branches and tortured wind. A voice foreign to her, but one she had no trouble placing. She'd seen those wreaths on the doors of the Casenna villages, heard the songs they sang: folk songs, drinking ditties, but most of all, hymns that praised him and begged for his mercy.

"Why did you come this far," the god of winter asked, "for someone who abandoned you?"

The girl drew a ragged breath. Coughed. "She was my mother."

Her tears froze in the wind. She reached forward, clawing for something that was not there.

"Do you want to live?" the god of winter asked.

Yes. Yes.

But the girl was no fool. She knew the old tales of the god of winter. "I don't need anything from you," she gasped.

"But I want you to live."

The truth. For in that moment the god of winter pitied her, this human who travelled so far searching for a mother who never loved her. His pity reined in the snowstorm, quieting the winds just a little.

He descended toward her on wings of ice. Cupped her face in his ancient hands and tried to breathe life back into her. But his breath was cold and only pushed her further into death. He tried to pluck the arrowhead from her chest and close the wound, but her skin shrivelled and blackened at his touch. He was the god of winter, destined to take life and not to give it back.

So he did the only thing he could: he inhaled, then breathed out over her heart. His breath was snow and wind and crystallized solitude, and it spun a cocoon of ice over her heart, enclosing the arrowhead, the wound, and her death.

The girl opened her eyes. Sat up. She stood and began to walk, no longer stumbling, instead moving with such grace that many would swear she floated. Not once did she shiver, even as the winds resumed their howling and her legs sank knee-deep into the snow. She did not glance back at the bodies. She did not tire, even as the sun set and rose, even as the landscape changed from plains to forest to village.

On the second day of the Winter Reverence, Telzo trudged down the snowy path toward a house at the edge of the village. Alsen had ordered metal clasps for his flute case, and after more restarts than Telzo cared to admit, the clasps were finally ready. While Telzo hammered away at the metal, the blacksmith had grumbled about something as superfluous as a flute needing so finicky a part. But when Telzo presented the completed work, the blacksmith had grunted and nodded. About as much approval an apprentice could expect.

As Telzo neared Alsen's house, a fluttering black flag in the distance caught his eye. He stared, blinked, stared again. No, not a black flag. A girl dressed in white, her long black hair fanning out in the wind.

Her steps, lithe as a faerie of folk legend, carried her toward the village, toward Telzo. Her expression was serene, not like someone who'd braved the Winter Reverence snows. As she drew closer, Telzo noticed the reddish-brown stain on her coat. Blood.

He ran toward her, stumbling in the thicker snow beyond the path. "Are you okay?" he called. "Do you…"

She glanced at him. Their eyes met, and Telzo forgot his original sentence. "I—I'm gonna find the doctor, okay?" he said. "Wait here!" He took off, half-convinced he'd imagined the girl. Blood… A beast, perhaps? But her coat was not ragged or torn.

Doc Shozo was in his fifties and walked with a limp, so when Telzo returned with him other villagers had already emerged from their houses and gathered around the girl. Strangers drew crowds here, even more so when they were lone, bloody girls appearing in the middle of winter.

The villagers followed, chattering, as the doctor led the girl back to his hut. Shozo gave the crowd a disapproving glare before he shut the door.

A few minutes later he emerged, shaking his head. Telzo ran over to ask what was wrong.

"Nothing," Doc Shozo said. "That's the strange part."

"What d'you mean?"

"Lass told me she's fine. Like any doc with a brain, I point to the blood. So she takes off her clothes to show me."

"What?" Telzo yelped, flushing with embarrassment.

The doctor shrugged. "I'm used to 'em lasses being shy, but this one… Mayhap she's from somewhere with different traditions, or mayhap she's used to takin' them off…"

"No way!" the apprentice found himself shouting. The doctor's suggestion drove a spike of anger through him, though he couldn't say why.

"Well, you're probably right, kid. No sense in me judgin' her. Anyhow, ain't no scratch on her beneath the blood, so you can rest easy."

When the girl emerged from the hut, the villagers surrounded her though none came too close. Perhaps it was the blood still staining her clothes. Perhaps it was the wintry calm in her eyes.

"You from around these parts?"

"Wha' happened?"

"How'd you get here?"

"I don't remember," the girl said. "I don't remember anything."

So that night they called a village meeting to decide what to do with her. She had been left with Doctor Shozo for the day; he grumbled at first, but when the meeting came around he had shown up willing to take her on as an apprentice. He was old, his last apprentice had run off with some travelling troupe, and he had tested the girl with a few tasks during the day. She seemed smart and obedient, if a little strange.

A few muttered about extra mouths to feed, but Ms. Limbard voiced her support. The girl could live with her and earn her keep, lending an extra hand with the farm work.

So they gave the girl a place in the village and a name to call her by: Inara, after a heroic wood spirit from "The Song of Grey Leaves." Telzo felt an odd sort of triumph. He had spoken on the girl's behalf, though he was only the smith's apprentice. No matter how dismissive the villagers had outwardly seemed, surely his words had helped a little.

A week passed. Doctor Shozo called the girl a good assistant. She never complained, never seemed to tire. Ms. Limbard said she was "quiet and helpful, but distant."

Telzo glimpsed her every day as she went about her chores, but he could not work up the courage to talk to her. What would he say? Ramblings about his days spent working the bellows and hammering iron? Questions about the world beyond—the world she could no longer remember? For now, he contented himself with watching.

He noticed the girl had a ritual: every morning, she would stand at the edge of the village, raise her arms, and feel the rush of wind and snow.

On the last evening of the Winter Reverence, Ms. Limbard rang the village bell.

It had been a cold winter, and the villagers had gathered to sing their songs inside the village hall rather than outside by the bonfire. But as the clear, urgent sound of the bell interrupted Lisa's fiddle, the villagers flocked outside, racing toward the square. The bell was saved for dire occasions, and the villagers had plenty to worry about that winter: the constant snowstorms, the Hydas beasts becoming more active, and rumours during autumn—before the last travellers were snowed in—about renewed trouble at the border with Vilocet.

The villagers found an angry Ms. Limbard and three tearful, shamefaced children. The children had run off into the woods on a group dare. They had lost their fourth member, Ms. Limbard's son, in the darkness.

The villagers formed search parties, lit torches, grabbed weapons. Telzo was about to leave with his own party when he caught sight of Ms. Limbard yelling at Inara.

"Don't just stand here! Can't you see my son is missing?"

"What do you want me to do?"

"Look for him like everyone else is doing!"

At those words, the girl headed toward the woods. Alone, unarmed, without a torch or weapon. Ms. Limbard, perhaps realizing her mistake, tried to stop the girl, but her feet sank into the snow and gave her no chance to catch up. Inara, as always, seemed to float.

I can't let her go. Telzo broke off from his group, and—through determination more than anything—overtook Ms. Limbard. He saw the tail of the girl's white coat vanishing into the trees and plunged in after her.

He shuffled through a veil of aspen, their white, reedy trunks jutting from the ground like the incisors of an impossibly large monster. He managed to keep the girl's coat just in sight, yet as they plunged deeper into the forest, among the dark, sweeping pines, he lost her. He held his torch aloft, a buttress against the darkness, but wondered with every step whether he should extinguish it. It allowed him to see beneath his feet, preventing him from tripping in the snow or getting caught in the traps set by their own hunters. But the light killed his night vision, making it impossible to see beyond its shaky circle. The bears would be in their winter torpor, but there were always the wolves—or worse, the Hydas beasts. They might hesitate to attack a search party, but a lone man…

He shook off his fears and continued walking. All the more reason to find Inara. At least he had a spear. She had nothing.

The snap of snow and twigs beneath his feet made an odd percussion to the wind's song. Each breath of cold air burned his lungs. Winter pierced through his skin and settled in the bones and joints of his fingers.

After wandering for an eternity, he had to admit defeat. He had found no trace of either Inara or Ms. Limbard's son. His hands had grown almost too numb to hold his spear, and every time he stopped, it felt like an invitation for a beast.

Feeling useless but resigned, Telzo made his way back to the village. By the time the trees cleared and he could see the houses again, a small crowd had gathered by the bonfire. The smith's apprentice stumbled up to the villagers, peering into the centre of the commotion.

It was Ms. Limbard's son, carried by Liam Harow and his brother Selz. The boy's face was pale, his left leg a bloody mess. The smith's apprentice caught whispers of "trap" and "accident" and surmised what he had worried about in the woods had happened to the boy: stepping into a trap set by another villager. He heard whispers of "the new girl." He looked around but could not find Inara.

The Harow brothers brought the boy to the doctor's house. Inara opened the door. Before anyone could ask questions, they were shooed away by Doc Shozo. Tired but too full of adrenaline to sleep, Telzo went home and asked his father about what happened.

"Well, that new girl found him," his father said. "Carried him outta those woods. Quite the sight, actually. Liam kept enough wits about him to ask her to give the boy to him and run ahead to notify the doc, to prepare and all."

The smith's apprentice knew he should ask about the boy: how badly was he hurt, whether he would recover. But what he said was, "How'd she find him?"

"Said she heard him calling. Me and the rest, we got no clue what that means. None of us heard a damn thing and the boy's passed out besides."

His father retired to bed, but Telzo could not stop thinking about the girl. She had strode into the forest with no worry, no fear. She had faced the winter night like she was greeting an old friend.

The snows melted. Old Joen, who continued to live in the low-lying house his mother had left him, once again experienced a flood. The villagers shook their heads in exasperation but dropped by to help him rebuild.

Inara continued to stare into the woods and sky every morning. But one day, as the last of the snows melted, Telzo saw a shift in her routine. Usually she held out her arms and closed her eyes, lost in her own world. But this day, a frown creased her brow. She opened her eyes and looked around in confusion.

Telzo, watching from his window, felt a pang of worry. This was the young woman who had walked into the woods alone with no hesitation. What could have disrupted her routine, made her show something close to unease?

He found himself outside before he realized how he got there. He clenched his fists. *Just go. Walk over. Talk to her.*

One step, then another. He stood beside her, shivering, even though winter was finally receding.

"Um, hi," he said.

Wonderful. Great first impression.

She turned. Blinked, as if returning from a dream. "I can't hear it," she said.

"What?"

"The voice."

He was not sure how to continue the conversation, so he just stood there while she stared at him.

"I—I'm Telzo," he said at last. "I live in the house over there."

More silence. Then she turned away, returning her gaze to the sky. Telzo wanted to say more, but every attempt died in his throat. So he left, heading for the smithy. But even as he traipsed toward another day of sweat and tedium, a new flame lit within him. He had spoken to her, been ignored, but it was not the end of the world. He would survive to try another day.

He joined her the next morning at the village's edge. He offered a quick greeting, but she did not seem to hear him. Her eyes remained fixed on the woods. He tried to start a conversation: the first traders of the year had arrived the day before, and they brought news. Vilocet soldiers had attacked Joma in the middle of winter, perhaps trying to catch the defenders unawares. By all accounts it was a massacre for both sides.

But he soon trailed off, as Inara did not respond to his chatter. Silence returned, and stretched between them like a tug rope.

Telzo shuffled from foot to foot. "Do you... do you mind?" he asked.

She finally glanced at him, as if just noticing he was here. "Mind?"

"Do you mind... me being here?"

She turned away. Then: "No, not particularly."

The day after that, he did not try speaking again. He knew he'd have equal luck holding a conversation with the metals he smelted. So he mimicked her position and looked out into the woods. Didn't she mention something about a voice? He listened, wanting to understand her world, but all he heard was the unintelligible howl of the wind.

The silence was awkward. Her actions, incomprehensible. But those few moments with her became the brightest parts of his day.

The villagers began looking at him the same way they looked at her: with distrust and mingled curiosity. Still, he had been born and raised here, his family dating back more generations than they could count. The villagers could not call him an outsider or exclude him from work or daily life. A few nudged him and asked why he liked her so much. He answered with a shrug and silence.

Silence. Time with her made him appreciate it. There was something comforting about it, and he pitied the villagers for their hurried lives, their inability to ever experience it.

The silence between them changed from awkward to companionable. He no longer spent every second thinking of what to say, nor did he feel like slapping himself every time she did not reply. He was content watching the woods with her, and sneaking occasional glances in her direction. Her long, dark hair streamed in the wind, and her eyes were like a calm lake. Was she beautiful by other people's standards? He did not know, nor did he care. He just knew he wanted to be beside her—the mysterious stranger, the doctor's apprentice, the quiet heroine who had braved the winter woods to save Ms. Limbard's son.

Spring changed to summer. Flowers bloomed then fell, replaced by fruit. Green leaves covered the tops of the incisor-like aspen trees; what had, in winter, resembled the jaws of a fallen monster now served as shelter for tenacious foliage.

One morning, Telzo made his usual trip to their spot at the edge of the village. No tree or house was close enough to provide shade, yet it felt pleasantly cool here. Inara was wearing a white dress that looked like it had once belonged to Ms. Limbard, stitched in places to suit her smaller frame. She seemed to be listening again, but she turned at the sound of his footsteps. And, to his surprise, she spoke.

"Can you hear it?" she asked.

"I..." He looked away. "No. Not right now. But I'm trying."

She cocked her head to the side. "I wonder, why has the voice deserted me?"

"Maybe you can ask when it comes back?"

She gave a brief nod. "I think I will." She gazed into the woods again for a moment. "I will need to head back now."

"Yeah, I need to head to the smithy too." Telzo smiled. "I hope Doc Shozo and Ms. Limbard aren't as grumpy as my master."

The girl actually seemed to contemplate his words. "I have no comparison."

Do you want to stop by sometime? But he dared not ask. "See you tomorrow then?" he said instead.

"Tomorrow," she said.

The Midsummer Festival came and went. Telzo had wanted to ask Inara to come with him, but his mother and older brother wanted to make the village's biggest lantern together. Telzo allowed himself to be roped along, glad for an excuse to delay a potential rejection.

Near summer's end, there was another accident. Old Ben was gored by a Hydas beast, and left a trail of blood as Alsen and Ryensil carried him to the doctor's hut.

Ben's family wept and begged but Doc Shozo refused to let them in. Too restless to return home, they paced in front of the door while the doctor and Inara worked deep into the night.

The door cracked open at dawn. Inara stood there, blood splattering her white dress, her hands, her pale cheeks. A foul stench leaked from the half-open entrance to the hut.

Ben's wife, son, and daughters crowded around her.

"Is he okay?"

"Let us see him!"

The girl looked at them. "He is broken. We couldn't fix him."

A wail rose from the group. Ben's children clung to each other and sobbed. His wife, her face ashen, turned to Inara. "You should've done more! There's no way… no way he's gone!"

But all the girl said was, "You're in the way."

She brushed past the grieving family who were too astonished to stop her. She walked to the wash house to rid herself of the blood, then went to her usual spot to listen to the voice she could no longer hear.

Everyone attended the funeral. There were prayers and tears and mutters of disbelief. How fragile life was. How Martha now had to raise three kids on her own. How much those horrid woods had taken from them over the years.

The girl was there. But she did not weep or pray.

"We should've kicked her out from the start! Our village doesn't need someone like that!"

"Martha, I know you're upset, but—"

"You didn't see the way she looked at us! I swear, she must be a demon! Every time she walks by the whole place gets cold."

"Y'know, Martha has a point. She dropped by my place on an errand, and I swear I saw frost creeping over the mantelpiece…"

"Enough!"

Doctor Shozo rose to his feet.

"What a load of hogwash," he said. "We damn well did all we could for Ben. Or d'you doubt me too, huh?"

Martha quietened for a moment.

"Inara's… composed, she is," the doctor said. "That ain't a bad thing, when it comes to healin'. Keeps her head clear in emergencies and lets her remember what's best for the patient, which ain't always easy."

There were mutters of disbelief, but Ms. Limbard was quick to speak up on Inara's behalf, reminding them of how Inara had saved her son. Several others nodded in agreement.

In the end, it was decided that Inara—demon or heroine, outsider or one of them—couldn't be left to the mercy of the wilderness. They dispersed from the village hall, and Telzo heaved a sigh of relief as he walked home.

Telzo was the first to arrive at their usual spot. Inara came to stand by his side a minute later, and he wondered if he should bring up Ben.

She spoke first. "Why were they yelling at me?"

He could only stare at her. *So she doesn't know. She really doesn't know.* "They were sad," he said. "Grieving. Someone they loved has passed away, and it's natural to look for someone to blame."

"Sad… Loved…"

She sounded out those words, as if they were a foreign language she had not yet mastered.

"We couldn't fix him," she said. "That is all."

"Well… He was someone they saw every day. Who Martha was married to for twelve years, who raised three children with her. He talked with them, worked the fields with them, made them laugh… Now he'll never laugh or talk again. It's like a piece of their lives is missing." He paused. "Can you remember anything at all? Anyone who was like that for you?"

The girl furrowed her brow. "No. No one I can think of."

In the coming months, the villagers' eyes hardened and their comments grew sharper. Toward Inara, yes, but also toward Telzo, for he continued to stand beside her each morning. “If you’re trying to understand her, then don’t bother,” the blacksmith said to him.

Telzo barely heard. His thoughts were on the Harvest Festival which was fast approaching. He needed to do what he hadn’t done at Midsummer: ask Inara to attend with him. Because otherwise he’d never dare ask. Because now more than ever, he wanted to show the villagers that Inara was not some cold-hearted monster.

Two days before the Harvest Festival, Telzo stumbled up to their usual spot. “Do you—I mean, I… You, you want to come to the Harvest Festival with me?”

“Harvest Festival?”

“There’ll be storytelling, music, dancing. Alsen said he’ll play a new song he learned in Elsach. Oh, and Lisa’s the best fiddler in southern Casenna. You need to hear her play ‘The Tale of Prince Kessand.’”

“Prince Kessand…” Inara’s eyes seemed far away.

Telzo’s heart skipped a beat. “You know the story? Do you remember something?”

“It’s the one with the ice palace…”

“Yes, yes! Merlida, Kessand’s true love, was imprisoned by the god of winter. And…”

He trailed off. Inara didn’t seem to hear him anymore. She reached out a hand, as if grasping something invisible that floated from the woods.

“Will you come with me?” Telzo asked after a moment.

“I want to hear that song,” she said.

On the day of the Harvest Festival, he found her waiting in front of his house. He hurried to the door, then paused, hand hovering over the latch. They had never met outside the usual spot before, he realized. His heart began to hammer.

Get a grip, Telzo, he berated himself and opened the door.

He barely managed a hello before she turned away. Wordlessly, she started walking toward the bonfire at the centre of the village. He followed, and despite her nonexistent greeting and stony silence, a grin broke across his face.

They joined the crowd that had gathered to hear Alsen play. As always, the flute looked like a toy in Alsen's big hands, but all that was forgotten when he blew the first note.

"Valeria," Alsen's new song from Elsach, stretched like a delicate, spiralling web, trills and crescendos mixed with softly held notes that had Telzo forgetting to breathe. When the last strains of music melted into silence, Telzo glanced over at Inara. Perhaps it was a trick of the light, but her lips seemed to curl in something close to a smile.

Then Lisa stepped forward with her fiddle. She plunged into "Swiftly Runs the River," and villagers rose to their feet. Telzo held out his hand to Inara, an invitation to dance. She took it; her hand was icy, but he did not mind in the least. They moved together to the bright, emphatic notes. She danced with a wild grace—not the precision of a practiced performer, but something more raw, unpredictable, like the pattern of dancing snow.

After a few more rhythmic songs, the villagers sat down. Drinks were passed around, and Lisa struck the first note of "The Tale of Prince Kessand."

The opening was mid-tempo, melodic. After a few moments Lisa took on the countermelody, and the villagers began to sing. They sang of Prince Kessand meeting Merlida, a palace dancer. Of him falling in love with her, and vowing to marry her despite the disapproval of everyone at court.

Here the villagers fell silent, and Lisa took up the melody again. The notes came slower, darker. For on the night of the wedding, a snowstorm swept through the palace courtyard. The god of winter, who'd also fallen in love with Merlisa, whisked her away to his palace of ice.

The villagers sang of Kessand's twelve years of waiting. And when Merlida finally escaped from the god's palace, she had lost all her memories. Telzo glanced at Inara, and saw her mouthing along with the words.

Lisa lowered her fiddle, and the villagers' voices told the next part of the tale.

Kessand treated Merlida with care, with patience. And eventually she fell in love with him all over again.

The song ended with their marriage festivities. Lisa's hands were a blur as she played the staccato notes, and the villagers clapped along. She ended the song with a flourish, fiddle raised high, then bowed. The villagers burst into cheers and applause, as if this were the first time they'd listened to her and sang with her. No one ever grew tired of "The Tale of Prince Kessand."

Telzo looked at Inara. She stared into the firelight, as if she could see Merlida and Kessand dancing within.

The following week, they spoke more than they had all those months before. They talked about "The Tale of Prince Kessand." She did indeed know the story, but in her version the god of winter hadn't loved Merlida. He'd locked her in his palace because he foresaw a terrible end for her, should she marry Kessand.

"And was he right?" Telzo asked.

Inara frowned. "I don't know. I can't remember how the story ended. I think… my father used to sing it to me."

That evening, Telzo paid Alsen a visit and asked about other versions of Prince Kessand's story. "Was there one where the god of winter didn't love Merlida, but was trying to save her?"

Alsen stroked his chin. "Now that I think about it, that's probably the most popular version in Vilocet." His face twisted. "I've crossed over a few times, before their Reunionists started chanting 'One Nation' and attacking our borders. Where'd you hear that version?"

Telzo made up a story about hearing it from a trader. He kept the truth to himself. It mattered little to Telzo which side of the border Inara grew up on, but it wouldn't be wise to let the villagers know.

The next day, Inara asked when there would be another festival, when they'd be able to dance again. Telzo's heart soared. If only the villagers could see her during those conversations… they would never suggest kicking her out, never see her as anything other than human.

The leaves fell and were blown away by the increasingly cold wind. Soon, the first flakes of snow began to fall.

Telzo walked toward the meeting spot, lifting a hand over his eyes against the stinging wind. He found Inara with her arms outstretched, her eyes closed. Her face took on its closest approximation to happiness, and he immediately realized why.

"You can hear it again?" he said.

She nodded.

"What is it saying?"

She opened her mouth and… spoke. Her voice was an incomprehensible howl. A cold blast of wind struck him, and he dropped to his knees, shivering.

He took a few deep, chilling breaths. Those words she'd spoken, they hadn't been human. He shook his head. No, no, he must've imagined them. She hadn't said anything; it was only the wind. He climbed to his feet and did what he always did: strained to hear the voice she was listening for. He heard nothing that sounded like words.

He found her the same way a day later. Not a fleeting reunion then; what she was listening for had returned for good.

A bittersweet taste permeated his mouth. Happiness for her, but sadness for himself at being left out.

"I have been thinking about your question," she said. "Something I miss, like Martha misses Ben… perhaps it's this voice? I feel incomplete when it's gone."

"But you don't cry or tear your hair out when it's not there," Telzo pointed out. For some reason, he didn't want to assign too much value to the voice.

"But I miss it." She turned her head, staring at him instead of the tree-lined horizon. "What if it goes away again?"

Telzo shrugged. "Maybe it only comes in winter."

The girl's gaze sharpened. "That is it. Why didn't I realize it before?" She stared out into the vast, snow-covered forest. "It's not as clear as it was last year," she said after a few minutes of silence.

"Maybe it gets louder as the winter grows colder."

Inara nodded. They came back to the spot every day, listening. Their conversations dwindled to nothing, except Inara's comments about the voice never rising above a quiet murmur. Telzo heard only the wind: an irritating howl, more wordless than ever. Sometimes it blew so hard that he could barely keep his footing, but Inara—light as a feather upon the snow—never seemed uprooted by the gusts. *If this winter's saying anything,* Telzo mused, *it's telling me to get inside.*

He took her to the Winter Reverence festivities. They danced, but she did not smile, did not sing along to any songs.

The days grew colder, then warmer. When the snows melted, Inara said, "It's gone again."

Telzo wanted to rejoice. The voice, his greatest rival, had finally peeled away from her. But he had never seen her so close to genuine sadness, and all he could say was, "I'm sorry."

Alsen and Lisa were wed in early spring, with a bonfire and music and dance.

Alsen, ready to settle down after years of travelling, grinned so wide his face must have hurt by the end. Lisa, beaming, picked up her fiddle to serenade the village and her now-husband. Telzo didn't know when they had fallen in love, but they suited each other, with their love of music, their liveliness, their good humour.

The marriage was a loud, rowdy celebration. Drinks flowed and bawdy jokes were directed at both bride and groom. Telzo feared Inara would feel uncomfortable amidst such commotion, but she stayed by his side the entire time. In the days after the voice's disappearance, she had started speaking to him more again. He hadn't even needed to persuade her about attending the wedding.

Before bride and groom were swept away by the crowd and chanted into their bedchamber, Alsen passed by Telzo and whispered: "It's your turn now."

Telzo could only manage a quick nod. He knew what Alsen meant, but could he, after seeing how the voice had stolen Inara away, allow himself to wish for something more?

Doc Shozo had to leave for a month that summer, handing the town to Inara's care. Jane Withers caught a cold while drinking outside during a rainstorm. After Inara administered some foul-tasting but effective concoctions, she made a full recovery.

Alsen cut himself with a kitchen knife while attempting to cook. Inara stitched his hand expertly while he muttered sheepishly about trying to impress his new wife. Inara did not understand what he meant by that, but at least he promised to be more careful in the future.

Both patients complimented Inara, saying she had learned a lot from the doctor and showed them a surprising amount of care. Martha sat through that village meeting looking like she was chewing gentian root, but said nothing as the other villagers nodded their approval.

One morning, after Doc Shozo's return, Inara asked Telzo, "I sometimes wonder, why do we wait here every morning? We know we can hear him only in winter."

Him? It was the first time she had gendered the voice.

"Well…" Telzo swallowed. "The truth is, I couldn't hear him from the start, and I never did manage to. I… had a different reason to be here."

He waited one, three, five seconds. Would she tell him to go away? Shake her head in disappointment? Gaze at him with incomprehension, at best?

But what she said was, "I understand what you mean. I can't hear him now, yet I still come back here." She stretched out a hand. "But… maybe we should meet somewhere else. And return in winter. While we're here so many of them stare at us, talk about us. There is much I want to talk about, to learn."

Telzo's world seemed to grow brighter, sharper, like he'd stepped from a cavern into sunlight. Was this an invitation to spend time together, finally, without that never-there voice occupying her mind? Could he show her his house, show her the smithy, work together with her during the harvest?

Grinning, he reached out and took her hand. Perhaps they were getting used to each other, for she felt pleasantly cool to him now, rather than cold as snow.

They danced at the Midsummer Festival. It was difficult to keep up with her easy grace, but it was a chance to hold her, to admire the sway of her body and the precision of her steps. Telzo caught whispers about how strange this was, that the cold-hearted Inara now danced with the hopeless smith's apprentice at every festival. Telzo felt a surge of pride: that he'd played a part in how Inara had changed, that he had been right all along about her.

The day after, the blacksmith pulled his apprentice aside before they could start their current project. "You're at that age," the blacksmith said. "Settle down with a nice village girl. Inara… she's plenty capable, and kinder than we gave her credit for. But she ain't right for you, kid. Not as someone you'd marry."

"We sing of Prince Kessand," Telzo shot back. "He married despite his family's disapproval and eventually got his happiness, even after twelve years of waiting."

"That's a song," the blacksmith said. "Ain't no pretty tales like that in our lives."

Inara stood in a room of candlelight and blood.

She heard Lisa's ragged breathing. She heard Alsen pacing outside, his footsteps crushing the fragile lives of ants and the last autumn weeds. She thought she heard the pounding of a small heart, a weak echo to Doctor Shozo's barked orders.

She heard the wind, and to her ears it was a wordless wail.

Her hands moved, but they never seemed fast enough. Her head spun as if she were the one bleeding. The tools took on a layer of frost, and Lisa's skin seemed to blacken where she touched it.

No, that wasn't right. Couldn't be. She was tired, hallucinating. *Concentrate, concentrate.* She didn't know if those were Shozo's words, or her commands to herself.

Her hands fluttered like a caged bird, eternally in motion and eternally futile. Blood was everywhere, the lamps and candles were never bright enough, and Lisa's heartbeat grew fainter and fainter.

Until it stopped.

Still Inara moved. She must do something, anything…

"Inara. Stop. You can't…"

Shozo gripped her chin, forcing her to look at him and nowhere else in the room. "Stay calm. Remember what I taught you. Always do everything you can, but sometimes…"

That is not enough. She stumbled outside, away from the heat of the candles and the ice that seemed to rise from her own hands. She heard Doctor Shozo follow her, saw Alsen's feet shuffle forward. She dared not look up. She knew she should apologize, but she couldn't look at him right now, couldn't speak.

She wandered through the village. She didn't know where she was going, only that her feet moved and moved until she stood in front of a door decorated with a red-leafed wreath. She knocked.

Martha answered.

"I'm sorry," Inara said, and with the word came pain. Pain spreading from her chest to her limbs, until she sank to her knees. "I'm sorry, I'm sorry. Back then, with Ben… I didn't know."

They sprawled on the grass beneath the stars. Normally it would be snowing by now, but winter was late that year.

"I couldn't save her."

A gentle touch on her shoulder, the only comfort he could give.

"I know there was nothing more I could've done. Doctor Shozo says we did well to save the baby. So why do I feel… guilty?"

The word hung between them. Undiscovered until now, like a patch of sky she had never noticed before.

"Alsen doesn't blame me, but I blame myself," she said. "Is it normal to feel like this?"

"Yes," Telzo said. "Of course."

"Why?"

"Because you care. And you wanted to save Lisa."

“It’s irrational.”

“It’s what makes us human.”

She ran a hand through the yellowing grass. “Afterward, I didn’t know what I was doing. I just… stumbled up to Martha’s door and apologized. I didn’t know, back then.”

Unsure of what to say, Telzo tried to distract her by pointing out the different constellations, their names and stories passed down for generations in the village. She asked questions for a while.

Then, softly, she began telling her own stories about the constellations. Different ones, or similar ones with details changed. “My father loved these stories,” she said. “He’d always say, wherever Mother was, at least we’d all gaze at one sky.”

The day the first snows fell, Telzo was not in the village. He had left on an errand to a neighbouring town, which turned into a two-week stay when they discovered his blacksmithing skills. The town had their own blacksmith of course, but he was sixty-eight and could barely lift a hammer on a bad day. The townsfolk asked Telzo if he would consider staying on a more permanent basis—he would have the winter to think it over, of course.

Upon arriving back at the village, Telzo dropped by the smithy and told his master the news. He stumbled when the blacksmith clapped him on the back.

“What luck! And here I thought you’d stay my apprentice ’til we’re both white-haired grandfathers!” The blacksmith’s eyes narrowed at Telzo’s silence. “Thinking ’bout her, are you? I tell you, ain’t no time to be throwing away an opportunity like this.”

Telzo knew. His master was still strong, still relatively young, good for a decade or two barring disaster. There were more opportunities in a bigger town. And yet...

The sun had slipped past noon when he emerged from the smithy, and Telzo did not think Inara would be at their old meeting spot. But the winter's first snow had come that morning, and it wouldn't hurt to check.

To his surprise, she was there. Not standing in silence, listening. Instead she sat, knees pulled toward her chest. She jumped up when she saw him and ran towards him, all her usual grace gone.

The winter sun lit the trails of her tears. "He's gone! I can't hear him at all!" She stretched out a hand, reaching for him as she had once reached for the wind and the voice. Telzo opened his arms, and she fell into his embrace. Her tears soaked his coat, and he felt her shudders spread through his own body. Her hands, her shoulders through her coat, felt cool. But her tears were warm.

A sudden blast of wind almost blew him to the ground. The snow, dancing around them, prickled his face like needles. But he was holding her, and she did not pull away for a long, long time.

"I'm… okay now," she finally said, lifting her head. Her eyes were red.

"Are you sure?"

"…of course."

"Don't worry. I—I'm sure it'll come back. It's just not cold enough."

She shook her head, hair swaying in the wind. "You don't need to lie. I know he's gone."

They returned to the same spot in the coming days. Telzo would tilt his head as a question, and Inara would shake her head in reply. The voice had not returned.

"Maybe next winter," Telzo said.

"I hope," Inara said. "But… it's okay, if he doesn't return."

The door to a nearby house opened. Alsen stepped outside, holding his child in his arms. Inara stared at Alsen, the woods and voice seemingly forgotten.

"I was also raised by my father," she murmured. "My mother… was a soldier. She was never home. Even when Father died, she wasn't there."

She stopped talking. Silence returned as their third companion. Telzo, unsure of how to break it, chose to change the topic. "What did the voice say to you? When you could hear it?"

"I don't know."

"You don't know?"

"I used to understand him. That first winter. Ms. Limbard's son, I found him because the voice told me where he was. But now I can only remember the sounds, not the meaning." Then she smiled. "Maybe it's strange of me to keep coming back here when he is gone. But this place is special to me."

He almost told her then. *It's special to me as well. It's where I met you. And meeting you, speaking with you—those were the best moments of my life. So come with me. Let's leave this village together.*

During the Winter Reverence, Telzo decided to ask her.

Music carried through the village hall, a countermelody to the wind outside. "The Tale of Prince Kessand" remained part of the festivities—now played by Alsen. His flute lent a more sombre note to the story, and even in the festive bits at the end, no one clapped. They just listened, teary-eyed. When Alsen finished, he too blinked back tears.

The food, removed in measured amounts from their stores, could not compare to what they had enjoyed during the Harvest Festival. But few had much appetite while listening to Alsen's lament.

Alsen struck up a livelier tune just before the villagers drowned themselves in their beer mugs. The hall was too cramped for the dancing to anything but bodies bumping into each other. Several couples sneaked out the door, arm-in-arm and speaking with hushed excitement.

"Let's go too," Telzo said to Inara.

She nodded and followed him outside. It was a cold, barely lit evening. Telzo shivered and was surprised to see her do the same. It must be even colder than he'd thought. He could not remember another winter that had seemed to touch her.

They arrived at their original meeting place at the edge of the village. But instead of looking into the woods, Telzo took her hands in his and made her face him. "Inara," he said. "I have something to ask you."

A shower of snowflakes drifted from the sky, landing on her cheeks and melting.

"There's a town nearby that needs a blacksmith," he said. "They want me to move there. And—I hope you can come with me."

She opened her mouth as if to say something, but stumbled from a sudden gust of wind. Telzo, nearly falling himself, ploughed ahead.

"I've been meaning to say this for a long time," he said. "I don't know what your feelings are. But I want you to know: I'm so glad you came to this village. You are the most precious thing in the world to me." Perhaps it was his imagination, but he felt her hands squeeze his in return. "Speaking with you, dancing with you, hearing you talk about the things you learned, the things you remembered… it's been more than I dared hope for."

Numbness spread through Telzo, and for a moment he could barely move his lips. But no, he had come this far. He would not let the winter stop him.

"I love you," Telzo said. "I always have, since the day I saw you walking towards the village. When you saved Ms. Limbard's son, when you took care of Alsen and Jane during Doc Shozo's absence… I admired you more and more. If you say you won't come with me, I will stay here and be an apprentice for the rest of my life. If you say you never want to see me again, then I will leave… but I will always be thinking of you, and I will return if you ever need me. Perhaps it's just a foolish dream, but I want us to spend our lives together. I hope you'll give me the chance to be someone special to you."

His breath made white mists between them. He watched her face the whole time, noting every flutter of her eyelids, every turn of her mouth.

"Telzo." She looked at him with radiant eyes. "You are already special to me."

Those words. Those few words.

"I've… changed," she said. "It's been hard sometimes. I started feeling worry, pain. Guilt. I started remembering, but in pieces I still cannot put together. But every time we spoke, you made me feel that it's okay, that it's all worth it. I realized, no matter what, I cannot go back to being empty."

Her smile was brittle as ice in the spring thaw, bright as sunlight on freshly fallen snow. For a moment his thundering heart drowned out the wind.

"I will come with you," she said. "I want to see where this takes us."

He wrapped his arms around her and pulled her close. "Truly? You'll come with me?"

"Of course."

The snow, the forest, even the distant sound of flute music disappeared. He saw only the road stretching before them, long and golden.

He pulled back for a moment, so he could see her face. Her eyes danced with hope.

He kissed her. Her lips were soft as rosebuds, and for a moment he felt like the prince of a story. No mazes, no dragons, no disapproving kings would keep her from him. She was warm in his arms, soft and human in a way she had never been before.

Then her grip slacked. Her head fell back. Their lips broke apart, and he opened his eyes. A scarlet stain covered the front of her coat.

He heard a distant scream. It was the sound of a thousand windows shattering. It was the sound of the earth ripping itself asunder. It was the sound of a storm and a weeping god.

The god of winter, with his wings of ice and voice of wailing death, watched the girl and the boy exit the hall.

He heard the boy speak. He blew, and snow swirled from the still-clear sky. He howled and the wind came, but he could not steal the boy's words.

He watched them embrace. He watched the foolish boy press his lips to the girl's.

He felt, more than saw, the last of his work being undone. The remaining ice in her heart melted and the old blood flowed, a vivid red wound that refused heal.

The god of winter screamed as she collapsed in the snow. She drew raspy breaths, clawed for something that was not there, but this time neither he nor the boy could save her.

The god could only watch as the boy ripped off his coat. Tried to bind her wound. Called out for the help. Cradled her still-warm body in his arms, and wept.

At least the boy could hold her, the god of winter thought, and cry out the last words she'd hear and understand. The god's tears, as always, came down as snow.

Inpsirations and Influences

Y.M. PANG

I WROTE *THE GIRL WITH THE Frozen Heart* sometime between Christmas and mid-January. On January 13th, I sent it off to my long-time friend with the message, Enjoy the heartwarming winter tale. *[insert smiley face]*

In retrospect, that smiley showed way too many teeth.

It snows a lot in wintertime Toronto. That's not news to anyone, though the rest of Canada probably thinks we have it easy. I had the image of a girl stumbling through the snow, bleeding. That's the beginning.

As for the ending... Let's switch gears entirely. Ever seen *Gankutsuou*? It's an anime based on *The Count of Monte Cristo*. With giant robots, just because. In the final scene... well, don't let me spoil two stories for you.

My third major inspiration, the one that ties the themes together: Snow White. Sleeping Beauty. There sure are a lot of fairy tales about true love's first kiss saving someone from a death-like slumber.

Let's go back to those robots. There are no robots in this story, but perhaps it mirrors their journeys, or at least the journeys certain authors assign to them. Someone previously unfeeling learns to feel. (*But why?* I wondered. *Why do we need to love?*)

I had my three characters. Inara, the girl with the frozen heart. The god of winter, who pities her and wants to save her. Telzo, who loves her and wants to save her. But can they? Can they really? I knew the answer before I started writing. You could say the answer inspired me to write this story.

So. Enjoy the heartwarming winter tale.

A Chat With Y.M. Pang

The Girl with the Frozen Heart **fits our Awakenings call for short stories beautifully. Can you tell us the ways that the story engages with the theme?**

There are many forms of Awakening. Realizing your destiny. Walking from incomprehension to understanding. The ubiquitous form of Awakening I wanted to address is the one where a previously heartless character begins to feel: the robot learns emotions, the alien chooses to spare humanity, the originally cynical protagonist falls in love (the domain of a thousand pop songs).

The Girl with the Frozen Heart is very much about that last one. But not all "Awakenings" lead to a happy ending. Sometimes it's worse than just a break-up song.

In many ways this is a cautionary tale about fairy tales and romance that ultimately subvert the idea of true love as salvation. Can you tell us a bit about these elements in your story?

"True love's first kiss" is an important concept in many fairy tales. Think Snow White. Or Sleeping Beauty. I keep thinking... If a kiss can have the magical ability to save someone, then can it not equally have the power to destroy someone?

Sometimes your love isn't true enough. Or, worse, your love is true and you try to do things right, yet things still don't turn out well. I want more stories like that. Not because I'm a sadist—okay, maybe a little—but because they're rare.

In terms of influences and sources of inspiration, what are your own favorite fairy tales and romantic stories?

I have a soft spot for "The Little Mermaid." I was (thankfully) exposed to the original ending in picture book format before watching the Disney movie. It was one of the first tragic endings I encountered (along with that infuriating scene at the end of the old Outlaws of the Marsh TV series); perhaps it's not framed as such, with her rising with the spirits and all, but to a kid it's hard to see her death as anything other than tragic. I also have fond memories of "The Ugly Duckling" and "The Emperor's New Clothes," though these days I sometimes write stories that subvert the former and often wonder if I am the latter.

Moving outside western fairy tales for a moment, one folk tale that has stayed with me is the Japanese story "The Crane Wife." It's a lovely cautionary tale, and I later had the chance to tell it to a group of younger children for a storytelling assignment.

Tell us about your experience writing short stories: what would you say are the advantages and potential pitfalls of writing short fiction versus a novel or novella?

Biggest advantage: Shorter timeframe between initiation and completion, quicker transition between writing and completion. I went through a three-year period of my life and writing going off the rails. I could barely write, and didn't know what else I could do. Short stories—and finding a good writing group—haves been what pulled me back. I am working on novels again, with one that is in the editing stage. But overall short stories can be mapped out and executed in a shorter period of time, and if done well you can maintain the same impact for your ending.

Biggest disadvantage: All that being said, I think I'm a novel writer at heart. Novel storyteller, anyway. My ideas tend to be large-scale, and plot or character driven rather than idea driven. I've heard writers describe short stories as being about a single idea or location or scene; that sounds almost crazy to me, since I don't think I've ever written a single-scene story outside of less than 1,500 word flash.

I've gotten better though. Back when I first started submitting, half my "short" stories were over 10,000 words long.

Finally, a question we ask all of our interviewees: We Book Smugglers have faced condemnation because of the sheer volume of books that we carry back home on a daily basis. As such, we have on occasion resorted to "smuggling books" home to escape judgmental, scrutinizing eyes. Have you ever had to smuggle books?

Growing up, the library was my best friend. I've been blessed with schools with good libraries, and living within walking distance to a public library when needed. The only books I owned were what my parents allowed me to buy as birthday and Christmas presents. The books I bought were ones I'd already read and loved (*Silverwing*, Harry Potter, ect.)

Of course, these days it's a different story. I have three bookshelves. They are all full. Some levels are filled with blu-rays or artbooks or French dictionaries, but it's mostly novels. I've had to set several rules for myself. Top of that list: stop prowling used book sales. (Note: This is not directed at anyone else. Just toward me and my dwindling shelf space).

As for smuggling books... I tend to smuggle the ones with the, ah, lurid covers. From judgmental, scrutinizing eyes, as you put it. It's not usually a problem since I can just place them face down. The problem is when the naked person is on the spine too. I'm looking at you, *Kushiel's Dart*.

Running

ITORO UDOFIA

I'VE GOT AN ANCESTOR ON my back.

She wades through whatever spirit filled world she inhabits to rest herself beside me while I sleep. She recalls every inane habit of mine, down to the wrinkle that forms between my brows when I frown. *What makes you different?* Her knobby fingers wriggle between mine, and she positions her mouth next to my ear. *A language? A country? A history? A prayer? I wanted to be you.* Everything I eat. Wear. Say. Think. Sing. Love. Hate. She knows. *I'm from your mother's side. I died about a four hour drive from her hometown. I know where her people rest and where they go to church. I visited them often in the summers with my aunt. They're still over there. Living and waiting.* When she tells me this, I know I need her on my back, sniffing out my trail. I need her watching me because I know nothing about these people she's visited. These people—she claims—wear the same face and frown that I do. I haven't seen them since I was two or three, and I may never see them again. No one speaks their names over here unless one of them dies, and if they haven't died, then I haven't heard of them.

Possibly, my mother had mentioned something about these people in passing. Like that time she was driving and talked about her girlhood days of getting water from a river with her cousins. Perhaps these were the cousins she loved so dearly in those pictures I've seen in our family scrapbook. She said they walked four miles to a river they called nature's mirror because it was so clear you could see all of nature in it. When she told me this story, I was barely listening. All I could think about was her driving fast enough to get me to the school dance while checking my cherry lip gloss and frosted eyeliner in the rearview mirror. My thoughts were of my failed attempt at beauty, despite my best efforts, I was sure no one would pick me to dance. Perhaps if I had grown up in her country, I wouldn't have been so distracted and afraid, and could've heard her story of a clear river with laughing cousins. But I've put too much of myself into surviving on *this* land, and if there›s a story I need, it's about making life work out here. I'm too much of an American kid, stuck in my American ways, and wedded to the personality I›ve formed here.

I fear that the country this ancestor spirit speaks of has something to do with my parents birthing their children in a slush of desperation and fear. My anger at their homeland makes me quintessentially American; I never care to ask what happened to their people or country. I only consider the fruit their country produces: the unforgiving faces and disjointed habits of my parents. And that, I can't forgive. I'm an American through and through. At least, I think I am. Americans like me don't bother to factor ourselves into the equation of any accountability. There'd be too much explaining and heartache that way. I'd rather point the finger, and forget there are four other fingers pointing back at me.

The ancestor resting beside me sniffs out my sentiments in the way I roll my eyes and scoff at her speaking of this so-called family waiting for me in another country. *I met you when you were real small. You wanted to play games nobody knew or cared to understand, so I left you sitting on the couch and took your sister to play instead. She was old enough, and the games we played were games we understood. I should have spent more time with you, maybe if I had, you'd think of coming back.* Her breath heats the tip of my ear. There's nothing to forgive in my mind because I don't remember a thing about a thing. She's telling the truth though, this much I know, because in the family photo album I see pictures of me, a little girl with beads in her hair and a scowling face staring at the camera. In the picture, I'm surrounded by people; they stare back at the camera with scowling faces, some dressed in school uniforms, head wraps or tunics. One of them puts their hand on my shoulder. Their eyes stretch out across their face as mine do. Are these the people waiting for me to visit? Surely the spirit knows we've moved on from those pictures. I now have a little brother they have never seen, and we've all grown taller and gained weight while the photo album gathers dust on a shelf of books together with wasteful trinkets we've acquired. I think those people should stop waiting, and this ancestor spirit should stop wasting her time visiting someone she couldn't even visit while alive. Besides, I don't recall seeing her face in any picture I took while in my parent's country. Who is this ancestor to me?

She recounts stories of her adventures roaming different worlds. Where she goes, she can ride on the back of a sound, and join spirits with dancing feet and swaying hips. These spirits—she tells me—were once-upon-a-time humans who now dance to a vibration that sits between wailing and praise. *I go to a place where spirits dance out their sorrow after a hard time on earth.* She traces my nose with her fingers. *When I come back here, I come back to learn.* "Take me with you!" I say, jumping in excitement because the spirit has finally said something that interests me. "I like to dance. I dance a lot in my room." She rubs her knee, a knee that›s as knobby as her fingers. *Anyone can dance for an eternity—but to live here on earth—that's not a task for the weak-willed. You my dear, are stronger than me.*

Later that week she visits me on a bad night. Bad nights consist of me hiding in my room while trying to scream into a pillow. This night, I get angry with myself because I'm too scared to even hear the muffled sound of my voice. When she appears, I try to gather myself and quickly wipe tears from my eyes, and snot from my nose. I'd never tell her that I'm happy to see her, but at that moment I can't help myself. I ask her through sniffles, "Please take me with you." She cups my face in her hands. *No.* I punch her, though my punches don't hit skin or bone, they just go through her, as if I'm punching air or trying to hold water. *I'm the one who's supposed to take you from this world into the next, and I won't take you anywhere until you are too old to be alive.* I lunge toward her, hoping to pinch her nose until she cries, but she curls into herself and vanishes. I lay there that night thinking to myself. Sometimes you've got to keep punching until a bone cracks beneath your fist.

She first appeared when I turned ten. I was too much of a coward to run away from home but I thought about it. I sulked in my room, trying to hide from the feast my mom was cooking. The smell slithered through the cracks of my door and found its way into my nose. It was the smell of palm oil burning, and it coated itself in my nostrils, causing me to sneeze. I could hear laughter over a preacher's voice blaring from the television speaking of God and salvation. My door muffled the sounds of the "I'm gonna get saved" music playing after the preacher's sermon. When the TV evangelist's voice thundered and Mom cooked while humming a hymn or a prayer, it was a good night.

About half an hour later, someone yelled from the bottom of the stairs, "Come down and eat!" I was the only one upstairs hiding, and I knew the decree was for me. I was a hiding kind of kid. The kid who failed to remember how to make goat meat pepper soup even though I had cut the meat, diced the onions, and burned my eyes slicing habanero peppers. My fingers usually looked like wrinkled faces after I washed the vegetables and meat because Mom would say, "Kill every germ you can with the water. I don't need any one of us getting sick." I was the kid who forgot the names of spices bought from the African market and boiled the yams till they turned to mush because all I thought about was hiding. That night I wasn't called to help cook, and I sat on my bed cursing the smell invading my privacy. Why can't we just have spaghetti? I wondered. That's what most kids at my school ate for dinner. Why can't we do the same? That night I ate afang soup with doughy Bisquick wishing a wormy string of spaghetti was sliding down my throat. A couple of hours later, the ancestor girl woke me from my sleep. She sat next to my bed, picking the crust from the corners of my eyes.

Her hair was shaved, revealing her jutting forehead and big eyes that left little room for a nose and mouth. I think she was seventeen or eighteen because she talked like someone who was ready to go out into the world on her own terms. But her shaved head made her look younger, like she was thirteen or fourteen. She wore a long dress that was lined with plain white buttons trailing down the middle. If she dared come to my school dressed like that, the kids would point and laugh. Even the *uncool* kids would point and laugh. If I had seen her walking through the hallways like that, I may have pointed and laughed, or just looked away. She rubbed my cheek and wiped the drool off my chin. Then she turned to a plate of spaghetti and meatballs sitting on her lap. The plate looked exactly like what I had craved for dinner. She let the noodles dangle from the fork as she took a bite. *It tastes ok. Soon you'll see that it's not the best.* I dismissed her visit thinking she was nothing but a pestering dream, but her touch on the side of my eyes and chin left a tingle on my face that lingered for the next day. A few days later she caught me on a bad night. It was a day when the evangelist preacher wasn't blaring from the television, Mom was asleep, and we children made lunch and dinner for ourselves, eating ramen noodles, chocolate chip cookies (the chewy kind) and leftover soup with rice. We watched morning cartoons turn to family-friendly afternoon movies to rated R night shows with kissing girls and boys we weren't supposed to watch. That day the TV shows bored me, and I decided to have some fun in my room. In my room, I'd dance, sing, and pretend to date a guy named John with blow-in-the-wind hair. I drew pictures of what I would look like in the future. My future self looks like a tall woman with large hoop earrings and a back that doesn't hunch. Her mouth is closed and though she'd never say it, I know she's not afraid. I'd turn on the radio and dance to the latest pop and R&B tunes. I let my body stomp and twirl in the room, doing a liturgical dance to the future. In my merriment, I jumped as if trying to fly across town, the state, or the country until I sweat. When I danced this way, trouble usually followed me upstairs. I learned in my room that trouble always followed if I danced to wish for something different.

He never knocked on the door, and the lock to my room never worked. He entered that day, giving me no time to gather myself back into reality.

"Didn't you hear me calling you?" He asked.

"Yes," I muttered. That was a grave mistake. You just don't answer "yes," when a parent calls you. You must address adults according to their position and title; I should have said, "Yes Daddy." He hit me over the head for that one, and I fell back on the bed with the left side of my head throbbing.

"Why are you so rude?" He raised his arm ready to strike again, but my feet started to kick the way they did when I danced and twirled in my room. He tried to find a limb to grab, but my legs kicked till I couldn't see them anymore. I gained momentum like a fan once it's turned on, and at that moment, I kicked until he turned to leave. I had won, but I knew once I went downstairs I'd pay for my disobedience. I played music and danced till I fell asleep. That night the spirit visited again. *So you all kick your fathers over here? Siii!* I turned away to the wall, but then she appeared lying next to me, with her broad forehead pressed against mine. "If you were me you'd kick him too," I said. *You should stop doing that. It is wrong for daughters to kick their fathers.* The ancestor took her forehead off mine and scowled, like the way those people in the pictures scowled in the family photo album.

"Is it wrong for fathers to hit their daughters?" I asked.

She scanned my face. I could tell she wanted to answer but she just sucked her teeth. *Why do you hide away from your family?* That night, I told her about all the things I heard from my room. Chairs thudding against the wall. Someone crying. Parents bickering in a language I didn›t speak. Occasional laughter and giggles, but mostly an overbearing preacher and gospel music playing from the family TV.

I told her about what happened in the house when I left the room. I told her about how each time I went downstairs, my chest tightened and my knees began to hurt. I told her the story about the time I saved my life before I had to eat dinner. I was washing a dish to eat with, and I must have done something to make him angry with me. When I turned around, I saw him with a softball in his hand. That was the softball my sister used to practice for her games, games that for some reason I never got to see. I couldn't explain to the spirit how he found the softball lying around in the kitchen. But that's the way it was in our house. You'd see a softball placed next to a fork, a bag of Cheetos, and a can of Raid. I watched him pick up the softball and aim it towards my forehead. Thankfully, something in my body reacted and my arm came up to block the collision from happening. I figured that if I was going to get out alive, I'd need to have my head intact. He tried to strike once more and I wrapped my arms around my head. Finally, he got tired of me covering my head and stomped away. It wasn't until he left that I realized the rest of the family was watching while they were sitting at the dinner table. We looked at each other, simply blinking for a moment or two until there was nothing to do but laugh. "Sorry." Mom said after a wave of laughter. "That would have been real bad if he had hit you."

"Yeah, that softball was coming for your head pretty fast." My sister said. I sat down with my dish, and we went on eating. That's why I hide, I told her. She rubbed my cheek. *I wanted to be you.* I tell her we could switch bodies. I assumed she had the power to make that happen. Dancing and flying between heaven and earth seemed like a treat. Maybe I wouldn't mind wearing a long dress with plain buttons. She could take my life and have my body any day of the week. But she didn't seem interested in switching bodies, all she wanted to do was ask me questions.

She asked if I knew the language my parents spoke and I told her the words I learned. Amesiere meant good morning, didia mkpo meant come and eat, dimi meant come here, and kopinwa meant shut up. Tears fell down her face onto her dress. I tried to wipe a tear away, but my hand just went through her. "Are you dead?" I asked. She sucked her teeth and sat up in bed. *They buried my body in a grave, and I have a tombstone.* I tried putting my hand in hers but it just went through her, and I finally stopped trying to touch her because I realized she wasn't made of bone or flesh. That night I learned she never got to visit America like she had hoped because she died during her last year of high school.

If I'm in my room, Dad won't hit me because he thinks I practice juju upstairs. Mom knocks before entering, and my brother and sister make fun of me from outside the door. They cackle saying, "She's talking to herself again," or, "She's jumping around again," or, "One of these days she's gonna break the floor." They say I'm bizarre. They don't know that sometimes the ancestor spirit dances with me. I taught her how to do the butterfly and tootsie roll. I draw pictures of what she could look like in the future, and she insists that I draw her in jeans and a tube top with her hair touching her elbows. I still say "Yes Daddy," eat what's on the table, and say my prayers. Dad still enters my room without knocking, but instead of yelling, he hands me a book to read. This time he gives me a book called, *The Souls of Black Folk.* All I know is that the book is thick and the author looks like he sits and broods all day. What do I care about the souls of Black folk for? Can't this man see I'm dancing? Dad teaches Africana Studies as an adjunct professor at a community college and loves books. "They pay us pennies." He says. "But at least I'm not driving a taxi like other immigrants I know with degrees but no options." Teaching is one of the few things that'll make my dad take a long shower, shave his beard, and leave the house whistling. It's the only job he'll work without a fuss. He refuses to work at any place where he has to punch in and out on someone else's clock. In his words, those jobs are mindless, and he didn't come to America to languish in a dank room watching a machine stamp a chef's knife. His eyes inspect my room.

"Your jumping better get you to Harvard."

I look at the cover and guess the book to be about five hundred pages or so. "Read this and have an essay to me by the end of next week. You should know who this man is." I'm fifteen. I care little for school, and even less for Harvard, though I read the books he gives me because I care for my life. I go downstairs to sit at my mom's bedside and complain. She lets out a small laugh.

"Read it. You all don't have my love for science, but you do have your father's love for words. Don't be like us with all these booksmarts but no money coming in. I want better for you than working retail and teaching part time like your old Mama here. Prepare your mind for Harvard. Ok?" She pulls the cover over her head to sleep. That night the schoolgirl visits me, rubbing my cheek and touching my braids. *Your mother really enjoys sleep. Why?* I shrug. She moves to take the latest book I must read off my desk.

"It's so dumb I have to read that," I say.

She thumbs through the pages, making a few grunts and sighs, perhaps showing a little bit of curiosity for the book. "It's alright." I say nonchalantly. "If you're into history it's not a bad read. The author writes like he's too smart to say things plain because educated people like to talk too much, but all he's saying is that nothing that our teachers taught us in school about this country are true, and if you're Black you really can't act the fool and lie to yourself." The spirit raises her eyes from the book and looks at me with a smirk on her face. *So your father isn't all that bad, huh?* She smiles almost wickedly, and in that moment I try to ignore the gnawing thought that tells me I hate her. *You will miss them when you leave here.* She puts the book down. *When you finish reading, I want to know everything. Don't keep good information to yourself.* That night I learn her name is Ekpewan.

It's my sixteenth birthday, and Ekpewan always visits on my birthday. For years this has been our ritual. She'll arrive flushed and out of breath because she's been dancing. Sweat will run from her forehead and she'll smile. *I dance over there the way you dance over here. I dance so we can find peace. It's coming. It's coming...* this birthday is different. I'm still too cowardly to run away but I'm old enough to know I will soon leave here. I'm also old enough to see that dancing and twirling in this world does not always mean things will change. I don't need a spirit who can't help me traipsing around here. We need a miracle. The snow-haired evangelist said if we believed and tithed more we would get one. We give ten percent to the church and keep the TV preacher speaking from morning till night, and still no miracle. Giving money to said preacher's church does not equal a miracle. For all the smarts my family says they have I don't understand how they came to accept such a ridiculous equation as a fact. The only benefit I've seen is our dollars and coins weighing heavy in the preacher's pocket while we kids continue to eat ramen noodles and stale bologna sandwiches for lunch. I'm sixteen and think like a true American. Miracles aren't handouts, a true miracle is bought. The miracle is in the racketeers pockets! I want to scream this at them. Take the velvet tithing basket and dump it into your purse. Pay your bills and get your miracle. You'll feel better waiting for God's light knowing your electricity won't shut off. I think this to myself whenever I see my mom's worn hands drop a check into the basket.

But if they were to follow me into my room and watch me when I shut the door they'd find me entertaining a spirit. If they found out that my closest friend was a spirit that went to another world to dance, I'm not sure they'd say, "Now there goes a girl with her wits about her. Let's put our faith in her." Maybe we're all untrustworthy in one way or another, because if I said the words, *I speak to spirits* out loud, I wouldn't trust myself.

Tonight I wait, sitting with the pillow against the wall, awake and ready. Ready to catch her. I can't tell if she flew through the wall, or door, or ceiling to get here, but she appears smiling. She always arrives like she never left, and it bugs me that I can never pinpoint how she enters my room. I straighten my back against the pillow and lean forward hoping my voice won't crack, "Unless you can bring us a miracle don't come here again." Before she can sit down to rest on my bed I say these words. "It's not fair that you get to go away whenever you want. You won't even bring me with you. That's a real shitty thing to do." She inches a bit closer, maybe wanting to rub my cheek or wipe a tear. "Don't come any closer, just stay away, please. I gotta get out of here, ok? I think I get what you're trying to say but you've got to understand what I'm saying too. They hurt me, they hurt me here, ok? They just do. I don't know how to say it, I don't how to prove it, but I know that it's happening. I got to leave. And I don't want to see you until I get out of here." She looks at me, not squinting her eyes in displeasure or anger, not looking like she might cry, but looking like she knew this day was coming. My right hand feels cooler than my left, and my intestines feel like they're trying to twist themselves into a bowtie. Nausea sets in. I get a sneaking suspicion I've done something wrong.

This is how I did it. The night I sent Ekpewan away I had decided to take the spirit world into my own hands. I knelt in front of my bed the way Mom had taught me to. I usually hated lowering my head before a man sitting somewhere in the sky that I couldn't see. Hadn't I wasted enough of my life bowing down, counting the scratches in wooden floors? *Women like us must bare it all behind locked doors over the comfort of our beds.*She'd tell me this whenever I'd frown in defiance having to sing another praise song or fumble through reading Psalm 63 before I could go to sleep. *On my bed I remember you, I think of you through the watches of the night. Because you are my help, I sing in the shadow of your wings.* I had remained skeptical about God, sweaty evangelical preachers, and whether or not Moses parted the Red Sea with his staff, but that night I clasped my hands together and thrusted my arms back and forth ready to call on a God of my own making.

A wooden floor mirror stood at the side of my bed. I had always wondered why it was placed there. I had rationalized that the room was too small for it to fit anywhere else but I wondered if it was there for me to say a prayer to myself. The God I wanted had a wide nose and skin that turned the color of eggplant in the heat of the sun. The God I wanted knew what it felt like to be chosen last for a game in her PE class and understood what it felt like to wish that the lock on your door actually worked. I didn't have much favor with a Santa Claus like man dressed in a flowing robe sitting on a cloud, but I could try to garner sympathy from the young woman staring back at me. I had nothing to lose that night.

I prayed that night. "Put me to sleep!" I shouted. "You hear me? Send me away." I groaned through tears and spit. "Take me to dance on a rainbow, or to sit on a star, or to fly through Jupiter, bring me there. Please…" I was pitiful, a blubbering fool, but the young girl in the mirror told me to speak. "Drain my body of every feeling, drain the joy, drain the confusion, drain the anger, drain the excitement." The words sputtered from my mouth like a sprinkler flailing about the lawn with no care for where the water aimed. "Take me out of this small town. Out of New England. I want something bigger, better, than here." The floor shifted from left to right and my arms pulsed faster. I looked at the young woman hoping I had said enough but she demanded more. I tried to unclasp my hands but it was as if gorilla glue had fastened my palms together, making it impossible for me to free myself. The young woman's eyes turned red and her forehead was glistening. She had more to say. "I, Artit Essien, ask for help. Help me. Please." The girl in the mirror settled into herself, eyes turning back to white and her hands unclasping. She became calm and I realized I was free.

A sudden craving growled in my stomach as my mouth watered. In that moment I had a taste for sugar; a chewy peanut butter cookie, creamy blackberry ice cream, a thick chocolate shake with shaved coconut on the top. A bitter taste sat like paste in my mouth and all I wanted was a sweet to hide the stench. If hunger was an entree filled with nothing but sugar I would have eaten it gladly with a knife and fork. Mom screamed from the bottom of the stairs. Shrill and persistent in her conviction to get my attention. "Arit, stop jumping around and come down here to eat!" Her message had come at the right time.

On any other day I would have pretended I didn't hear her and turn the volume on my CD player up, blasting the latest Aaliyah joint in my ears. But that day I felt no protest. "I'm coming!" I screamed. I think I had screamed, maybe I was too hungry to shout. I had decided that whatever was for dinner I'd eat it and pretend it was chocolate lava cake until I could get the real thing. I didn't shout or raise a stink with anyone for the next two years. All I cared about was finding a way to sweeten the hunger. I wiped the remnants of a young woman beside herself from my face and went downstairs to dinner.

I call home twice a week. Sunday I call because my family goes to church, and it's rude for a daughter not to call her family after service. Wednesday I call them because those are the days I must run to wash dishes between classes and homework. From morning until dinner I work shifts as a dishwasher, a gig I worked out with the financial aid office for work study.

I never see the faces of students placing their dirty plates in the dish trays. I do see their hands though. Hands with shiny rings, leather watches, magenta nails, all placing half scraped dishes in trays and utensils in soapy water. I study the hands of those of us taking the dirty plates to wash. Our hands are the color of dusk, tree bark, squash, pearl, and hazelnut. They spray half eaten food off plates into the sink. We're from the Dominican Republic, Los Angeles, Nicaragua, Ohio, Senegal, Massachusetts, New York, China, Mexico, Cambodia, Florida, and Barbados.

The wrinkles and sponginess of our dampened hands reveal we must wash dishes if we want to study here. Some of us pulling the lever to turn on the dishwasher are one of the first in our families to walk these hallowed halls our parents took low paying jobs for. Some of us take the dishes with satisfaction, knowing we will have our time to duke it out with the decorated hands that give us their filthy plates. We'll be ready for those hands in class, knowing that soon enough we'll give them their dirty dish back. When they ask why children from "underprivileged areas" never have their parents around, we'll say our parents are busy, busy washing the plates of people with shiny rings and watches. Busy scrubbing toilets, and wiping the asses of their ungrateful children. Then we'll say the things our parents couldn't say because they needed the money, for us.

We also have other perks that come with our parents' hopes and prayers, like the luxury of hopping from one dining hall to another and swiping our ID cards that let us eat with wild abandon. The grumble in my belly isn't all consuming like when I was home. There are other things to fill myself with, like staying up all night to write ten page papers for my African-American lit class or daydreaming about how I'll land a high paying corporate job and drive a Mercedes Benz by the time I graduate. From time to time, the gnawing chews my stomach and alerts me that I need a fix. College has expanded my appetite to a life beyond buttercream frosting and Arnold Palmers. Our cards give us access to noodle bowl nights, vegan food, spaghetti, ice cream sundae night, and good old hamburgers with french fries. If our families travel to dine in these hallowed halls, they must pay to eat. Non-ID carriers must pay for the five-star cuisine the school offers. Sometimes they can pay, other times, we take our Tupperware to the dining hall and stash extra food for our families. We also get to study abroad or cry in the college counselor's office when we're overwhelmed. No wonder when we visit home our arrogance prompts someone to ask, "Who are you?"

On Wednesdays when my apron is soggy, I call home to check on them. My parents still pray and give their ten percent to the church. My brother transferred to a new high school where the students are college bound and the class sizes are much smaller, which in layman's terms means he's at a predominantly white school with hapless teachers mispronouncing his name every chance they get. My sister's in her last year of college and is leading six different organizations while failing advanced calculus. They're my blood, and blood is supposed to ensure a sense of adoration and kinship, but I wonder if what binds me to them is a sense of the familiar. Like brushing my teeth every day because I don't want trashcan breath. I'm not certain that I check in on them because of that all encapsulating sensation called love. If I can make Thanksgiving or Christmas, I'll try, but I have no money to buy gifts or contribute to food for the holidays. If I want to see them, I better pick up another gig polishing silver for the fancy dinners the college president likes to host. One night, after I call my Mom, I can tell the schoolgirl, Ekpewan, is around. She doesn't reveal herself, and I don't think I have the sensitivity to see her anymore anyway. Studying for exams have replaced my days of dancing and drawing pictures of my future self.

The tingle on my ear gives her away. I'm not ready to see her, but I am willing to talk again. And listen. *If you leave them for good. Who will you become?*

The next morning I call Mom again. Her work schedule is more grueling than mine. She works during the day as an adjunct professor (they won't give her a full time position, though she works a full time schedule), and in the evening she works retail (meaning she never gets a chance to sit down). On Sundays she's energized from the rush of hearing the Word and more willing to share a few good words of her own. During our Sunday phone calls, I learn that she was once a girl (a fact that shocked me, since I thought she came out of her mother an exhausted woman), worked at a convenience store while she was pregnant with me, and believes there is God in science (How can you look under the microscope and watch those cells move and not see the work of God?, she says). She'll tell me stories about her mother and begins her sentences with, "My mother taught me…" or, "She was a wise woman." I think she tells me these things because she left her mother's house too, and maybe she didn't listen too much to anything her mother said until it was too late. When I finally left home, I learned that I couldn't fly on top of buildings, or pick up a car on my back like Superman, but I could move to a bigger town in New England, wash dishes, and study.

It's Thursday morning and I listen to Mom's sighs and murmurs of exhaustion. She has to finish prepping lessons for her classes and fix her mind on working a six hour shift selling furniture and appliances.

"I love you," I say. "I love you very much."

The line is quiet, and I'm not sure if I'm hearing her breathe or if there is static on the other side.

"I love you too dear." She replies, "And remember, God loves you most."

That night I lay awake in bed and pray. I won't bend over my bed to pray or read passages from the Bible. I lie in bed, ready to talk about what I remember. I whisper to myself, knowing a young girl with red eyes and eggplant skin is listening, until I fall asleep.

Here, you must choose sides. In the land of the free and the home of the brave they could care less whether you're Yoruba, Igbo, Ijaw, Galambi, Efik, Ibibio, Calabar, from the north or the south, multilingual, or the daughter of a chief. They don't care if you puke out the colors red, white, and blue, or love their founding fathers more than they do. When you go outside they don't see your tribe, or the garb you so proudly choose to wear or not wear; they see skin.

"We're not far from the dark ages here." I tell her. "Here, your skin is currency."

When you're walking down the street no one asks who you are, where you're from, where your people are from, whether you're rich or poor or somewhere fledgling in the middle, you're Black. And Black skin means you're a perpetual foreigner. Here, they shoot first and ask questions later, if they even ask them at all. I tell this to Ekpewan.

She eavesdrops on conversations I have with friends, all of us Black women, with our legs and arms crisscrossed with one another so we can fit on my twin-sized bed. They're from Atlanta, Arkansas, and Pasadena. They've been born and reborn in this country for generations, much longer than I have. Lisa, my friend from Arkansas, tells us about the high school sweetheart she left in the South.

"Down there, white folks can laugh with you over a glass of lemonade, but the next day they'll call you a nigger if you step out of place. They'll laugh with you till they're beet red so long as you know they're white and you're Black. When I started dating Bryant, his parents kicked him out of the house for a week. They wanted him to stay at his grandparents' house, but his grandparents didn't want to take him in, so he had to stay at his uncle's place in the next town. His dad went to see him and had a 'good ole boy' talk with him, saying that before he got married, he also had a case of 'jungle fever' before he settled down to have a respectable life. His dad was like, 'I'll let you back in the house because this is gonna end.' Can you believe that?" One of us rolls our eyes and lets out a sigh before giving an answer.

"Well, after listening to white people say they're not racist after wearing blackface for Halloween... it definitely is within the realm of possibility."

Ah-ah! The whites like to paint their faces Black over here? But why!? Ekpewan. She always interjects into our conversations. I hope she doesn't reveal herself and scare my friends away. They'd run out of here so fast. We giggle, letting our arms and legs shake with our laughter. I suspect Ekpewan might have found a little space on the bed, or sat leaned over in a chair, laughing too.

"Why would Bryant tell you this?" I ask.

"'Cause he felt guilty like they always do when they know they're not gonna do shit. He said he was in love with me and wanted to get married. The southern girl in me said 'of course I'll marry you,' but if I wasn't even allowed in his house, how would we work out? We didn't last too long after that."

Ekpewan's voice stays with me throughout the day, following me into the shower, my classroom, dinner, and bed time, trying to understand the conversations I have with my friends. *These friends you have are good. They have guts. You need guts to live on earth. But what about your other sisters I see walking on campus, the ones coming from Africa? You never sit with them. Why?*

I murmur back to her while turning towards the wall.

"I don't know my language, I don't talk much to my parents, and I can't stand the Nigerian gospel songs they play."

What does that have to do with saying hello and eating lunch with somebody? Though I can't see her, I guess she's lying next to me tracing my nose with her finger, or moving about the room dancing.

"Let me break it down for you," I pull myself upright in bed.

"The Africans and Caribbeans don't cross into the Black Student Union, and Black Americans don't really cross into the African & Caribbean Association. Sometimes we'll go to each other's dances or movie nights, but overall, we stay in our lanes. One side thinks the other is lucky to be in America because their homelands are barbaric and their cultures need to be modernized, and the other side thinks the other is lazy, and they don't want to be guilty by association when they get here, so... it's easier not to associate."

And what of you? She challenges, as if wagering a bet to see if I'm quick enough to match her appraisal. *Are you not African?*

"I was born here." I snap. "As far as I know, I'm American made." She does not say anything after my thorough explanation. I feel a tickle of satisfaction, triumphantly lying back in bed. I have outranked her somehow because I understand something more than she does. That night, a dream comes. Or perhaps something more like a memory. In the dream, I'm dancing with my siblings and some distant cousins that came to visit us from Connecticut. The fact that we moved into a three story house was cause for a party. I must have been eight or nine. One of the aunties brought dollar bills to shower the children with while we danced. I remember grabbing the floating bills and dancing to some song with a good beat. In the dream, I had more time to observe the smiles forming while we danced, and hear my parents say something about spraying us with money on our wedding day. The next morning, I wake up and write about everything I remembered about my life before I left home. I'm ready to talk frankly to the God I saw in the mirror that night.

To the God who looks like me,

I used to get hit and called a lot of names at home. My dad used to say I was a loose girl, a crafty kid, and a fool. My mom stood and watched him, and when she was too tired to watch she went to her bed and took a nap. It hurt me but one day I prayed to you and didn't feel pain anymore. You got me out of there and now I'm asking you to help me again because in three years I don't want to go back and live with my parents. I want a good paying job and a Mercedes in a nice neighborhood where people walk dogs with silly names like Periwinkle. Take me to California where there's no snow and the weather is nice. Help me put my degree to good use, after all, I go to an all girls college and we're supposed to be the leaders and the voices of the future. Give me a big voice with a lot of money.

Thanks,

Arit

On Sundays, I clean my apartment. I begin with my room, going through the closet to find unworn sweaters and pants I swore I'd wear months ago. If it turns out the hangers wore a shirt or pair of itchy jeggings more than I did, those clothes go in a box for donation. Then, I clean the bathroom, scrubbing the floor, toilet, and tub till I see their surfaces glisten. My mom said the two cleanest places in a home should be the kitchen and the bathroom. So I sweep every corner, mop as far under the refrigerator as the Swiffer will let me, and polish my forks and spoons until I see myself in everything I've touched.

I live on a street where Chinese immigrants walk under bright umbrellas when the sun gets too hot. Police cars speed down the street during the day, and during the night they speed down the street with their bells and whistles ringing. When you walk further down, you'll see bright walking umbrellas change to people hanging on the corners or sauntering across the road, letting cars swerve around them while drivers honk out their frustration. Selena's bidi-bidi-bom-bom blasts onto the street, giving people a bit of nostalgia for a woman wearing a bustier with silver sequins, unafraid to sing the songs of a resilient people. The week before a 90s R&B girl group blared from someone's storefront, causing a passerby to yell to the owner, "Man, you're playing all the slaps out here!" A stocky man with a baseball cap sells bags of cut watermelon and mango with chili and lime juice on the street to people on their way to the bus, to the hospital, to the store, to their homes.

When I finish cleaning my studio, I walk the street. On these days I wear gold hoop earrings bought for $5.99 and rub my skin with shea butter. I never intend to go to church on a Sunday, but I make sure to wear my Sunday best, which means a modest dress that stops a couple of inches below my knees with a cardigan sweater tucked in my purse in case it gets cold. Further down the road women and girls with short skirts and Brazilian weaves walk up and down the block waving to cars passing by. Some of them wear jeans and a t-shirt, or a dress that stops a couple inches below their knees like mine. They look like everyday people doing everyday things until a car slows down and they get in. I remember a friend giving me unsolicited advice about my neighborhood, saying, "If you see little girls waiting on a corner, just know they're not waiting for the bus." I've got to be careful walking the street because many times I've been stopped. I try to convince myself that I'm different from the other girls on the street. I found a job at some non-profit teaching kids from neighborhoods where the streetlights flash on and off, and there's a check cashing store on every block. The job keeps me eating rice and beans all week but at least I'm doing some good. I think this to myself as I step out the door. But every thought I have gets put to the test on the street, where the chill of the Bay Area sweeps up all our skirts just the same and you never know who's peeping. One man followed me for twenty minutes and finally stepped out of his car to ask if I needed a ride. I looked at him in disbelief and said, "Sir, I've reached my destination!" This isn't a walking kind of neighborhood. Not for a young woman alone. But on Sunday, after I clean, I walk. Not all people that drive slow or hang onto their street corners do that—follow people that don't want to be followed. Some call me sister, or queen, or give a nod of recognition as I walk. I never hold a glance for too long though. On this street, it's best not to linger. I've tried to walk to the end of the street, but really, it's one of the longest streets in the city.

When I walk, I know that Ekpewan walks with me. She's always there, the flea that won't stop buzzing in my ear. I hear her footsteps tapping beside me, and her voice leaves a tingle on the tip of my ear. She notes the trash strewn across the street, cluttered with candy wrappers, half eaten cheeseburgers, plastic red cups, bras, and even a used tampon. We watch cars drive around potholes taking up the entire street. We pass children playing in front yards with not much room to run because everywhere is fenced in. *Why do you live here?* She asks. These days I find myself snarling back at her in every exchange.

"Why do you follow me?" I ask this not wanting to know the answer but she offers one anyway. *Because I love you and I don't want you picked off the street. Something similar happened to me when I lived on earth and I tell you it's a suffering greater than anything I've ever known.* She drones on and I keep my eyes shifting about the street, taking in new sights and colors I didn't catch before. I'm getting tired of her in my ear. I didn't move across the country to entertain a wandering soul. I've got my own to save.

On one walk, we happened upon a Nigerian restaurant. There, I ate fufu that reminded me of my mom's cooking, jollof rice with dodo, and a meat pie. After we had found the restaurant (and felt satisfied with the food), we started going there as part of our Sunday walks. I met a man whose voice sounded like the TV preacher I watched as a kid. He turned around to look at me while he was waiting for the cashier to ring up his meal.

"How are you?" He asked.

"Fine," I replied.

"You sound like you were born here."

"That's 'cause I was born here."

"Do you visit home often?"

"Nope."

"Why not?"

I shrug.

Another man—I suppose his friend—turned around to join the conversation. He grabbed a greasy bag of chin-chin from the cashier while staring back at me,

"Are you not an adult? Why don't you go home? There's no excuse now."

"True," I answered.

"Leave her alone, brother. We all choose what we choose. Besides, it works better for me that my children don't know my language, and have never visited Nigeria. They were born in Sacramento, and all they know is Sacramento. When they ask me why my accent is so funny, I tell them, this is how Black people from the South sound. And when I talk in Yoruba, they never know what I'm talking about. They don't know a damn thing, and it works better for me this way. Children asking too many questions is not a good thing."

The man with the TV preacher voice and his friend laugh.

"My children are confused-o!"

I walk to the restaurant to cry and eat. Once, a woman wearing a large hat with purple feathers caught me shedding tears while stuffing rice with red sauce down my throat. She first sat across from me, peering over her plate of rice and beans to observe me wipe my eyes and eat my meal. Finally, she picked up her plate and walked over to my table, sat herself down and asked, "Sister, why do you weep?" I don't know what I told her, probably nothing, because in that place, people talk-talk-talk without listening, and laugh so hard that they may not hear what someone else is saying. I don't think there was enough room for me to explain anything because she took a bible out of her purse, recited passages from Psalms, and told me the importance of giving my life to Jesus.

"He will solve it all!" The woman stretched her rough hand to touch mine, "I tell you, you must give your life to him. Give your life to him, and you won't cry anymore, my dear." Ekpewan weighs in. *If I were alive I'd have given my life over to Jesus Christ but I don't know what he'd say about what I've seen in this country! She makes good points. If more people gave themselves over to our Dear Savior, then they would know to put their trash in the garbage. Little girls would not sell their bodies and would go to school, and the police would not be so corrupt. You wouldn't come to a restaurant to put all your business out for the world to see and cry without reason. I think I agree with this woman here. What are your thoughts on this Arit?* I say nothing to the woman holding my hand or to Ekpewan tugging at my ear. They don't care that I'm in love with a God that looks and sounds more like me than it does them. I wipe a tear from my eye. I should have known that it's best not to cry on a Sunday.

I always brace myself for the walk back home, which is all uphill. I should take the bus, but I hate waiting. Sometimes I think Ekpewan works her magic to push me up the hills a little faster. I always make it back to the apartment before the streetlights go on. Before I go to bed, I think about the day, and all the chores I've done to clean the tiny studio. Usually, I am satisfied with my handiwork and might sit back to watch reality t.v. But this Sunday night is different. I sit up straight in bed, with the pillow wedged between my back and wall, waiting just like I did when I was sixteen... for her. My ear tingles and I know she's near.

"Ekpewan?" I say. No sound comes back, but I know she's listening.

"It's time for you to go." There's no response, but in my belly I know she's there. She might be squinting her eyes in discomfort, or pulling on one of my braids, whatever she's doing I keep speaking,

"You're from my mother's side, you died when you were too young, and your life was hard. I'm sorry for that. I hope when you dance you find peace, and I hope you've learned what you've come here to learn, but I'm ready to move on now. I like my doors and gate locked, and I want to know who's in my room and why they're here. That wasn't the deal between you and me before, but it's got to be the deal we have now. So I'll see you when I'm too old to be alive, and you can take me from this world into the next, but for now, my life is my life. Go away."

I stare at the floor I scrubbed, the table I disinfected with Lysol, the mirror I wiped down with white vinegar. I sit until something shifts in my belly telling me she's gone for good. That night, I turn on pop and R&B music and add some Fela and other songs I heard in the restaurant to my growing playlist. I twirl and stomp on the floor. I look up different spices online that I will use to make an okra soup similar to my mom's. Later that night, I draw another picture of my future self. This woman is still tall, still wearing hooped earrings, with box braids hanging past her shoulders. I draw dimples under her cheeks and give her firetruck engine red lips to add an extra punch to her picture. The fear she has known is slowly draining out of her body, that's why her knees don't ache so much. She has sturdy legs, and she'd rather use them to walk than fly. I put the finishing touch on the woman, I draw her with her mouth open rather than closed. This time around, the woman on the paper has something to say. Under the picture I write, I, Arit Essien, ask for help... I feel satisfaction at my handiwork. The woman I drew is a woman made of her own efforts. She is made from sweat and elbow grease. I bask in this. Until... a feeling. My right hand, the hand I use to draw this woman turns cold. My intestines twist and tighten making me want to faint. My face heats up, reminding me of the many blows I endured as a kid. My leg twitches, as if it is ready to run leaps and bounds or dance forever. But I won't let this part of myself take over. I'd rather curl up in a ball and wish for everything to go away. The only one who knows this part of me, the part that wants to dance between two worlds is the ancestor I cast away. Ekpewan.

I will bind myself to her
wrestle with her
Swallow her whole
if she dare think
she can wipe me out
Unless she peels off her skin and burns her flesh
She is part of me
Her face and gait do not belong only to her
I'll be seeing her again.

Inspirations and Influences

ITORO UDOFIA

I DREAM OF A WORLD that dreams me.

Like most Black girls growing up in the 90s (I'm assuming), it was rare to see someone with my life experiences reflected in fiction. In school we read from the usual suspects, Steinbeck, Hemingway, Ray Bradbury, Shakespeare, and Charles Dickens. They weren't terrible writers. There were invaluable things to learn in terms of plot, craft, and mastery. The issues with constantly reading from these types of writers was one of perspective and value. These old white men were considered the pinnacle of all that was good and true in the world, and my dilemma with this unspoken idea was that my young Black African girl self did not exist within their realm of the good and the true. Thus, the problem.

Introducing works from people of color, let alone Black people, was treated as an addendum to the already stellar work of the founding fathers of American literature. We got Sandra Cisneros, The House on Mango Street, during Hispanic

Heritage Month, and Toni Morrison's, Jazz, during Black History Month. Those are the few writers of color whose stories I remember reading as a young girl, and I clutched to these stories like it was a lifeboat because they gave me a glimpse of something different.

I had predominantly white teachers who were crafty in nurturing their own intimate biases about the habits of people of color through fiction. Case and point. The required reading for my high school political science class was Richard Wright's Native Son. My teacher wanted her bright eyed students to learn about the mind of a criminal. What better way to do that then to read about the main character, Bigger Thomas, and study his natural tendencies towards criminality? That was one of the few books I had read where the main character was a Black man. When I reflected on this educational experience—about ten years later—I broke down into tears.

I've always written, I've been scribbling words on paper since I was four and can tell you most of what I wrote as a kid was rubbish because I was writing with no aim or intention. But as I got older and began to articulate these contradictions I felt as a girl in high school, I picked up the pen to write a world where someone like me could exist with dignity. Reading the works of Toni Morrison, James Baldwin, Ama Ata Aidoo, Nella Larsen, Gloria E. Anzaldúa, Amy Tan, Edwidge Danticat, Zora Neale Hurston, Isabel Allende, W.E.B. Du Bois, let me know that there are worlds within worlds to explore. In order for us to know these worlds and figure out the conversations we need to have, those of us on the margins must have the audacity to create in any way we can. The erasure of us is real, and in our creation we can find a way to make a world that includes all of us, in our full complexity and ordinary-ness. At least this is the intention with which I approach writing. My stories tend to have elements of the speculative and magical in them, as well as themes of familial relationships, identity, African-ness within a U.S. context, and gender. I'm very concerned with how people deal with difference and complexity, and I do think this propels me to write with a sense of immediacy because right now we need even more stories that gives our humanity back to us.

My story *Running* comes out of this urgency to create. The main character is trying to find her place within a world where she constantly fantasizes about escaping because she feels invisible. She lives within the rigid world of her family, which is a world filled with survival and denial. Then, she must grapple with the world of the ancestor spirit she meets. The ancestor's world is more mysterious and alluring, yet the main character finds tension in this world because the spirit is invested in her own limiting beliefs about how life should work. So the main character, Arit, is on a search for a world that has space for how she chooses to show up in it, and in many ways she's running away from these worlds to find her own truth. The lesson for Arit, is the same lesson I had to learn as a young girl coming of age hoping to find some space for herself: You can't run forever, and one day you're gonna have to make sense of how these worlds come together. Even if you choose to let pieces of your life go.

A Chat With Itoro Udofia

***Running* fits our Awakenings call for short stories beautifully. Can you tell us the ways that the story engages with the theme?**

I feel that *Running* is about a woman's coming of age, her awakening into herself and how she relates to her larger identity as the daughter of Nigerian immigrants. The protagonist, Arit, faces many mini awakenings throughout the story. The first notable one, is her realization of a spirit world that goes beyond the limitations of her conditioning of God. The spirit she meets dances between many worlds, as opposed to the God that has been given to her by her parents, and given to them through the colonization processes they went through in their homeland, this God is white, male, domineering, static, and sits judging everyone on a cloud. I think another way Arit's story is a story of awakening is when we see her engaging with the physical world. Though she is first generation Nigerian, we see her slowly develop consciousness around her Blackness in America. This has a profound impact on how she moves in the world and negotiates her shifting identites. Overall, the story is about a woman's awakening into herself, and how she both resists and allows the transformation to occur.

When you first submitted *Running* you mentioned that it was part of a larger body of work that follows the lives of Nigerian women across four generations. Can you tell us a bit more about it and how that meshes with your experience as a first generation Nigerian writer?

This story belongs to my novel in stories called *The Soil Below*. *The Soil Below* follows four generations of women grappling with spirituality, ancestral trauma, conformity, mental health, abuse, and change. Tensions arise amongst the women as they try to make choices outside of familial and societal expectations. I can relate to a lot of the characters I write about (of course!). In many ways, I've had to grapple with some of these themes and decide who I wanted to become in the face of what appeared as insurmountable odds. I think the reason why I write is to make sense of the historical forces many of us do not have immediate control over. For example, how does one deal with a God that is steeped in centuries of colonialism, exploitation, white supremacy, and plunder? What happens when this is the God you must wake up with, pray with, and end your night with? What happens when this is the God that was given to you? How do you begin to parse out all this history and legacy that has become so intimate and braided into your way of being? These are the questions my stories explore, and this is what I as a first generation Nigerian writer and human being grapple with every day. Negotiating and renegotiating the terms of my history, while doing my best to live a life that honors where I come from.

In terms of inspirations and influences, what are the works and authors that have inspired you the most when writing *Running* (or your writing in general).

Anything Edwidge Danticat for sure, reading her work changed the game for me. Toni Morrison, when I read her novel *Jazz* sophomore year of high school, I remember thinking, I want to write this way. Marie Vieux-Chauvet's *Love, Anger, Madness* was another sweeping novel that took my breath away. *The Rapture of Canaan* by Sheri Reynold's was another book that shifted my perspective on the ways a coming of age story could be written. Isabelle Allende's *The Island Beneath the Sea* shattered my world. Anything James Baldwin puts me in a contemplative mood. Nnedi Okorafor, *Who Fears Death* and Mariam Ba's *So Long a Letter*. Junot Diaz's *The Brief and Wondrous Life of Oscar Wao*. These stories in particular shifted me into exploring new terrain in my writing. I think whenever I write, I have these authors in mind. I also love reading great non-fiction pieces, Martin Luther King Jr., Janet Mock, Howard Thurman, Ta Nehisi Coates. Growing up I appreciated Steinbeck and enjoyed reading Judy Blume books. And finally, I'll read anything by playwright and actress, Dael Orlandersmith.

Tell us about your experience writing short stories: what would you say are the advantages and potential pitfalls of writing short fiction versus a novel or novella?

I've always liked writing short stories because it felt more digestible to me in terms of writing, but in the past year I've had more to say, and I'm exploring what it would look like to write a novel or novella. I think short stories are a true craft and art form in and of itself, you really need to distill the story down to its essential parts and keep the plot moving. I think if you're a lover of brevity this might be a great way to go. I used to be in this school of thought, but these days I find myself wanting to linger more on characters, their settings, and motivations. I think this is the advantage of a novel or novella, it can give you the space to go deeper into the narrative. I think with either form there needs to be a balance. It's a dance between saying too little or saying too much.

Finally, a question we ask all of our interviewees: We Book Smugglers have faced condemnation because of the sheer volume of books that we carry back home on a daily basis. As such, we have on occasion resorted to "smuggling books" home to escape judgmental, scrutinizing eyes. Have you ever had to smuggle books?

I try to smuggle books. When I travel I usually travel with a bunch of books. When I was in the airport security line my bag was pulled because it was suspicious that I had all these books in my bag (I think I had more books than clothes). I did face judgement and pure bafflement from the person looking inside my bag that day. But I decided that one way of smuggling would be to order books online so they can come right to my home or to wherever I'm staying at that moment. I haven't come up with a plan better than that.

Phantom Limb

REIKO SCOTT

AT FIRST GLANCE, HOW CYBERNETIC do I look? Can you tell my face has been reconstructed from a mold or that neither of my arms are made of flesh and bone? Cut them and you'll see—they shed sparks, not blood. But you probably already noticed the seam in my neck and the color of my skin. There's only one way to get skin as white and flawless as mine.

"Naomi, where're you heading?"

I slip my tablet into my jacket pocket and clear the remnants of my lunch from the desk. Taste hasn't been the same since my jaw replacement left me with a synthetic tongue and I've left most of my dessert untouched.

"I've got a lead on a place on Bleecker," I say. My voice is my own, though barely. It's too difficult to recreate the minute variability in vocal cords from scratch, so they salvaged those from my organic throat and stitched them into the folds of a fabricated larynx. The timbre has a metallic echo, though I'm told I'm the only one who notices.

"University kids, huh? Sounds about right," Williams says, hoisting his bag onto his shoulder. "I'm heading downtown too, want to grab a cab?"

I received my first cybernetic arm when I was eight years old.

All I remember from the crash was the wail of tires and a sound I associated with a tin can of soda being crushed underfoot. After that, nothing. No yelling, no sirens, no sobs. But that's what the mind is meant to do, right? Forget?

If it had happened ten years earlier, the doctors would have tried to save the limb. Patched the tattered meat back together and left the scars to grow like vines over what was left. It would have been ugly, but it would have stayed mine. Instead, my parents insisted on fine-tuned silicon and steel, the best of what medicine had to offer.

"The somatosensory system is equal to or better than organic skin," the nurse had explained when running through orientation to my new limb. "Electronic mechanoreceptors are more finely tuned at the fingertips than any bio-receptor can be. Pain is also cut off at a threshold."

I rubbed my shoulder where metal met skin. The attachment process was more agonizing than the accident itself—if only because I remembered it—but I didn't tell the nurse. It wasn't what she wanted to hear.

The Bleecker street lead is my first breakthrough in weeks. There are rumors of an underground cybernetic clinic selling mods—memory enhancements, sensory acuity adjustments, that sort of thing. There's need in a city like New York that runs on firsts and bests, and community health center prescribed ADHD stims don't cut it. I get it, it's hard to compete against the first-chair violinist when her cochlear implants give her perfect pitch and her wrist has been replaced after a bad case of carpal tunnel. It's tempting to want to program one or two fewer hours of sleep with just the flick of a dial. Cybernetic equal opportunity.

It's just my job at the NYC Department of Health and Mental Hygiene under the Cybernetic Registry to make sure that doesn't happen.

The apartment is retrofitted to look just like any doctor's office. The waiting room has bland couches and mag-tablets spread over the particle board coffee table. A metal plaque inscribed with "Min-ji Kim, MD" is tacked over the door. The receptionist stares at me, his eyes roaming over the top of a book that's fallen loose in his fingers. Politeness, or the appearance of politeness, tends to make people look away from my implants. This man truly stares. My clothes hide most of it, but he lingers on the subtler tells. The bump of the seam between shoulder and torso that makes the fabric of my jacket fall strangely, the thin scar that ghosts along the bottom of my jawbone toward my ear.

"Water?" he says, slow and careful, like the words have spines.

"No thank you." I take a seat, grab a mag-tablet and wait.

Screen after screen of modded men and women in the ads flash in my face. The desired body is the perfect body. No wonder there are so many pop-up cybernetic shops. I fiddle with the screw on my knuckle as I put down the mag-tablet and stare at the patterns in the rug instead.

When Dr. Kim finally emerges, I see she is a thin woman, dressed in loose fitting black slacks and button down floral shirt. She wears her white coat and stethoscope with the air physicians always do, as if they need to remind you of the power they have over you and your liver and lungs and veins and teeth.

"New patient?" she asks. "You need to fill out your forms with Mr. Cortez."

"I'm just here to talk," I say. "Can we go to your office?"

She taps her heel into the carpet. "We can speak here."

"Dr. Kim, I'm from the DOH."

The receptionist, Mr. Cortez, puts his book down.

"No," Dr. Kim says. "You need to leave."

"We have reason to believe—"

"I'm fully registered," she says. "Up to date with my licensing."

"We have reason to believe," I try again, "that you are signing off on prescriptions for cybernetics in unqualified patients."

Mr. Cortez rises from his seat and walks to Dr. Kim's side. His eyes glide from the line at the edge of my jaw to the screw on my knuckle I'm still playing with. When he opens his mouth, he speaks to the metal of my palm. "You don't understand how hard it is for people like us."

"Francisco, be quiet," Dr. Kim says.

"I'm sorry, but I'm going to have to take you in for questioning," I say. "Mr. Cortez, you are free to go."

"No," he says, placing a protective hand on Dr. Kim's shoulder. "Dr. Kim doing the work that the hospitals won't. Not all of us can afford the so called qualifications."

"Francisco."

"Dr. Kim," I say. "I'm giving you this chance to come without fuss. Please."

I wait. Somewhere, a phone chimes. A door slams shut down the hall, neighbors bickering over the crinkle of plastic grocery bags. Dr. Kim doesn't move, so I reach for my handcuffs, collapsed under my belt.

Mr. Cortez grabs my wrist first. The intrusion is quick, sudden—the man's hand on mine before I blink—but even as he twists, trying to wrestle the cuffs from my grasp, I don't feel the pain. I step back, turn, and press my chest against his, restraining him. The unwanted sensory input of skin against skin against fabrication is a bolt of lightning over my nerves.

He writhes. He can feel it too. "Fuck. Is any of you real?"

Dr. Kim doesn't struggle when I escort her out next.

In my first year of university, I contracted meningitis. One week into my hospital stay, drugged and tubed until I felt I had become one with the hard plastic of the bed, the doctors decided it would be best to restructure the lining of my central nervous system. I wasn't awake when my parents signed me off to be a test subject for the radical procedure.

They wanted the best for me, and if I was qualified for new cybernetic upgrades, how could I say no? Memory mods would get me further in life. Sensory acuity enhancements would allow me through more doors. It would make me better. It wasn't my first cybernetic procedure since the arm. I had one for my vision (nearsightedness) and some spinal reconstruction (scoliosis), but this was the first procedure that made me wonder how much of me was still Naomi.

Am I like the ship of Theseus? If I replace each part of me one by one, will it still be the same me?

You could say the same for the life cycle of cells, I suppose.

When I went back to university for my second year, I started to notice the changes. I could remember better, yes, but I saw it more in the tip of the head of a professor after a didactic. In the lips of the first boy who slept with me, grin fading from giddy at the beginning of the evening to half-formed sneer afterwards. In in the greedy twist of words from the well-known bioengineer I applied to do research with, studying the neural links of synthetic limbs. Under "skills" I had put down my cybernetic enhancements. I was given the position because I was told I would be easier to train.

That's when I stopped trying so hard to hide my arm in public.

I learned about cybernetics on my own, reading papers and tweaking my hardware whenever I had a chance. When I didn't know if I could call this synthetic arm *my* arm, I reconstructed it to be mine alone. When I didn't know if the thoughts that started racing through my mind over sleepless nights belonged to me or the flickering feedback of circuits embedded in my temporal lobe, I decided it didn't matter. I used the extra waking hours to devote to computational models of neural networks.

"When are you coming home?"

I was talking to my mom over the phone on a hot June day of my third year. I'd elected to stay at school over the summer to work in the lab, finals week running into long, humid nights with no air conditioning in my dorm room.

"I have a week off before starting the semester," I said.

"Will you be able to make Kimi's wedding? She told me she wanted you there."

"In August, right? Sixteenth?"

"It's a weekend, let me find the invitation. Oh, I can't read it in this light, give me a moment."

"You should think about the new visual implant they put on the market," I told her, listening to the far-away rustling sounds of my mom searching her desk. "You can stop complaining about needing reading glasses."

"I don't know about that," she said. "I've had reading glasses forever, it isn't bad. I'm not like you, Naomi, adapting to all this new technology. Oh, here it is. Yes, the sixteenth."

"It's a walk-in procedure, you'll be approved immediately. Uncle Ken had it done last year."

My mom laughed and it sounded tinny across the line. "I'm fine how I am," she said. "Now, tell me more about that project. I can't believe your advisor is letting you take that on yourself. And you said there's a conference…?"

I didn't end up going to that wedding. I didn't find time to visit home at all. Another opportunity popped up, an experiment my Principle Investigator needed to finish before she could submit to a journal. It was the first time I got my name listed as an author on a paper.

Instead of getting angry as I thought they would, my parents told me they were proud.

It doesn't go well in the interrogation room back at the DOH.

Dr. Kim's is just a small clinic, but it's the closest we've come to rooting out the ring of suppliers that serves the tri-state area in a while. Two years of work—of dead ends and dropped calls and shit luck—flash in my mind. Reports of untraceable cybernetics on patient discharges are piled on my desk next to pages of contacts in the major hospital in all the boroughs. Stories of stashes filled with forgotten limbs scatter across tales of stripped corpses and I'm left to untangle the whole mess.

We need concrete information to arrest the guys in charge, dates and locations, but Dr. Kim won't speak to any of the investigators about her suppliers.

Detectives Williams and Parker call me over after two hours with no headway.

"We think she might open to you," Parker says. "Since you're—I mean, you're the one who brought her in." He coughs, swallowing the remnants of the words still on his tongue. I know what he's implying. Mods and implants aren't the only thing people aren't comfortable talking about out loud. Not the only thing that prevents people from looking me in the eye.

"Room two?" I ask.

"Go ahead."

I bring a bottle of water and an apple I nabbed from the kitchen in with me and slide them both across the table. As I sit, Dr. Kim reads my name on the badge that's now clipped to my shirt pocket. She laughs. A quiet little puff of air, just barely a chuckle and very far from real amusement.

"When I first saw you, I assumed you were just another one of those entitled brats," she says. "White trust fund kid from the Upper East Side, daddy's connections getting you cool gadgets. Hungry for more."

No, I'm not any of those things, but I'm familiar with the impression I give.

Drumming my false fingers across the table, I work to keep my fabricated face steady. If she's comfortable enough to start speaking, maybe she'll say something of use. There's a click in the knuckle of my middle finger whenever I move it. I noticed it a couple days ago, but haven't had a chance to go in and fix it yet. I fiddle with it again. Drum, drum, click, drum, drum.

"But you're something else, aren't you? A machine," Dr. Kim says. "They made you into a machine. And now, look at you, you're perfect."

I stop drumming and she stops talking. The fan bolted to the ceiling rotates lazily and the lights hum overhead. Dr. Kim doesn't touch the food or water.

I walk out after fifteen minutes of silence.

"Sorry, Parker," I say. "She's not going to cooperate."

"She said something when you—"

"Nothing of importance to the case," I say, but he notices the way I stiffen. Reactions are reactions, no matter how synthetic the neural impulses are.

I think he's going to let it go, but instead, he leans in, as if we're buddies. As if we talk like this all the time. "Don't worry.

You did well today, Ms. Shimizu. Really well. The boss is going to be happy."

To my parents' confusion and disappointment, I didn't go into academics after college. All the hope they had stored in me since we immigrated to the US from Japan—the dreams they had cradled and fed me for years—disappeared the moment I graduated. Instead, I applied for a job at the New York City Department of Health.

On some level, I deserve what happened. I took the ship they built out of their faith and sailed it into a storm. And in that storm, my body fell apart.

I had tracked the location of a lab conducting unregulated testing of performance enhancing implants. They were applying new materials to old cybernetics, seeing if they could change out the energy storage systems in the fluid musculature of synthetic legs. The scientists knew the risk. As soon as I cornered them, they overloaded one of their own prototypes, sending flammable gas, shards of metal, and live wires cascading toward where I stood, a freeze still caught in my mouth and a hand too slow to shield my face.

It was pain like nothing I'd experienced before. There was no shut-off mechanism, no override. It was organic pain, so my pain alone, and I was sinking. The doctors must have told me what parts of me were dying—the flesh of my chest and shoulders and face that couldn't be saved—but I couldn't hear them under the sound of rushing water in my ears and the thudding of my own heart.

I was drowning.

If they ever asked me if they could change my body like they did, I didn't hear them. I never said yes.

Sure, it was actually easier to have two cybernetic arms instead of just one. I got used to that very quickly.

The face? It took me months to get used to that. They evened out the shape of my ears so they would be symmetrical, enhanced the little freckles on the tip of my nose that only used to come out in the summertime, lightened the color of my eyes a few shades, because who wouldn't want to see those beautiful eyes pop? They sparkle wide under the eyelid fold and defined brow ridge I never had before. It was all an improvement, they said. All to be just like those models in the mag-tablets.

After I got out of the hospital, I cut and dyed my hair so I could be in control of at least some of this new me. I ran my fingers through my short, blue bob and stopped looking in mirrors. After that, I could deal a little better.

My new metallic-tinged voice, though, I never got used to.

Mr. Cortez lets more slip in his interview than Dr. Kim does and it's enough to give us a lead on Kevin Yang, the younger of a pair of brothers running the Manhattan branch of the cybernetic suppliers.

His information leads me to a little shopfront in Washington Heights. The faded yellow and red lettering on the awning says Home Supply, but the metal grates over the doors and windows are shut. Inside, the store is empty except for a few shelves of paint and a lonely checkout counter. It's easy to find the back entrance, easier to break the lock with a lazy twist of my government-issued cybernetic hand. I take a breath and look up the stairwell. The dust hasn't settled like it had through the foggy window of the shop. It's been disturbed recently, the metal steps cleaned with the feet of frequent guests.

I ascend.

As soon as I make it past the third story, I hear voices.

"The doc down on West 103rd is looking for attention mods," a man says. I recognize his voice from the vids I studied over the past couple months. Yang, my target.

"CNS mods are tough. Skulls aren't forgiving."

I take a cautious couple of steps toward the open door of the office. The shadows of two men spread like spilled ink over the floor.

"There's a pediatric neuro clinic attached to Mount Sinai that runs through those like candy. Dumpster dive, for all I care."

I crawl closer, ear to the wall.

"I don't—"

"Shh. I hear something."

I hold my breath, knowing that the mechanical drone of air around my synthetic larynx would give me away. There is total silence for one, two, three seconds. And then, I know I'm found.

Before I can react, Yang leaps forward, slams the door shut, and throws his chair against the handle with a clatter of wood on metal. Without hesitation, I smash my fist through the glass of the door to unblock it, disregarding the criss-crossing wires that would have cut flesh. My fist can't bruise or bleed. The chair clatters to the floor and I burst through the entrance, but Yang has already climbed out the fire exit, his partner following behind.

I leap after them, the rickety metal ladder shaking so hard I think it'll collapse. When the pavement nears beneath me, I jump, ankles buckling, but the two are already half a block ahead of me. The light streaks over the line of parked cars and my legs burn with effort, fatigue coursing through my last organic limbs. My arms can only pump in a whir of useless motors and circuits. Yang leaps into the driver's seat of a black Toyota.

I gasp and call, "Stop!" but they don't hear me over the thrum of the engine starting.

It's over as soon as they start driving. They'll head straight for the George Washington bridge into New Jersey where there's nothing I can do to catch them. The tires skid as they pull away and all I can do is shout after the headlights whipping around the corner.

One week in May, after my first year with the DOH, I'd garnered enough time to stay with my parents for a week.

"Just in time to see the flowers bloom," my mother said in Japanese as I kicked off my shoes in my parents' genkan, ignoring the pile of slippers in a basket by the door. I liked the feel of bare feet on wooden floors, toes free to stretch and curl.

"Just in time to have me work in the garden," I teased back in English, leaning into the hug she was waiting for. It had been eight months since my surgeries and my mom still couldn't meet my eyes, instead fixing her gaze somewhere past my right shoulder. She visited me right after the accident, when she had pressed her palms on either side of my face, searching for something in the ridge of my nose. She said nothing, only nodded, like it was all so normal that her daughter no longer shared her wide set mouth or crooked canines. That nod wormed its way into my mind again and again, like a wave crashing on the shore. Like an error message in code, a loop I couldn't escape from. I didn't know what it meant.

"Dinner first. Help me cook."

My dad waved at me from the living room with the same look that slipped right by me, like water over a duck's back. It passed by the electronic photoreceptors in my eyes and tracked across the signal replicators under the synthetic skin that allowed me to smile and laugh and frown. The look ignited something, a tic in my circuits that shorted and cracked, and I could feel myself grimace.

I retreated to the kitchen and took the knife from my mom's waiting hands. I'd never been able to wield it with the same deftness as her, but I always tried my best to mimic her precision. Out of practice, even with my enhanced reflexes, the scallions were torn to shreds and the onions diced into uneven chunks.

"Who taught you to cook like that?" my mom joked, though we both knew the answer.

The joints of my hands froze. I sent commands to them to keep moving, but some signal got lost in the electric jumps between brain and fingers.

"Sorry."

"It's all your new technology," she said. "Makes you forget all the important things." She stole the rest of the vegetables back from me and started chatting so quickly I could only catch half of it, my fading command of Japanese dropping words and phrases. I hadn't spoken fluently since I was little. Little and whole. Maybe when they cured my meningitis and enhanced my memory, they did so at the expense of my language centers. Now, whenever I reached for Wernicke's area, it was like there was a file I couldn't access. When I tried, all I got in return was a buzzing sound at the back of my throat and shame electrifying my spine. "Remember when you were six? All you did was follow me around when I was cooking. What happened to my little girl?"

I didn't remember.

My right arm started to hurt.

I was afraid that when they fixed me, they reorganized my episodic memory too. That they picked through my thoughts and chose which ones I was allowed to keep before stuffing them all back—that my memories were tainted by surgical hands. I'd never dared voice this fear with the synthetic throat they'd given me.

Something I did remember: the ship of Theseus was remade to honor the hero's trip home. The Athenians had built it strong, over and over, to preserve the legacy of their past. What was I but a thing my parents made? Carefully constructed, over and over and over.

"Sometimes I wish you were still that little girl," my mom said.

I wanted to scream, but my traitorous voice was soft and full of static. "You wanted me to become like this."

The phantom pain in my arm grew worse. The nerve endings to the spinal ganglia had all been connected to the cybernetic limb, but I was simultaneously processing false data from my lost organic. For a moment, I felt like I had three arms—the two still cradling the knife, and the third, a ghost. My arm flared up in the agony of an impossible feedback loop, growing and growing before shorting out. I gripped the right limb with my left so it wouldn't spasm. I was pitching forward. I was losing the vision at the corners of my eyes. I didn't want my mom to notice.

She was still speaking quickly, but I didn't have enough processing power to listen.

"Wakaranai," I said, because it was the only piece of broken Japanese I could manage. I don't understand.

I call into the DOH to report what happened with Yang. My boss tells me I was impulsive. That if I knew what I was doing, I would have waited for backup.

"Shimizu, I expected better from you."

I know. I told him I could do it and I made myself a liar.

I end the call as I drag myself back up to the empty distributor's office, hoping to find salvageable data on any tablets left behind, but there's nothing. The men are gone and that's what matters. All the effort, wasted. The extra time I put in updating my cybernetics. The holidays I missed because I needed to catch up on my reports. Working on January first? My mother had asked. That's a bad omen for the new year. But I still need to prove myself. I need to catch these guys and show that my education, that my body, wasn't a waste.

I look out the window, at the rusted fire escape, and know that if I had been just a little faster, a little stronger, it would have ended differently. That I could plan all I wanted, but it came down to a race that I had lost.

I stick my head out, then my torso, and finally curl my legs out into the fresh air. Four stories doesn't seem too far. What if I could have jumped?

I rub my organic legs, feeling the prickle of hair that I hadn't shaved in a couple days, the scars on my knees from when I was nine and fell playing tag in the yard, the goosebumps that perk up when a cold wind blows my way from over the Hudson. I squeeze my shins, feeling the release of lactic acid makes them ache. Sweat comes off in my palm. I look down again.

I know why there are unregistered clinics all over the city. I know why people who have the means pay double or triple the uninsured prices on cybernetics. I even know why MDs, who devoted their lives to making others well, making others better, would risk their licenses to serve people who couldn't afford the implants they wanted.

I know.

The fire escape shakes as I stand, though it might just be a reverberation from the trembling of my knees. My organic heart races as my cybernetic fists open and close. I shut my eyes, imagining myself on a ship, salty air whipping through my hair as I prepare to enter the sea. I hold my breath as I jump, feet first.

There's a Japanese equivalent to the ship of Theseus. Shinto shrines, in a ceremony of renewal, are rebuilt every twenty years with entirely new wood. There are festivals to celebrate the reconstruction, the gods as their witness. The building is still sacred.

But is it the same?

At the hospital, they fit me with state of the art legs, more perfect in every way. Indestructible, two inches longer, blemish free, hair free, and milky white.

Inspirations and Influences

REIKO SCOTT

I WROTE ***PHANTOM LIMB*** **WHEN I WAS** a little bit angry. I'm still not sure if angry is the best mood to in which to write a first draft, like it's not a good idea to go grocery shopping when you're hungry or start an argument with your significant other after a bad day at work, but I know it did get the job done. Maybe it's akin to "write drunk, edit sober." Write angry, edit calm.

Anyway, I was angry at the live-action remake of *Ghost in the Shell.* Specifically, the whiteness of Scarlett Johansson who played the Japanese main character.

This got me thinking about the "shells" we all have and how at many points in my life, I've felt uncomfortable in mine. Whether that be the physical body I inhabit—its race or its shape—or the ones I've put on—white coats, team athletic gear, or makeup. Writing science-fiction allowed me to take that idea to the extreme, influenced by *Ghost in the Shell* and its use of synthetic upgrades, but set in a world more like my own. Naomi must come to terms with how each one of her synthetic modifications changes how others interact with her, and therefore her perception of identity morphs as her body does. This was how I wanted to specifically address what I *Ghost in the Shell* failed to, the cognitive dissonance an Asian woman would feel to be "upgraded" to a white form.

I took my current studies as a medical student and my past life living in New York City to create the setting in *Phantom Limb.* A little bit of midnight studying stress and the wish that I could just make myself smarter with an implant, a little bit of amazement at what we already can put into the human body. A city where it would be common that students would seek out mods instead of Adderall.

And finally, I thought about a conversation I had with my mom after we both read *Pachinko* by Min Jin Lee. We were talking about emigrating and immigrating and I told her I was amazed at her resilience in following my dad to America and thriving in her new country. How she responded surprised me. "I've always thought it was harder for the next generation. Immigrants come to make their lives better, but then their children have to live up to their expectations."

When we chase other's dreams we always fail because the expectations of others are amorphous, changing things. They are phantoms and our fingers will go straight through them.

A Chat With Reiko Scott

Phantom Limb was submitted for our Awakenings call for short stories. Tell us, how do you see the story engaging with this particular theme?

There's a certain degree to which we awaken to a new version of ourselves every time we meet someone new. We are forced to see ourselves from another point of view—ask ourselves what we must look like to this person. For Naomi, this constant reinvention becomes a literal event each time she awakens from a new surgery. With every new modification, she needs to meet a new version of herself and she needs to relearn how to navigate how everyone else sees her.

It is a tiring process to constantly reinvent oneself for other's benefit. I feel it as a half-Asian woman each time I feel I'm not Japanese enough, or not white enough, for other's tastes. It changes depending on the context of the environment, but the impression is the same. Who I am is never enough.

Phantom Limb was my way of expressing the frustration that no matter how hard we try, we can't ever marry conflicting desires for who others want us to be. That sort of awakening can destroy us.

When you first submitted *Phantom Limb*, you mentioned you wrote it as a response to the recent cases of whitewashing in media – please, elaborate.

I wrote this story a few months after the release of the live-action remake of *Ghost in the Shell*, starring a decidedly not Japanese Scarlett Johansen as Motoko Kusanagi. At first, I was more perplexed than annoyed, because hadn't Hollywood realized that every live action remake of an anime with a white cast has failed spectacularly? But when the movie reviews started coming in, I realized there was something much more to my frustration than just another face that should have looked like mine replaced by someone the movie industry believed more marketable. It was the very idea of the augmented humans in *Ghost in the Shell* implied that "Perfect," in this movie, is white. Specifically, when a Japanese woman is upgraded, she turns white.

It reminded me of every small moment growing up that I wished I were only white and nothing else. Still now, there are many things that would be easier if I could be society's version of perfect, or neutral, even if I wouldn't give up my heritage for anything.

There's more nuance to whitewashing and representation in media than simply having a diverse cast to check the boxes. There are stories that are unique to those specific points of view, such as Japan's hunger for economic power during the late 1980's when *Ghost in the Shell* was first written, or the feeling of being caught between worlds in an immigrant family, that cannot be effectively told with a "colorblind" casting. *Ghost in the Shell*loses its depth as a story because of the blasé way it treats the philosophical foundation that holds up the action scenes. It wasn't made by people who understand the underlying struggle.

In terms of inspirations and influences, what are the works and authors that have inspired you the most when writing *Phantom Limb* (or your writing in general)?

The idea for this story came about from a conversation at VONA – Voices of our Nations workshop for writers of color. Marjorie Liu was my instructor, someone I'd admired for her ability to tell complicated and nuanced Asian-American stories through speculative fiction, especially in *Monstress*. We were reading Kelly Link short stories and talking through one of my fellow writer's pieces on robots and identity and I realized what I had wanted the *Ghost in the Shell* movie to be. One part Marjorie's incredible bravery to put her heart on the page, one part Kelly Link's perceptive strangeness, and one part inspired by the writer across from me as we learned to be honest through our stories together. (And perhaps one last part Ursula K. LeGuin, just because I want her to be in everything I write.)

Tell us about your experience writing short stories: what would you say are the advantages and potential pitfalls of writing short fiction versus a novel or novella?

I've always thought of the split between short fiction and novels as the way they tackle the underlying theme of the work. Short stories ask a question, while longer works attempt to answer that question through the experiences of a character. For me, it has always been easier to finish a short piece because of that reason. I had the ability to leave the ending open and not feel like I'd let my characters down.

Novels, however, haunt me. I've been working on one piece for years because I feel like I owe it to the characters I've created to do their world justice. They speak to me in my dreams and tell me when I've misinterpreted their desires. I've committed their whole lives to the page and I can't get myself to let them go.

In the end, when I sit down to write a new piece, it usually comes out somewhere in between, and I'm staring at 20,000 words trying to figure out if it is a question I want to ask or answer.

Finally, a question we ask all of our interviewees: We Book Smugglers have faced condemnation because of the sheer volume of books that we carry back home on a daily basis. As such, we have on occasion resorted to "smuggling books" home to escape judgmental, scrutinizing eyes. Have you ever had to smuggle books?

In the home I grew up in, there was a never ending war of the bookshelves. Stacks of books would fight for space, toppling over onto the floor or under the coffee table, or ending up in a drawer that used to house batteries and rubber bands. My parents and I attempted to find order, laying out specific areas for my mother's Japanese language books or my father's extensive collection of books about the Apollo space program, but it never lasted. I lost novels under piles of cookbooks and eventually resigned myself to purchasing doubles of works I knew I already had but couldn't find.

So, my version of smuggling books was smuggling them out of the house (because our logic says when one space is freed up, at least two books can be shoved in its place.) I loved making my home a library of sorts, lending out my favorites to my friends so we could talk about them together. Even now, I've kept up that habit. I have a sticky note stuck to the back of the shelf in my apartment with a list of who has what book out of my collection, just so I can keep track and not buy three copies of the same book. (Though for gifts of these books to my friends, maybe I still will.)

Timshala

LEAH CYPESS

1

WE SAT IN THE SHADOWS waiting to die. There were five of us: the royal secretary, the two handmaidens, the music master, and me. The tomb was dark and musty, shadows pressing around us, darting into the flickering circle of light.

It was ridiculous to be afraid of ghosts when you were about to become one.

"It's an honor," one of the handmaidens said. She had said it five times already, more firmly each time. Her fellow handmaiden turned a chiseled profile toward her in annoyance.

That one believed it, and therefore didn't have to say it.

The two men in the tomb didn't believe it at all. Unlike the handmaidens, who had been offered at birth to serve the Empress, they had fought their way to their positions. Around the purity of the Empress's inner court was a mass of scheming and plotting and endless deceits, not very conducive to religious devotion. Both the music master and the secretary had spent years struggling through it.

Silence filtered in again. I kept my eyes down, but I could feel them looking at me—all except the taller handmaiden, the one with the sure and quiet faith. None of them knew why I was there.

Well, I thought, *that makes five of us.*

The tomb felt almost peaceful—or rather, the little circle we sat in, lit by four torches, felt peaceful. Beyond it, in the darkness where the Empress's corpse lay drenched in perfume, with her scrolls and her clothes and her favorite things laid neatly around her, was darkness and fear and a terrible stillness.

I had once wondered aloud, with one of my maids, what happened in the tombs. Did the people wait to die, quiet and accepting? Did they scream and try to dig their way out? Did they kill themselves, to end the waiting?

"Maybe they fight and kill each other," my maid had whispered, eyes alight with the scandal of discussing this, and I had looked at her blankly and asked, "Why?" I had never understood people very well. Not until it was too late to do me any good.

"An *honor*," the shorter handmaiden said again.

With any luck, if we did start fighting, she would be the first to go.

For now, we sat still, not looking at each other, and not looking at the spot in the darkness where I could almost feel the Empress's casket pressing on the earth.

Surrounded by all her favorite things.

But I had never, really, been one of her things at all. She had borne me and pushed me out onto the earth, it was true, but then she'd handed me to a nurse and washed off the blood and gone back to being Empress. I had seen her twice in fifteen years.

And then, in my sixteenth year, every day. She had started coming to my quarters, just to watch me—at lessons, at embroidery, at rest. I had not understood it, and had not been happy. I had long ago abandoned any need for a mother, or so I'd thought. Seeing her made me feel a sharp longing, a painful ache that was as impossible to fill as ever.

She must have known she was dying when she remembered that she had a daughter. She had already chosen my father's new wife, a girl my age who would presumably bear him lots and lots of round-faced sons. I met her, the future bearer of sons, right before the funeral—a pale, lazy-looking thing, though perhaps I wasn't at my most objective. I had just found out about another of my mother's decisions.

"It's a—" the shorter handmaiden said, then stopped. I looked up. Something long and thin and dripping protruded from her chest. A jagged dark circle rose around it, staining her white silk robe.

The music master twisted the knife and pulled it out, casually lifting the handmaiden's trailing sleeve to wipe her blood off his blade.

Her body hit the ground with a thud.

I let out a strangled sound, and clamped my lips firmly together before it could turn into a scream.

The other handmaiden looked at the corpse gravely, then turned her head and gazed at the music master.

"We're all going to die," he snapped. "It makes no difference, except now we won't have to listen to her whining."

The taller handmaiden pursed her lips. She had one of those classical faces, all dark eyes and raised cheekbones. "You didn't know she would be like this. She didn't start until after we were buried."

"So?"

"So why did you bring a knife?"

The music master sneered. "You don't think we'll need knives in the Afterlife?"

Her eyebrows went up a deliberate fraction. "You don't think she'll be angry at you, in the Afterlife?"

"I'll keep the knife." He slid it back into his boot and returned to his chair.

The brief excitement died. Eventually blood stopped spreading from under the handmaiden's body, and became a still, stagnant pool, uninteresting to watch. I watched it anyhow, because it was better than watching the others. Especially the music master, who had his head tilted back, as if he was more bored than ever.

The music master, I knew, had spent time in the Cthonian port—on the Emperor's orders, of course, but that didn't make him any less tainted. Clearly, it had skewed him somehow, and everyone had sensed it. In the months since his return from the port, no one would step within arm's length of him. Even now, the other chairs were set apart from his.

Even now? *Especially* now. The Afterlife was practically touching us, and there were no more cleansing rituals possible.

He had killed the handmaiden knowing that. She was so still, so dead, with the pool of blood around her.

Not that it mattered, really. We would all be that still, that dead, very soon.

I wished it had been the other handmaiden, the calmer and more beautiful one. I hated the half-smile on her lips. It reminded me of my mother.

The most beautiful woman in Timshala. So the songs said, and I had always believed them, not knowing that any empress would be declared beautiful by the bards. They were saying the same thing about my father's new wife, now, somewhere up where the sun shone and the air moved. The wedding was probably over by now, somewhere up where the sun shone and the air moved. They couldn't do it until the old Empress was buried, but my father would not have waited an extra second. He needed sons.

There was no requirement that he wait until his *daughter* was dead.

I wondered if he had fought my mother over her decision. Probably not; I doubted he remembered my name. Arguing would have been pointless, anyhow. She had the right, by law, to choose five of her subjects to accompany her into the Afterlife.

The remaining handmaiden had stopped smiling, and was gazing thoughtfully into the darkness. If there had been light, she would have been staring at the stone wall slanting over our heads. Not that it mattered....

"What are you looking at?" I asked.

I was surprised by the fact that I had spoken, and even more surprised by the edge in my voice. It was panic. I hoped it sounded like irritation.

The handmaiden turned, her eyes large and calm. I was sure she would refuse to say anything, or spout some mystical nonsense. Instead, she said, "I think there's something moving in here."

The music master sat bolt upright. My fingers dug hard into the seat of my chair.

"Don't be ridiculous," the secretary said. "It's just the four of us."

The music master was on his feet. "What did it look like?"

"It didn't look like anything," the secretary snapped. "It's pitch-black, and there's nothing there. Sit down."

"Now I hear something," the handmaiden said dispassionately.

"I heard something, too," the music master said. I hadn't seen him draw his knife, but it was back in his hand.

I forced down my fear. I couldn't afford to be afraid, not now, not until I was much closer to death. If even a tiny bit got through, it would all come flooding in, and I would scream and weep like a madwoman until the moment my breath stopped.

"Everybody sit down," I said.

They all turned to look at me, and for a moment I thought they were going to obey. Then the secretary raised an eyebrow, the handmaiden looked back at the darkness, and the music master said, "You're not a princess anymore, Siara. You're just a sacrifice like the rest of us."

Nobody except my nurse had ever called me by my first name. While I was speechless with the shock of it, the secretary said mildly, "That's only temporary. Surely you realize that she'll still be a princess in the Afterlife? You should watch how you speak to her."

There was something underneath the words, something that mocked me despite the complete absence of mockery in his tone. Whatever it was, it turned my shock into fury—and that was when I realized I still had faith. Despite my anger, despite the way I had lost control at the end and screamed at them to please, please not bury me; despite the fact that for the past few hours I had sat and stared at death as if it was a black wall with nothing on the other side. I still believed it was right that we were in this tomb, that the Empress should be escorted into the Afterlife. That *we* would escort her into the Afterlife. That we would die, and it wouldn't be the end.

For a split second, I understood why the handmaiden was so calm.

"It's still there," she said.

The second passed. "*Be silent!*" I snapped.

The handmaiden looked right at me, for the first time. I hadn't noticed before that she was avoiding my eyes. "It will still be there if I'm silent, Princess."

"There's nothing there," the secretary said.

And then it stepped into the torchlight.

What was it? Large, and clawed, like an animal. But there was no fur, no heavy, breathing flesh. It was made of darkness, as if the night had wrapped itself into form and detached itself from the shadows. I think it had no eyes.

The silence was broken by the handmaiden's scream. She knocked over her chair as she stumbled out of it, backing all the way to the end of the dim circle of light. The—*thing*—moved, and she screamed again. It was pure panic, not mixed with hope or faith of any kind.

It makes no difference, I told myself. *It's just another type of death.* But the only reason I wasn't screaming was because my breath had frozen in my throat. The thing had no eyes, but it was looking at me.

Dimly, I was aware that the music master was still as a statue, that the secretary was on his feet. The thing had no eyes, but it was looking at me. It moved toward me, in a way no living thing should move; blackness flowing into new space, forming new limbs.

And then it was upon me.

My scream ripped through my throat. It had weight, but not heat or feel or smell. I was on my back and it was on top of me, but it was like being attacked by a gust of wind. I couldn't move, and I couldn't feel why.

The handmaiden was screaming. So was the music master.

The secretary was not.

Cold sliced into my chest, cutting off my screams. There was no pain, only a terror so deep it was worse than pain.

"No!" the handmaiden shouted, and the creature was thrown off me. I had a quick glimpse of a long polished object—a spear—jutting from its side, and then the darkness swallowed both the creature and the weapon. I rolled over and scrambled to my feet, gasping and sobbing, just as the secretary threw a second spear. It missed its mark completely, thudding into the wall.

"No," the handmaiden said, in horror.

I raised a shaking hand to my throat. The cold was completely gone, as if it had never been.

"Princess," the secretary said. He backed away from me, into the center of the flickering circle of torchlight, away from the darkness where the thing that had attacked me either lay dead or stalked toward us. No way to tell; it was pitch black, and the creature had been soundless.

The handmaiden was shaking. "Defiler!"

"Shut your mouth," the secretary snarled.

My mind lurched and started working again. I stared at the spear that had hit the wall, then to my left, toward the darkness where my mother lay surrounded by her favorite things.

It was much debated, among priests, whether one needed weapons in the Afterlife. The general consensus was: better safe than sorry.

"You used her spear—" It took my voice a moment to work properly. "You violated her death-state!"

"I saved your life," the secretary snapped.

"I am here to die." I managed to say it steadily.

"Not like that."

I opened my mouth, then shut it, recognizing both the stark truth of his words and the enormity of what he had done. He had wrapped his hand around spears dedicated to the dead, his skin coming into full contact with the smooth wood. He could not become more defiled, not if he walked over to her casket and touched the preserved body itself. And he was about to die, and there was no priest here to cleanse him.

"Do you think it's still out there?" The shrillness of the handmaiden's voice gave me a mean sense of satisfaction.

The secretary glanced around the circle. "No."

"Is it… dead?" The shrillness of my voice didn't bother me. I had just been attacked by a creature that shouldn't exist. I had a right to be shrill.

"It can't die," the secretary said. "It sneaked in from the Afterlife." He reached down and, deliberately, picking up the death-touched spear.

The rest of us stepped back, eyeing the secretary warily. The secretary looked from the handmaiden to the music master, lips pursed. The handmaiden stepped away from him, closer to the darkness.

The secretary took two quick paces in and drove the spear under the music master's heart.

The music master didn't scream. He gurgled, lifted his hands, and dropped them. The secretary yanked the spear out, and the music master staggered backward.

This time, I managed not to scream.

"Sorcerer!" the handmaiden gasped, and only then did I realize that the music master's body wasn't falling to the floor. It stood, swaying slightly, blood and—other things—spilling over its white robe. The secretary chanted under his breath, fast and furious, and a faint light surrounding the death-spear he held.

Something moved near the edge of the darkness. I tore my eyes from what I was seeing—foul sorcery, desecrating my mother's tomb—and focused instead on a spot near the edge of our circle of light, where the darkness was thickening.

"We don't have much time," the secretary said. He had followed my gaze. "There's more than one of them."

"What are they?" My voice was beyond shrillness now. "What are *you*?"

The handmaiden must have been even more shocked than I was, but she still managed to focus on the most pertinent question. "Not much time to do what?"

The secretary spoke to me, as if she were invisible. "To get out of here."

"We can't get out of here!" I said. My voice rose, despite my best efforts to control it. "It's a tomb! The only way out is through the Afterlife!"

"Exactly." He tossed me something. I didn't react fast enough—I didn't react at all—and it fluttered to the floor: a strip of cloth. "Blindfold yourself."

"This is blasphemy!" the handmaiden gasped. "You are stealing from the dead!"

Behind me, something growled—a growl I heard with my mind, not my ears.

"I can't put down the spear," the secretary told me. "I can't put on the blindfold for you. Make a Choice."

It was in the briefest inflection of the word: *Choice*, not *choice*. He thought this was one of my Choices, a decision I actually had the power to make.

If he meant to make me move faster, he had miscalculated. My heart pounded in an uneven staccato against my ribs. Terror choked me; all I wanted was to get away from the things in the darkness. But if I truly had a Choice, could I let *this*—betrayal, desecration, theft—be the action that defined me forever?

"I think," the secretary said, "you should hurry."

I found myself bending and picking up the cloth. The secretary was wrong; this wasn't a Choice. I was completely ruled by my terror. I could not possibly do anything but follow his orders.

The cloth was silk, but covered with dust; once, I would never have let it touch my face. As I tied it on, with fingers that shook so much I could barely manage the knot, I said, "Why do I need a blindfold?"

"Because we're going through the Afterlife. Here, take his hand."

The hand that reached for mine was warm and soft. By the time I realized whose it was, the dead fingers had closed around mine. I opened my mouth to scream, and was interrupted by the handmaiden's voice. It sounded even shriller now that I couldn't see her face. "How can you do this? She's your mother!"

Rage ripped through me, and I accepted it as a gift. I turned my face in the direction of the handmaiden's voice. "What sort of mother asks her child to die for her?"

"It is your duty!"

I knew she was right, but I didn't want to die. I said the first thing that came to my mind, knowing it was a rationalization, not caring. "It is my duty to die when air or food runs out. It is not my duty to stay here and be ripped apart. That was not my mother's intent."

"You don't care about your mother's intent!"

"Stay here, then," I snarled. "The creature came for me, but I'm sure it will be just as happy to take you."

"No," the secretary said. "That will only give it strength. You will come with us."

"I can't." Her voice hitched into a sob. "It's impossible."

"People can do the impossible. Trust me."

"But I *don't* trust you."

I felt the secretary's body move, a sharp jerk. I couldn't tell what he did, what weapon he used. I knew only that the handmaiden screamed once, and then was silent.

"To be fair," the secretary murmured, "she was right not to trust me."

The dead man lurched forward, and I stumbled after him. My foot hit soft dirt, and everything around me changed. The air burned my skin. I opened my mouth to ask a question, and my breath seared my throat. The dead hand pulled me forward.

Everything around me was wrong, wrong, *wrong*. Shifting shadows moved across my blindfold, and I closed my eyes tightly, but I could still see them. My skin hurt from the inside out.

"How much—" I tried to say, and heard my voice come out in a series of growls, as if I had become something else. Something not human. Panic overcame me, and I tried to yank my hand away. The dead fingers held on tight.

I tried to scream, and nothing came out of my mouth. I tried to breathe, and nothing came in. My mouth worked frantically, attempting to suck in air that wasn't there. The dead man pulled me forward.

Faintness whirled around me, and I gave into it, with a feeling that was almost relief.

As I lost consciousness, I took my terror with me into the blackness.

2

I WOKE IN A LOW mat bed, in a small room, with a soft breeze drifting between the slats in the walls. I'd had a dream—a terrible nightmare of a place shifting and cold, where I had wandered for hours while my skin slowly faded away. The terror of the dream still gripped me, and I lay rigid and still, trying not to breathe.

A gust of air brushed my face, bringing with it the scent of grass and water. I opened my eyes and realized that I was alive.

I ignored the fact that I shouldn't be. For now.

I got out of bed and pushed aside one of the room's sliding walls. It let me out onto a covered porch, and before me lay the world. Craggy mountains retreated toward the horizon in green waves, then faded into misty gray peaks. A waterfall, thin and clear, rushed down from the rocky heights. When I tried to see where it fell, and couldn't even make out the mist, I knew the mountains were farther away than they seemed.

Footsteps hit the wooden floor behind me. The secretary stepped onto the porch, wearing a short, embroidered robe over baggy riding trousers. He bowed from the waist, very properly, his gaze averted from my face. "Princess Siara. Your servant, Keijan."

"What are you," I said, "and what did you do back there?"

He straightened and smiled.

"Answer me!" I snapped. And, when that accomplished nothing: "You owe me an explanation."

He looked me straight in the eye, a presumption that stopped me cold. "I don't owe you anything, Princess. I just used my only Choice to save your life."

My skin prickled. I had heard people say it before, of course, despite what we had all learned as children. Minor blasphemies: *This has got to be a Choice. At least I know this couldn't possibly be a Choice. Let's hope I used up all my Choices long ago.* But I had never heard it said with such certainty.

In my confusion, I fell back on what we had all learned as children, though the secretary had surely been a better student than I. "We can know how many Choices we have, but never what they are, even after we have made them. Only a fool tries to figure out the unknowable."

He twitched his shoulders slightly, as if I was a persistently buzzing fly. It was the most disrespectful move anyone had made toward me in my life. "When I was born, my divination revealed that I would have only one Choice. And that, in the tomb, was it."

An old saying ran through my mind, in my nurse's soft voice: *There is none so dangerous as he who thinks his Choices are all made.*

That, some cynics said, was why we were taught that it was impossible to know when our Choices were made. There were, in truth, ways to figure it out; but the knowledge was too dangerous. Every person had to believe he had Choices left, that there were consequences for his actions, that he would suffer in the Afterlife for his sins. Without that, society would collapse.

Most of a person's life was like a stone rolling downhill, predetermined and unchangeable. The choices we thought we made, from the small to the large, whether or not to take a walk, which robe to wear, whom to marry, were illusions. Forces within us and around us steered us inevitably into the course we took. No matter how agonizing the decision seemed, most of the time, we really had no choice at all.

Most of the time.

There were a few decisions in each person's life that were true Choices; moments where the forces of nature and society were equally balanced, and the decision one made was truly one's own. There was no way to tell when those moments were, to distinguish them from the thousands of illusory choices made every day. The Choices could be small or large, made in a split second or agonized over for months. But they alone were the actions upon which, in the Afterlife, a soul's worth would be weighed.

It was generally agreed that we had to treat each choice as if it was a *Choice*, not to distinguish between decisions; because we couldn't know which ones counted. It was only with reluctance that the law allowed priests to divine the number of a person's Choices at birth. And the same law absolutely forbade a priest from divining a person's Choices ever again. A man who had made his final Choice at the age of seven would never know it.

Because if he did, he would also know that for the rest of his life, he could do whatever he liked, and it would make no difference.

There is none so dangerous as he who thinks all his Choices are made.

Except perhaps one who thought that *and* had powerful death-fueled magic at his disposal.

I looked away from the secretary, so he wouldn't see my fear, and stared out at the landscape. I had never been so close to wilderness before. At first, it looked like a picture—one of the paintings that hung in my room, with quick dark lines creating a river and trees and distant mountains.

Even when I saw the rider coming, he seemed part of the portrait, six horses winding their way along a riverside. Only when the horses came close enough for me to make out the features of the man riding the first did the landscape seem suddenly real: a vast, wild, uncontrolled space, stretching all around me.

I could see the line of gray dust the horses' hooves kicked up, a thin cloud that followed them across the valley. Two were clearly pack animals, loaded down with bags. But even the saddled ones were far more heavy-boned than the horses in portraits, or than the elegant mare I had occasionally been allowed to ride.

A wave of disorientation washed over me. Since the moment I had stepped into my mother's tomb, I had accepted that my old life was over. I had done unthinkable things–gone unveiled before men who were not my relatives, spoken to people of lower ranks as if they were my equals, even been ignored by them. Still, I froze at the thought of exposing my face to that rider. I reached for my veil, but of course it wasn't there. One did not go veiled into the Afterlife.

I gestured at the line of horses. "Who is that man?"

“He’s a priest.” Keijan leaned both his elbows on the railing. “And a friend.”

A priest? I looked again. The rider’s sleeve had fallen back, revealing a red swirl tattooed around his wrist and forearm, liked a graceful wound.

I went cold, as if the shadow I stood in had suddenly darkened.

“He is a *Bechirian* priest,” I said accusingly.

“Ah, so people still recognize the symbol.” Keijan sounded pleased.

“He is not a priest,” I snapped. “Not anymore.”

Keijan made a *tsk*ing noise with his tongue. “You have walked through the Afterlife, and you still think priesthood is made and unmade by your father’s word?”

I had no answer to that. And so I said no more, as the man who should not have existed galloped closer.

No one knew why the Emperor had ordered the destruction of the Bechirian Temple, the oldest and wealthiest order of priests. This in itself was not unusual; nobody knew why my father did most of the things he did. It didn’t matter. He was the Emperor.

The Emperor, unique among mortals, had no Choices at all. Everything he did—*everything*—was predestined.

It had to be that way. No man could change the tide of time. A person who embodied a nation would, of necessity, have his will subordinated to the destiny of that nation.

So the Emperor could do no wrong. Even when what he did seemed clearly immoral, it was the only thing he *could* have done. There was no point in wondering about his reasons.

And, for the most part, people didn’t. It was a saying not repeated often, because we needed no reminding: *The Emperor has no Choices.*

The destruction of the Bechirian Order had been different. Both for the suddenness and savagery with which it was carried out, and for the great respect in which its victims were held. The muttering carried even into the women's quarters, for years after the massacre.

I myself had never seen a Bechirian priest. One had divined my Choices when I was born, but by the next time I left the royal compound—at the age of ten—the Bechirians had already been destroyed.

Only it seemed the destruction had not been as complete as reported.

I kept my head down as we rode away from the travel house, daring only the occasional sideways glance at the impossible priest who had brought the horses. He was not precisely handsome—in fact, he was the opposite of handsome, with hair that clung to his head in tight curls, and an unusually strong-boned face. But there was something oddly compelling about his rough, raw appearance. I had never seen anyone like him before.

But then, I had spent most of my life in the women's quarters of the palace, and everyone there was chosen for their beauty. They had all looked the same.

We climbed the path upward, into the mountains. I kept my eyes on the ground right in front of me, focusing only on the grass and mud, trying not to think about anything else. For weeks, all thoughts of my future had ended with my imminent death. I didn't know what to do with the sudden vast unknown stretching ahead of me.

I didn't know where we were going. I didn't know anything. From the moment the ex-priest had ridden up, I had been too afraid to say a word. Keijan had greeted him calmly, as if he had expected him–which clearly he must have, given the two saddled horses.

My horse's shadow lengthened to a sprawling, elongated grayness before we finally stopped. I was relieved; I hadn't ridden in a year, and my thighs were in agony. But I remained where I was. Despite wanting nothing more than to be off my horse, I didn't know how to manage it. At the travel house, there had been a mounting step; here, the ground seemed miles away. And Keijan, who had helped me mount, was busy untying one of the saddlebags, and seemed unaware of my dilemma.

Finally, the priest came over, linking his hands together so I could step into them. I revealed more than my ankles in my desperate scramble out of the saddle, and as I rearranged my robe, flustered, I caught the priest staring at me. His rough-hewn face was expressionless, but something in it made my stomach tighten. As soon as I was on the ground, I turned my back on him and looked around.

I knew where we were immediately, though I had never been here before—at least, not since I was three days old. A stone stairway, gray and pitted, led up to a low, flat plateau littered with half-broken white pillars. Tree roots snaked across the ground, but there was not a single tree left standing, and the ruins were baked in sunlight.

I drew in my breath. "My father said no one was to step foot in this place for a hundred years."

Keijan removed a brown pouch from the saddlebag. It was tightly closed, but I could make out the faint, sweet-and-sharp scent of incense leaking out. "Your father also said that you were to die in your mother's tomb. We seem to be breaking a lot of laws today, Princess."

I could hardly argue with that. "Why are we here?"

Keijan re-tied the saddlebag. "We are here because I need to be cleansed."

I couldn't argue with *that*, either. He had desecrated the dead, practiced sorcery in a tomb, and opened a path through the Afterlife. "The Bechirians can't cleanse you. They no longer exist."

"One of them brought us here."

The stranger had finished hobbling the horses and was watching us, his deep-set eyes like smoldering coals. "He is no longer a priest."

"Why not? Because your father said so?"

Until the day of my death, the royal court had been my whole world. There had been excursions, occasionally, in silk-sheathed carriages and litters; I had seen mountains and trees and temples before today. I had been taught languages and history and art.

And I had been taught that all the Bechirian priests were dead. But one of them was staring at me, so hard his eyes were darts of fire in my back.

"There's no *temple* here anymore," I said finally. My father had certainly accomplished that.

"It's not the temple that's important; it's the site. And Parun knows the rites. It will take an hour, no more."

And then what? I said, "Parun?"

"An odd name, yes. His mother gave it to him." He hid a smile, and I could tell he planned to shock me again. "She was Cthonian."

Despite being braced for it, I couldn't control my expression. Keijan let his smile out. "Don't look so repulsed, Princess. It's impolite."

Cthonian. That explained both the priest's strange name and his strange looks.

A Cthonian had come to my father's court once, to negotiate the expansion of the Port of Foreigners, the only spot in Timshala where Cthonians were allowed to remain overnight. But I hadn't seen him. The women and children had stayed in their quarters that day, for fear of attracting one of the evil spirits sure to be trailing him. But we had watched him through the windows as he left the castle and headed back to the port.

"Be reasonable," Keijan said. "Going strictly by tradition, you should be dead right now. An unorthodox cleansing seems like a small price to pay for passing through the Afterlife."

I remembered the dark forms brushing against me, the shivers of fear and fury that had swirled around me. I pushed the memories away, and was left only with an uncomfortable disquiet in the pit of my stomach.

"How *did* we pass through?" I asked. "How am I still alive?"

"I don't know."

"But you're the one who did it."

"I was given instructions, and I followed them."

"Given instructions by whom?"

Someone cleared his throat behind us. I turned and saw the half-Cthonian priest—*ex*-priest—standing right behind us. I couldn't tell, from his face, how much of our conversation he had overheard.

"I'm ready," he said. "I'll cleanse the girl first—"

"You will not," I snapped. "I'll wait for a real priest."

His face didn't change expression. He looked at Keijan, as if nothing I said could possibly be important enough to merit his attention.

"You should allow it," Keijan said. "If nothing else, it will settle your mind."

I drew the tatters of my dignity around me. "No one has ever been cleansed by a priesthood that shouldn't exist."

"And no one has ever walked through the Afterlife and come out sane." Keijan shrugged, his robe rippling with the movement. "Just because no one ever has, doesn't mean no one *can*."

That was assuming we had come out sane. Which I did not consider a settled fact.

I didn't quite dare say it, but I didn't have to. Keijan smiled, a bit ruefully, and turned away. "You only can't if you *think* you can't. Consider that, Princess. Meanwhile, I will take on the impossible." He untied the pouch, and the warm scent of incense—of security, and home—filled the air for the briefest of moments. "Again."

I didn't watch the cleansing ritual. It would have felt wrong, watching a priestly rite performed by someone who was not—no matter what anyone claimed—a priest.

Besides, I had undergone the ritual myself, plenty of times. It would have been both wrong *and* boring.

The two men disappeared behind a huge fallen pillar, its elaborately carved base inscribed with green and black mold.

It occurred to me that they had left me alone with the horses. The path into the valley was a dusty brown ribbon. The clouds' shadows drifted over the mountains, shifting patterns of dark green. If I wanted to escape…

The thought didn't last more than a second before reality shredded it into wisps. I didn't know if I could get on a horse by myself, I had no idea where I was, and I wasn't even supposed to be alive. *Escape* was not a real option.

Though it hadn't been an option in the tomb, either. Until Keijan had violated the dead and ripped open a path through the Afterlife.

Shadows under my skin. Soft, dead fingers around mine. No air in my lungs, no sound in my mouth….

I shook my head furiously and pushed it away.

I wondered what it was Keijan was being cleansed for. The touch of the spirits, creatures with no souls and no Choices? The touch of the dead—a human body stripped of soul and Choice, even worse than spirits who had never had them to begin with? Or the loss of his own Choices, which caused the greatest uncleanliness of all?

Surely, he was correct; what he had done in that tomb was a Choice. There was no upbringing, no temperament, that could compel a man to do something so unthinkable.

And what *I* had done? Taking his hand and letting him lead me into the unthinkable? Was it really true, as I'd told myself, that my fear had ruled me too entirely to leave me a Choice? Or had that been one of my Choices—in which case, I *did* need cleansing?

I couldn't know. No one could, which was why we all got cleansed once a year, in case we had used up a Choice since the year before. It was futile to waste time worrying over it.

The clouds' shadows drifted over the mountains, shifting patterns of dark green. Every once in a while, I heard one of the high notes in the ex-priest's chant, or smelled a faint waft of incense. The horses occasionally slurped water from an old cistern, and a few flies buzzed around their hides. Eventually, I curled up on a patch of grass and closed my eyes.

Exhaustion washed over me, a black wave. But the ground was covered with rocks, and my mind was worse, ricocheting between jagged thoughts. For the first time in my life, I had no idea what the next day would bring, or even what the purpose of today was. I didn't even know who I was, now that I was neither a princess nor dead.

A week ago, when the servant had come and told me of my mother's command, I had thought my life was over. I remembered every detail of that moment: the color of my veil, the marble floor cold beneath my bare feet, the shocked and titillated gasps of my handmaidens. In that moment, I had grown a dozen years. I had tilted my head, conscious of the handmaidens' eyes upon me–they were from noble families, every one, and my response would filter back to my father–and said calmly, "Of course. Thank you."

The priests say that death, looked upon correctly, is not such a terrible thing. I had tried my hardest to believe that. I had amazed even myself with my calm, talked myself into the role of willing sacrifice. Until I stepped out of my litter at the tomb site, and saw the taller handmaiden serene and smiling, and recognized that she was calm and I was not. Until I saw the wet earth crumbling around the entrance to my mother's tomb, and disgraced myself by fighting my fate.

I would not break down again. I would make up for the way I had been forcibly dragged into my mother's tomb.

But though I forced my eyes wide open and bit my lip, the tears came, wet and salty and unstoppable.

I told myself I was letting them come—the illusion of choice giving me comfort. I wept until I had drained myself dry.

And then, finally, I slept.

The next morning dawned gray and humid. I woke with a sheen of sweat covering my skin, and, over that, a thick woolen blanket. Someone had covered me in the night—Keijan, or Parun.

Whoever had done it would have seen my tear-streaked face.

I sat up slowly. My bones felt as if I'd spent the night in a torture pit. When I tried to look around, a painful spasm went up my neck.

The men were both awake, and had been for a while, judging by the red embers of a campfire and the saddled horses. Parun walked over and handed me a long brown stick of travel bread.

Was a girl who had escaped her legal death by walking through the Afterlife permitted to partake of food served by a priest who shouldn't exist?

I bit off a piece and forced myself to chew. The ex-priest smirked at me, as if I was a child who had learned to pick a flower, which irritated me so much that I handed back the bread. It wasn't much of a sacrifice. The single piece I had swallowed lay in my empty stomach like a stone.

Keijan helped me mount, and nobody spoke as we rode back along the path, our horses' hooves thudding rhythmically against the dirt. I was glad of the silence. Yesterday's ride had been uncomfortable; today's was agony. My thighs chafed with every motion, and my hunger grew into a painful, gaping ache.

I focused on that, and not on my fear. By the time the sun was high in the sky, adding burning heat and prickling sweat to my discomfort, I was no longer thinking about what lay ahead, or my doubts, or my unveiled face. All I cared about was getting off the horse.

"At some point," Parun said to Keijan, "are you going to tell us where we are going?" His voice was a beat too slow, like he was thinking over whether talking was worth the effort.

I flicked a sideways glance at him, just long enough to see the sharp curve of his mouth, the glitter of his black eyes.

"We are headed for the Hikaras' northern castle," Keijan said. "We'll be there by nightfall."

"The Hikaras?" My voice was high and thin, but at least I didn't sound panicked. "My mother's family?"

Keijan shrugged. "Blood calls to blood. They might be interested in keeping you alive."

"But my mother was the one who–" Tried to kill me. I could have said it–I didn't need to surround the truth with poetry–but he interrupted me.

"Let's hope it wasn't on their orders."

My mother was the Empress of Timshala, and followed no one's orders save those of the Emperor. The suggestion was ridiculous–wasn't it?

My stomach tightened. Could it be? That she had not wanted to kill me, but had been forced to do it?

I looked away from Keijan, staring instead at the purple wildflowers that rose in clustered spikes along the side of the road. I didn't want to think too hard about why my mother had ordered my death. Thinking made me care, and I didn't want to care.

But the priests had a saying: *Understanding the past is essential. The past is a stone rolling downhill, flattening the present and shaping the future.*

Something sharp pricked me, a poisoned sliver of hope. Maybe, with my mother's family, I would find more than safety. Maybe I would find answers.

3

IT WAS WELL BEFORE NIGHTFALL when I saw the Hikara castle looming ahead, the triangles of its rooftops jutting against the fading sky. The sun was going down in a swirl of blue and pink, casting a golden light over the neatly symmetrical building, making it look more regal than it had a right to be.

A clatter of hooves alerted me, and I turned as Parun pulled his mount up beside mine. Immediately, I averted my eyes, but his gaze remained on my face. My tension communicated itself to my mare, who snorted and shook her head.

My face felt prickly and naked. Parun was watching me with that expression again, the one that made my stomach twist. I looked straight ahead, tilting my head forward so my hair veiled my face.

"Come, Princess," he said. "We're in between palaces at the moment. On the road, you can deign to look at me."

"And you, apparently, can presume to talk to me." I kept my eyes on the peaks ahead. "How very tiresome."

"Is it?" His mount trotted a few step forward, so that he was slightly ahead of me, which made it harder not to look at him. His voice went on in that irritatingly lazy cadence. "I would think you would find freedom more… interesting."

"You call this freedom?" I said, against my better judgment.

He shrugged. "In the palace, your every move was dictated, wasn't it? Your schedule, the tea you drank, the way your flowers were arranged. Everything decided months in advance and overseen by a dozen people. All within the same walls and screens you saw every day, and would see every day until you died." He swept an arm out, his sleeve trailing against the sky. "Here, there are no walls. You can spur your steed down any path."

My mare's hooves plodded in the mud, clump-slide, lurch-suck.

"Where would I go?" I heard myself say.

His eyes brightened, as if I'd handed him some sort of victory. "You have options. The capital is three days' ride behind us. You could go back, confront your father—"

I made a strangled noise low in my throat. He said, "Or you could escape. The Port of Foreigners is at the edge of the peninsula, and beyond even the emperor's jurisdiction. It's two days' ride away, if you can manage on your own that long."

I couldn't, and he knew I couldn't. Just as he knew I couldn't go back to my father's court, when I should be dead; just as he knew I couldn't enter the Port of Foreigners.

He was taunting me.

"It's not that terrible, the port," he said. "I've been there."

I knew what he expected to see in my face, and did my best not to oblige him. I couldn't tell whether I succeeded; he laughed scornfully without even looking at me. "It was the only safe place to hide, after your mother destroyed my home. And now you need to hide, don't you?"

I wanted to say no. That I was done hiding, done cowering in the dark. But it would have been a lie; and I had never been stupid enough to pretend I was stronger than I was. The girls who didn't understand how helpless they were, who thought their beauty or noble birth could give them power, were the ones who ended up dead.

So I said nothing, enduring Parun's smirk—I had endured much worse—until the trail narrowed, beginning its ascent, and he dropped back to ride behind me.

The trail soon became a treacherous switchback, winding up between gnarled trees and dark patches of ferns. I clung to my horse's mane and did not look down. Up ahead, the Hikara castle rose into the mist. When the trail turned, I could see the sea, far to the east, and the Port of Foreigners: a black, viscous blot against the sweeping curve of green and blue. A blight on our nation, a scab that contained the pus but still itched.

We were met at the castle gate by a stern-faced woman, her gray hair arranged in the elaborate braids and black pearl beads that marked her as a widow. Her eyebrows were shaved in the old style, but she managed to look surprised anyhow. "Your Highness?"

I glanced at Keijan.

"Siara," Keijan said. There was a small sigh in his voice. "This is your grandmother."

When my mother became Empress, she had renounced all former ties; and even if that renunciation was more official than real, she had never traveled anywhere with me. So I was fairly certain I had never seen my grandmother before. Even so, I bowed and said, "My apologies for not recognizing you."

She snorted. "That's the least of my concerns right now. Will you apologize for being alive?"

I started to say yes—I *shouldn't* be alive—but something in her voice made me think that wasn't what she wanted. I straightened and looked her in the eye. She might be my grandmother, but I was the one with royal blood.

"No," I said. "I will not."

She snorted again, and not with the approval I had half-anticipated. "Follow me, child." This time, when she turned into the castle courtyard, I didn't look at Keijan. I strode after her.

The old woman led me into the castle, down a long corridor, and through a translucent drapery into a massive domed hall populated entirely by women. After one quick glance at us, the women went back to what they had been doing—weaving, painting, talking.

My dread unclenched, the tiniest bit. This was not the women's court of the emperor's palace—it was a quarter the size, the floor was plain white marble instead of colorful mosaics, and the perfume that filled the air was far less subtle. But it was familiar enough.

A group of young girls were sitting on an arrangement of rugs near the center of the hall, all colorful robes and braided hair. They looked up and went silent as my grandmother led me in, and I was sharply aware of my creased, stained robe, of my disheveled hair, and of the reek that must be wafting from me.

My grandmother turned her head, and the girls quickly looked back down. As we drew closer, I saw what they were occupied with—sets of small wooden rectangles with red and black symbols etched into them.

I had heard of gaming, of course—a vice brought to our country by the Cthonians, that had spread like the plague despite the priests' constant harangues. In the palace, it was not exactly forbidden, but custom and sentiment made it worse than forbidden. What if you lost your Choice in a decision made in a game of chance? But these girls went on playing, apparently unconcerned by either my grandmother's presence or the danger to their souls.

I tried to decide whether to smile at them. But my grandmother swept by without stopping, and after only a moment's hesitation, I followed. It seemed easiest.

The perimeter of the hall was ringed by rooms, and my grandmother led me into what was, apparently, my room. It was smaller than an attendant's quarters at the palace but had an adequately-sized bed heaped with pillows, and a sectioned chest for clothes.

"I thank you," I said, after a short silence.

My grandmother smiled, as if I had said something amusing. "You understand that you are to tell no one who you are."

"Of course." I wasn't about to admit that I *understood* absolutely nothing. "What should I tell them?"

"Keijan will work out the details. He'll be here shortly to tell you about them."

My sense of familiarity vanished; apparently, I didn't know the rules after all. "*Here*? In the women's court? How is that permitted?"

"I suppose he'll have to come up with a story to explain that, too."

And with that, she was gone, leaving my next question—if I had dared voice it—to wait for Keijan.

It took him long enough to show up. There were no hourglasses or time-marked candles in my room, and I had nothing but my mounting anxiety with which to measure the passing time. It felt like hours. The occasional giggle or squeal reached me from the hall, but I didn't dare go out, not until I knew what story I was to tell.

It occurred to me, as I lay draped over the bed, that I could go out anyhow. My grandmother hadn't actually instructed me to wait, and I knew the rules of the women's quarter more than well enough to handle myself. I didn't have to wait for Keijan to come with answers, or lies. (Or both.) I could walk out on my own and start looking for the truth.

I stepped over to the door and stood before it. A shard of excitement went through me, but on its heels came a wave of fear.

That terror in the darkness, in my mother's tomb, had been the culmination of a lifetime of a gentler, more bearable fear. I had always known my life was controlled by people and forces far beyond my reach, that I could be deemed expendable at any moment. I had always known the safest course was to be pliable and easy to control.

And where had that gotten me?

I lifted my hand to the dor handle, just as a rap sounded on the door. I startled, backed quickly up to the bed, and said, "You may enter."

Keijan walked in, with Parun on his heels. I felt a rush of relief.

Parun shut the door, and the room felt immediately overcrowded. Also, it stank—apparently, neither of them had been given time to bathe or change, either.

"Well?" I demanded. "Am I going to be allowed to stay here?"

Keijan lifted a shoulder. "That's up to your grandmother."

"You didn't ask her?"

"That wouldn't be wise. If she thinks I've taken too great an interest in you, she'll make sure I'm not in a position to do you any good."

I tilted my head up to get a better look at his face. "Do you want to do me good?"

His expression was unreadable. "I saved your life, didn't I?"

"But I still don't know why." And that should have been my first question, asked long ago. *The past is a stone rolling downhill, flattening the present and shaping the future.*

Keijan sighed. "You are my niece, Siara. I am your mother's brother. Half-brother, actually—your grandmother is my step-mother, and has no particular fondness for me." He considered. "Or for you, probably. Or for anyone. I'm not sure she loved even her own children."

She had certainly never bothered to come visit me. I had always assumed that was my mother's doing... but I didn't want to think about my mother. Things were confusing enough. I focused on Keijan.

Perhaps it should have mattered to me, that he was my uncle; but I'd never seen any evidence that people acted differently toward me just because they were related to me. Instead, I focused on the important part of his revelation. "You're a Hikaran? But you're—" I stopped, not quite in time, and felt red flood my face.

"A sorcerer? Yes. I thought my family would find a sorcerer useful." He grimaced. "The family... did not agree."

Had he really thought they would? Sorcery drew its magic from death; it was a powerful profession, but not precisely a respectable one. Certainly not for someone of noble blood.

"Now that we've all had this history lesson," Parun drawled, "can we come up with the *pretend* history that explains who she is?"

He cocked an eyebrow at me, as if waiting for me to suggest an idea. Since I didn't have one, I fell back on haughtiness. "I suppose you have a suggestion?"

Keijan smiled, as if he saw through the haughtiness, but didn't mind it. "Let's keep things simple. Your name is Nekudat, and you are my illegitimate daughter by a maidservant."

"You want me to be a *commoner's bastard*?"

Parun rolled his eyes. "Aside from *Emperor's undead daughter*, is there any story that would satisfy you?"

Keijan flicked a hand at him, and Parun went mercifully silent.

So did I. Because Parun was right. I wanted to be who I was—who I had been: the Emperor's daughter, the second-highest ranked woman in Timshala. I wanted to walk out and have all those beautiful, giggling girls know that, no matter how alone I was or what I looked like, I was above them. I wanted them to curry my favor, not the other way around.

But I couldn't have that. I was unwashed, powerless, and completely dependent on strangers' hospitality. There was no story we could tell, other than the truth, that would change my new reality.

And we couldn't tell the truth.

"All right, *Father*," I said. "But for how long—"

"As I said." Keijan turned. "Tell your grandmother."

"I intend to," I said.

A smile touched his lips, briefly, before he opened the door. "Good luck."

4

MY GRANDMOTHER WAS NOT AN easy woman to find. First, she was on a tour of the estate, then she was holding an audience, then she was deep in her weekly meditation. I started every morning by asking my maid for a meeting with her, only to get a vague answer, soft as a brush stroke, delivered with lowered eyes. I was sure the maid was secretly laughing at me, but there was little I could do about it.

On the fourth day, though, my grandmother came to the women's quarter—a surprise but not unexpected inspection, judging by the other girls' resigned panic. By then, I knew the hierarchy of the women's court and my own place in it—low, but temporarily so. I allowed the higher-ranked noblewomen to direct us into a line, and to do the talking. I lowered my eyes as my grandmother passed, and her gaze passed over me as if I was nothing to her, no different from the other girls whose lives she directed and protected.

That neither surprised nor angered me. But as she turned to leave, having delivered a few curt words of praise and a far longer list of reprimands, I lifted my head.

The silence around me was soft and thick as a wedding veil, and every bit as inevitable. Even the act of looking up had earned me a few sidelong glances. I felt my throat close, and when I forced my mouth open, it was dry as sand.

"Honored Lady," I said. "May I speak to you?"

Everyone turned to stare at me, and the closer girls drew slightly back. But all their combined scorn was nothing compared to my grandmother's. Her eyes flickered in my direction, as if I was a slug she had found in her morning tea.

"No," she said. "You may not."

She left without looking at me again.

On the first morning of the fourth week, we were working on paintings when we heard the quick slap-slap of sandals on marble, coming from the other side of the entrance to the women's court. The entire hall was already taken up by hanging scrolls and vats of brushes, and a maid had just finished mixing the paints. We all groaned.

A maid scurried out through the draperies, then scurried back. "It is Lady Nekudat's father, here to see her on an urgent matter."

More groans, as the women began cleaning their brushes and retreating behind screens. A few shot me reproachful looks, which made my stomach tighten. I had barely begun recovering from my shocking behavior toward my grandmother; almost half the other girls were willing to talk to me again. *This* was going to set me back.

I did my best to smile. "Of course."

The maid set up a screen and bench near the entrance, and I hurried over, my silk robe brushing against my ankles. I could see Keijan's form through the blinds as I sat and tilted my head.

Keijan's voice shook, but he kept it low. "We just received word from the capital. I regret to inform you that the Emperor is dead."

No one could see my face, so I didn't bother pretending grief.

"He died of the wasting disease." Keijan spoke slowly and carefully, but I wasn't sure why; the wasting sickness, which had also killed my mother, was a common enough occurrence. "After the three weeks of mourning, he will be buried."

Buried. Understanding hit me, and I sat bolt upright. "Where will he be buried?"

"In the tomb of his first wife."

My mother's tomb. Which would, of course, have to be prepared before it could house an Emperor's corpse. Expanded, probably, filled with more and greater things. Cleaned of dust, and impurity, and corpses.

Except they would find the tomb was two corpses short.

"What are we going to do?" I whispered.

"We have to talk." He lowered his voice. "But not here."

A scrap of paper slipped between the blinds. I opened it carefully. His writing was beautiful, of course, his script impeccable.

Jade Garden. Dawn.

Come in travel clothes.

In the Hikara household, I had no servants bound to me, who could be killed at my word and thus trusted to be discreet. There was no one I could ask to wake me before dawn.

To keep things simple, I never went to sleep.

In the dim silence, I had too much time to think about my past and my future, about the creature in the tomb and the clatter of my mother's defiled swords, about the handmaiden's short, cut-off scream. About the sounds and sensations that had swirled around me as I walked through the Afterlife, a dead man's fingers clenched around mine.

Keijan had helped me escape once, and he would help me again. I knew that, but not through calculation. It was a deep still sense that was so new to me, it took me half the night to realize what it was.

I trusted him.

That was stupid, but I didn't push the feeling away. Instead, I held it close. Everything else was cold and black, the world so empty and aching that at one point, with no one there to see me, I buried my face in my pillow and sobbed.

I knew what Keijan was going to say: *Run.* And I didn't want to run. I didn't want to have to escape. I wanted to stay here, safe and cared for, in a place where I knew the rules. Where I wasn't alone. Where everything made sense.

Eventually, when the melted wax had crept halfway up the lengths of the candles, I decided that I preferred to wait for Keijan in the gardens. A small, meaningless disobedience, but it was the only escape I could see from the bitter emptiness inside me, or the tangled knot of terror and grief flowing into it. I left my room and walked as quietly as I could through the court. The draperies across the entrance felt heavier than I remembered, brushing over my arms and shoulders, then falling thick and silent behind me.

Something moved in the shadows, and the memories flashed through my mind—the moving darkness, the impact of the tomb floor on my back, the cold shadow crouching over me. I opened my mouth, and a meaty hand clamped over my face.

All my coiled tension exploded, in a terror that was almost relief, and I fought.

I shocked myself with my own savagery, as I kicked and bit and clawed at whoever had grabbed me. I shocked my attacker, too. He was much stronger than me, but he yelped and let go.

I could have run. Instead, I flew at him in a blind rage, barely aware of what I was doing. One of my hands wrapped itself in a thatch of hair and pulled, hard. My knee came up, even harder, and the yelp turned into a scream. He went down.

A wave of fierce satisfaction swamped me, even as the scream washed away my haze of fury. If somebody heard it… I stepped back, ready to do the sensible thing and run.

At the same moment, I recognized his voice.

I dropped to my knees on the marble floor, and, while he was still curled up on the ground, reached for the blade at his side. The dagger was still sheathed, which meant he hadn't been going to kill me, at least not right away. I pulled it out; his hand slammed down on the empty sheath, a moment too late to stop me.

I straightened and took two steps back, glad it was too dark for him to see how inexpertly I held the knife. "Explain yourself, Priest."

Parun moaned. I waited. Finally, he said, "That wasn't necessary, Princess."

Even now, his voice had that lazy sinuousness to it, which made my palm itch to slap him.

"And grabbing me was necessary?" I said.

"I needed to make sure you wouldn't yell."

I knew better. He had enjoyed asserting his strength over me, proving he could control me physically. Just as I enjoyed having the upper hand now, standing there with his weapon while he was unarmed.

I knew I would pay for it, eventually. But for one ferocious moment, I didn't care.

"It seems," I said, "you would have done better to worry about your *own* yelling. How did you know I would be here?"

"Keijan told me. It's–may I get up?"

I liked that he had to ask. "You may sit."

"Thank you." I did *not* like the mocking undertone in his voice, but there wasn't much I could do about it. The outlines of his form shifted as he raised himself into a squat. "Spirits! I'm going to be sore for a while."

"I hope," I said, "you're not waiting for my apology."

He laughed again, this time with an edge of nastiness—just enough to remind me that he hated me. I gripped the knife tighter, though no more efficiently. "I'm not expecting anything. And you have a lot more than my bruised backside to apologize for, Princess."

"Why?" I said. "What do I have to apologize for? I've done nothing to you."

"You took my Choice away."

Which was not only insulting, it was heretical. "How odd. You'd think I would remember doing that."

In the dimness, his eyes gleamed black. "Do you know how I escaped the Bechirian massacre, Princess?"

"I don't—"

"There were two of us, hiding in a crack between two rocks. I sneezed, and they came looking. Malik—my friend—he must have been as terrified as I was. But I was in deeper—I had found the crack first. He tried to scramble around me, to hide better, and I…." Parun drew in a breath. "I pushed him. I pushed him out, far enough that when they found him, they didn't look any farther. When they killed him, the blood sprayed on the rocks, but none of it got into the crack."

"How old were you?" I said, but I knew it didn't matter. Children, generally speaking, had *more* Choices than adults did, because they hadn't yet used any of theirs up. And a child's Choices were no less important than an adult's. A child is a rock at the top of a hill; a slight nudge can make all the difference in where he lands.

"I'm sorry," I said, then rallied. "I'm sorry, but it still has nothing to do with me. I am not responsible for my mother's sin."

In the deep silence that followed, I could hear the faint sound of crickets through the walls. Then Parun said, "You don't know."

"That seems likely. What, specifically, do I not know this time?"

"At the Temple, when you kept talking about the destruction of my priesthood—I thought you knew. I thought you were being vicious."

My eyes were adjusting to the light; I could make out the flicker of his eyes toward my face, the spasmodic clench of his jaw. Just for a moment, he looked at me as if I was a real person, not a manifestation of an old, bitter memory.

A person never knows their own Choices. But sometimes, you can see someone else's. In the moment of their making them.

I saw the moment when Parun let his hesitation go. His mouth formed a straight, hard line, and he said, "The Bechirians were massacred because of you."

He tried to be angry, when he told the story. But it must have been clear to him that I had never heard it before; that I was already as horrified as he wanted me to be.

It was a simple story—at least, it was the way he told it. When I was three days old, my mother had taken me to the Bechirian priests for my divination. The visit had officially never happened, because officially the royal family did not countenance divination. There was no public ceremony: just my mother and me and the high priest.

Afterward, they had retreated to the high priest's office and spoken for hours. When my mother left, she announced that the high priest was meditating and should not be disturbed.

The next morning, my father's soldiers came and massacred everyone.

"Even the high priest?" I said. I had figured out, by now, that the high priest must have been Parun's father. It explained not only Parun's presence at the Temple, at such a young age, but the ferocity of his grief after all these years.

"No." Parun's rigid lips curved, into a smile that wasn't a smile. "When I saw the soldiers coming, I ran to his office."

"But he was medi—"

"He was not meditating." Parun's laugh, also, was not a laugh. "He was dead. He was on his couch, and his throat had been slashed. The blood was already dry and stiff on his robe."

My heart climbed in slow, careful beats up my throat.

"Your mother killed him," Parun said. "After he divined your Choices, she killed him, so he wouldn't tell anyone what he saw in his divination. And then she massacred the entire Temple to cover up her crime."

I stepped back, my fingers slippery on the dagger hilt. "You think she did it to protect *me*?"

"Yes."

"You're wrong." My mother's face flashed into my mind, her thin aquiline nose and sharp chin, the way her kohl-lined eyes had always flicked past me. A hundred times, she had turned her head a fraction, shifted her gaze sideways, as if I wasn't worth a stray thought. "My mother didn't care about me."

"I think she did."

"Oh, do you?" I laughed, and it came out sounding like a sob. "My mother had me *buried alive.* In case you missed that."

"You're *not* buried alive," Parun pointed out.

I snorted. "No thanks to her."

"Wasn't it Keijan who saved you?"

"Yes, but—"

"He is her brother, Siara. You don't think she was behind his presence in the tomb? You don't think he was there specifically *to get you out*?"

My mind flashed back to that darkness, the dank, dusty smell I tried so hard not to think about. To the creature made of shadows, and the way Keijan had been the only one of us not screaming.

It sneaked in from the Afterlife, he had said, right before picking up my mother's spear.

He had known where it came from, because he had already opened the entrance to the Afterlife, in order to take me through it. He had let in the creature by accident, and then he had killed it to save me.

I was given instructions.

"She knew you would be in danger," Parun said. "From your father's second wife, probably. Or from someone who suspects whatever the Bechirians divined for you. So she arranged for you to escape. She arranged it at the cost of her own eternity. Don't tell me she didn't love you."

"But she *didn't.*" A whisper swallowed by a sob.

"I saw her," Parun said. "When she brought you to the Temple. You were swaddled in violet silk, and she held you tight." He swallowed. "She loved you. I was only four years old, but I know what I saw."

I thought of my mother's still dead face at the funeral, surrounded by burning rushes, cold and remote as it always had been. I had been angry at myself, then, for feeling grief. What, I had asked myself, was I grieving for?

"You want proof of your mother's motives?" Parun said. "I want that, too. We can help each other."

I didn't see how I could help anyone. Living princesses had little power. Officially dead ones had even less.

"I know you're going to talk to Keijan," Parun said. "*He* must know the truth. Let me come with you, and let's ask him together."

He thought I had power that I didn't. He thought I could refuse.

Which meant I could.

I looked at him. My eyes had adjusted enough for me to see the plea in his eyes, the anger around his mouth. Not aimed at me… or was it? Could I trust him?

I wanted to trust him. Maybe that meant I shouldn't.

It felt like a Choice. But I had always believed Choices were clear decisions between honor and shame, between your nobler self and your baser instincts, between what you wanted to do and what you were supposed to do. Could it be a real Choice if I myself didn't know what the right thing to do was?

I wasn't sure. So I did what I wanted, without really understanding why I wanted it.

And as it turned out, what I wanted to do was nod my head and say, "Come with me."

5

THE SKY WAS A FADED rose petal when we stepped out of the castle, into a garden so perfect it could have been in my father's courtyard. A small, asymmetric pond filled most of the center, half-covered with thick mats of water lilies. A flat wooden bridge spanned the pond at its narrowest, ending at a raised boulder shaded by the branches of a twisted pine.

I blinked at the boulder, which seemed expressly designed to have someone sitting on it cross-legged, robes draped over the jagged edges, exuding wisdom and calm. The Women's Garden back home had a rock exactly like that, and the head mistress used it to speak to maids who needed correction or advancement, or who had caught the eye of a nobleman.

But this rock was bare. Instead, Keijan appeared around a curve in the cobblestone path, his robes flapping around his ankles, his forehead gleaming with sweat.

"Where *were* you?" he gasped.

"I—"

"Did anyone see you?"

"I did," Parun said, in that slow, lazy voice I hated.

Watching it be used on someone else made the purpose of the voice obvious. It was irritating because it was *designed* to irritate.

And I had fallen for it, every time. But Keijan just nodded. "Good. You can help. Anyone else?"

"I don't think so," I said, at the same time that Parun said, "Help with what?"

"Help Siara escape," Keijan said. "She is in great danger. The Hikaras want to use her, and the Emperor's spies will soon figure out why. But if we get her to the southern provinces, she can hide from both of them."

I don't want to hide, I thought. But no one was asking me—and besides, it wasn't really true. I was tired of being scared, but *scared* was probably my only alternative to *dead.*

I opened my mouth to say it anyhow, but I never got to. I was distracted by a movement—a whisper. A sudden rush that didn't belong in this garden.

I looked, just in time to see two shadows detach from the trees, black-clad men with silver blades too bright for the gray dawn. Keijan blinked at my expression and turned just in time to see his death arcing toward him, but without enough time to avoid it.

"Stop!" I shouted.

Two blades froze inches from Keijan's throat.

It took me a moment to recover enough to speak. I had not really expected them to obey me.

"Leave him," I said, and my voice fell naturally into its old, regal intonations. Power settled around me, like a warm familiar cloak. Not much power, I knew that; no woman had power in the wild roads outside our palaces, and no human being had power in the shifting foreverness of the Afterlife. But in this garden, to these men, I had power. Right now, that was all that mattered.

"Step back," I said.

The guards remained where they were, blades shining near Keijan's face.

Then the bushes rustled and my grandmother stepped into the clearing, and I realized whom they had really been obeying.

"Before you decide to spare your uncle," she said, "perhaps you should know what he is hiding from you."

Before *you* decide. Meaning it was my decision? A Choice?

I didn't know why she would give me that power, when clearly it belonged to her. But I knew enough to accept her terms. I nodded.

"Tell her, Keijan," my grandmother said.

The two guards stepped backbut did not sheathe their blades.

"Tell her," my grandmother said to Keijan, "what was divined for her when she was born."

Beside me, Parun sucked in his breath. I stepped away from him. I needed to focus on my grandmother, and my uncle, and the truth they knew about me.

“Have you figured out,” my grandmother said to me, “why your mother had the Bechirians killed?”

“It was because of me,” I said. “But I don’t know why.”

“She did it *for* you. To save your life.”

“She hated me,” I said. And discovered that, despite what Parun had told me, I still believed it.

My grandmother tsked. “She… had some trouble dealing with her guilt. You were a reminder to her of what she had done, and she found it hard to look at you after that.” I flinched. “Your mother’s Choices were divined at birth, too, and she had only one. She believed the massacre was it, that it had condemned her to eternal servitude in the Afterlife.”

No wonder she hadn’t cared about defilement afterward.

“And she blamed me?” I said.

“Of course not. She blamed herself. But part of her fault, she believed, lay in loving you too much.”

So she had tried to stop loving me at all.

I’d told myself my mother’s abandonment had stopped hurting me. But it had merely curled up tight, a contained knot deep within me; and now it was unfurling, scraping me raw, like I was once again a child who didn’t understand why she wasn’t loved.

I forced it down, to seethe deep within my gut. None of this mattered right now. It *couldn’t* matter. I had to think. I knew, I almost knew, what my grandmother was saying.

Your Mother’s Choices were divined at birth, too.

Too.

She killed him so he wouldn’t tell anyone what he saw.

“How many?” I said. I looked at Keijan, whose life I had just saved, who owed me. Who cared about me. “When the Bechirians divined my Choices, how many did I have?”

Keijan looked past the knives, past the guards, straight at me.

“You had none,” he said.

An Emperor has no Choices. Because no man could change the tide of time.

No *man*.

It had always been a man.

But my father, the Emperor, had killed all his brothers before they could bear sons. And my mother had given him only a daughter.

A daughter who now had the right to rule.

But when the Bechirians had told my mother that I would be Empress, she had known she would bear no sons—which meant the divination had placed us *both* in danger.

"Revealed *how*?" I said. "She killed them all. There's no proof."

"She did not," my grandmother said, "kill them all."

Parun stepped even farther away from me.

But my grandmother was already looking at him, her skin stretched tight over her bones. "You were there," she said.

"Not at the divination," Parun said. "I don't know what they saw."

"I think you do." Her voice was low, steady, and sweet. "I think your father told you, before he died. And I think if you tell the people that, they will believe you."

Parun swallowed.

"You will go with her," my grandmother said. Her voice was calm and inexorable; it was clear, as her will poured over me, that nobody in this garden had any Choices right now. "Our soldiers are waiting in the capital. We've infiltrated the palace guard and the street patrols. Once we have control of the city, you and Keijan, together, will tell what you know. You will proclaim my granddaughter Empress."

"And if we don't?" Keijan said. His voice shook, but he got the words out—the defiance I had, just a second ago, believed impossible.

“Then I will have to kill you after all.” My grandmother let out a small sigh. “I probably should, anyhow, for your disobedience. Not to mention your stupidity. Did you really think you could get her away?”

Keijan’s jaw tightened, but he said nothing.

“What if *I* don’t obey?” Parun, too, was speaking the unthinkable—though it was less unthinkable now that Keijan had said it. “What if all three of us refuse to fall in with your plan?”

My grandmother shrugged. “Then no doubt, she will die.”

Parun looked at me. “Siara. What do *you* want?”

Now that they *both* had spoken, it was easy for me to. But unlike them, I didn’t know what to say.

“It’s not up to me,” I said finally. Which was so obvious I felt immediately stupid. *Nothing* was up to me. Including what I did, or said.

Within the next few days, I would either become the first female Emperor in all of history, or I would be dead. There was nothing I could do to affect the outcome, either way.

I had no Choices. I’d never had any. I couldn’t even pick out a color robe to wear. Only in my imagination did my thoughts, my choices, or my will have anything to do with what I decided.

“I think,” Keijan said, “that we should give Princess Siara time….”

“Time to *what*?” I snapped, and the viciousness in my voice shocked him silent.

I might have felt bad, if the viciousness had been something under my control.

My grandmother gestured imperiously, and we all followed her across the garden and through the ornate iron gates to the stable. Five horses were saddled and ready.

"It's a four-day ride to the capital," my grandmother said, as we all mounted. "There are new mounts waiting for you at every travel house on the way."

Parun grinned, white and sharp. I gripped the reins hard, breathing in the scent of horse and leather, so oddly familiar. As if I had always been a traveler, and my stay with the Hikaras had been only a dream.

The guards saluted. Keijan nodded. As the castle's outer gates opened, I found myself leaning forward. When the horses broke into a canter, I leaned into the smooth, rolling motion and let out a little sigh.

As if, without knowing it, I had been waiting for this all along.

6

I HAD NEVER DREAMED OF being Empress.

Okay. That's a lie.

I had dreamed of it all the time, when I was a child. Cosseted, pampered, protected, and ignored. Every time my father passed without a glance, every time my maids yanked combs through my hair and ignored my whimpers, every time one of my handmaidens accepted a suitor.

But I knew it was impossible. I always knew.

And yet, as we reached the end of the switchback trail and turned south, slowing to a walk between a thick mosaic of autumn-leaved trees, there was a stillness deep within me. I should have been shocked, terrified, conflicted; and I was all those things, on the surface. But deep down, where the feelings would have hurt, I felt only calm.

As if some part of me had always known this was my destiny.

It wasn't until the sun passed over our heads and sank into the woods, drawing all the colors of the sky down with it, that I truly understood why none of this felt like it mattered.

Because none of it *did.*

At some level, I must have known all along that I was never directing my own fate, choosing my own path. When I'd put my hand in Keijan's and stepped into the Afterlife. When I'd let myself sink into the familiarity of the Hikara household. When I'd waited up until midnight, when I'd accepted Parun's offer, when I'd come to the garden. I had been weak and foolhardy and scared, and I hadn't striven to overcome those things because *it didn't matter.*

It had never mattered. Whatever I did, it wasn't *me* doing it. My thoughts, my decisions, were illusions. Every last one.

Which meant that as we moved forward, over the leaf-strewn trail and down the corridor of my life, I knew that there was no turn, no passage out, no door leading somewhere else. I had felt that way in the past, convinced I had no Choices left. But I had only been guessing. There could have still been a Choice ahead of me, unexpected and unpredictable. I hadn't *known.*

"Hsst!" one of the guards said, and we reined our horses in. The sun had already set, but pink-rimmed clouds were still coiling toward the vanishing horizon; in the trees around us, darkness gathered to wait out the night. In the distance, I heard the crash of some animal racing through the underbrush, and the long high call of a bird. "I think—"

We never found out what he thought. He toppled sideways off his horse, an arrow sticking out of his chest.

Parun wheeled his horse around and slammed it into mine. Another arrow whizzed over my shoulder, so close I heard the whine as it went by, and then the thud as it hit the ground behind me.

The dead guard's horse reared. There was a horrible crack as his hoof came down on his rider, but no scream. The rider was already dead.

"There must be two of them," the second guard said. He drew his blade, his words coming sharp and fast, his eyes darting up at the dark-gnarled tree branches. "That was a crossbow, so we have a few minutes while they reload. Princess, get down—"

The knife hit him in the back, a low sickening sound. His death wasn't as silent as the first guard's; he screamed, then thrashed, craning his arm back to try and reach the hilt in his back. His horse snorted and turned—these mounts were battle-trained, obviously, or they would have bolted by now—and he slid off.

By the time he hit the ground, he was dead.

My mare did not move, but I felt her trembling. Probably because she could sense my fear, the way my blood roared in my ears.

"Open a portal!" I shouted. "Keijan, get us out of here! We can go through the Afterlife—"

Keijan's voice was high-pitched, but his words were steady. "I can't, Princess. I wasn't close enough to guards' deaths to take power from them."

"Then let's *run*—"

"No!" Parun reached over and grabbed my reins. "They'll be prepared for that."

Keijan wheeled his horse around, facing the dark trees. "Stop!" he said loudly. "Declare yourself. We are on the Emperor's business."

Something rustled, and a voice spoke from the forest. "As are we."

I narrowed my eyes at its source, wishing I had a knife to throw. Or that I knew how to throw one.

A different voice, from a different spot in the foliage. "We are here to escort the princess home. Give her to us and be on your way."

They must have had time to reload the crossbows by now. What were they waiting for? My shoulderblades prickled, and I heard again the whine of the arrow, passing over my shoulder....

I looked at the ground, where the arrow that had been aimed at me still quivered among the leaves. Next to it lay the first guard. The arrow jutting out of *his* back was perfectly still.

I replayed it in my mind: the speed and force of the arrow, Parun knocking me sideways, the arrow whizzing past my cheek.

Parun hadn't been fast enough to save me. Not if the arrow had been aimed at my heart. I would be as dead as those guards if they had been aiming to kill.

They were telling the truth. They wanted to take me alive.

But how *much* did they want me alive?

Hope and terror coiled within me, so tightly I could barely tell one from the other.

"Be on *your* way," Keijan said, "or face the wrath of your Empress, once she ascends the throne."

The wind carried a throaty sound, like a snicker. And then another, more ominous sound: a series of short, sharp clicks.

I had never heard a crossbow being drawn. But I knew what that sound was.

Keijan sat his mount in the center of the path, his body outlined in the dusky light. My foot twitched toward my mare's side. A few steps, and I would be in front of Keijan, blocking his body with mine. If they really wanted me alive, they wouldn't shoot.

If.

We stood frozen in that tableau for what felt like minutes, but must have only been seconds. Long enough, if my heel had actually nudged my mare's side.

I didn't move. And then the thick wooden snap, and Keijan fell back on his horse, still holding the reins, the arrow in his chest pointing straight at the sky.

"*No*!" Parun screamed.

Keijan didn't scream. He grabbed the arrow shaft with one hand and gestured sharply with the other.

The clearing lit up, an unearthly red light, like the blood that was drenching Keijan's hand. His own life's blood. He was using it to summon magic.

The trees around us erupted in screams. And then there was silence.

The red light faded, leaving behind a faint glow. Enough to wash Keijan's face with pink, as Parun lowered him off his steed. Parun was sobbing, his face contorted and wet.

I slid off my horse with no awareness of how I had done it. My feet hit the ground hard, and I stumbled and fell, then crawled over the twigs and ferns to Keijan. He lay silent on the leaf-strewn ground, looking at me with an expression that made my stomach twist.

I'm sorry, I tried to say, but discovered that my throat had closed up. Which wouldn't do at all; I had to stay in control.

I drew in a gasping breath, but it didn't quite make it all the way out, and I still couldn't speak. Which was for the best, because I couldn't be *sorry*. This had nothing to do with me. I couldn't have stopped it even if I wanted to.

It didn't matter if I was brave or weak, if I was selfish or self-sacrificing. It didn't matter. I would do what I would do, and then it would be done.

And nothing—not the act, not the consequences that followed—were my fault.

Keijan's eyes closed, and I heard a rasping, painful sob, and realized that it had come from me. Parun slid back, away from the corpse. He looked up at me, tears still sliding down his cheeks.

"We have to go," he said. His voice was thick. "There will be others."

I nodded. It was all I could manage, with everything in me splintering apart.

"We can't go straight to the capital," Parun said. "They know we're headed there; they're looking for us. We'll go to the Port of Foreigners. From there, we can take a ship around the coast to the capital. It will take longer, but no one will be expecting us to come from the sea."

"We can't," I managed to say. "We'll be defiled—"

"I'm a priest. I can cleanse you." My face must have shown what I thought of that, because he actually grinned, just for a second. "It will be all right, Siara. Really. Cthonians won't touch you, if you ask them not to."

I turned my arms sideways, looking at my pale wrists. I imagined pressing a blade against the narrow purple veins. *Everyone's Choice*, the songs called it: death with honor when life offered none. The priests said that was heresy, but people still sang the songs.

I turned my hands back over, curling my fingers tighter around the reins. The priests were right; it was not *everyone's* Choice. I knew there was no way I could ever do it, cut through my own skin and blood. Even thinking about it made my stomach clench.

"Come on." Parun glanced at Keijan's body. His face twisted, and then he got himself under control. "If we ride without stopping, we can be at the port before dawn."

Dizziness washed over me. I wondered what would happen if I just gave up. If I lay myself down on a mat of leaves and closed my eyes and slept.

But of course, I couldn't do that. I wasn't doing it. Instead, I was letting Parun help me remount, then gripping the front of the saddle and leaning forward. The horse moved beneath me, and the black night thundered by, and I hurtled helplessly toward whatever fate had in store for me.

7

WE REACHED THE PORT OF Foreigners well before daybreak. By then, my horse was shivering uncontrollably, and Parun's mount had flecks of lather on its neck. We had probably ridden both horses to death; I felt a twinge of guilt, before remembering how irrelevant guilt was.

"Follow me," Parun said, and of course I did. We rode through narrow streets that twisted too often, in sharp, *wrong* ways—as if Cthonian aesthetics were not only different from normal people's, but the opposite of it. The buildings that threw the streets into shadow were also repellent, not just ugly but misshapen, with haphazard construction that made me feel like the walls we passed were about to tumble down on us. I did my best to ignore that, until we passed a heap of rubble, with pieces of wooden furniture sticking out of the stones, and I realized my feeling was entirely accurate.

After that... I went on ignoring it. What else could I do?

The city seemed deserted—the Cthonians lived most of their lives on their ships, and only dwelled here when they had to. The air was thick with the smell of brine and seaweed and something else, a stink so intense it made me gag on my own breath. It seemed the rumors about Cthonian hygiene had been not only true, but unexaggerated.

I ignored that, too.

The city ended abruptly, at the edge of a cliff. From here, steep stairways wound down to a flat, narrow beach, where the waves crashed against the sand over and over. Several wooden boardwalks extended from the beach into the sea, and beside each was a ship with vast, rectangular black sails.

Parun swung off his horse, and after a moment, I did, too. My actions felt thick and slow, and so did my mind. Everything about this place was wrong and dangerous, as if things could come at me from directions I didn't know about—*things*, things I couldn't anticipate and would never understand. It made my skin crawl, and freeze, and then crawl again.

The worst part lay ahead: the sea, blue-gray rippled with black, moving constantly but going nowhere, where lost spirits attached themselves to any warm-blooded creature they could find. I would require two days of cleansing, after getting off a ship. I wondered if people enacting a coup had that much time.

Though surely overthrowing the government would require killing people, and I would need cleansing for that, too?

Parun's eyebrows drew together as he watched me. He had been on alert since we entered the port, his body rigid and his eyes darting from side to side, but he was clearly not as terrified as I was. "Siara?"

He should not be addressing me by name. I would be Empress soon. Or dead.

"What are we going to do with the horses?" I asked.

His shoulders lifted and fell. "We'll have to leave them here."

Which was unthinkable disrespect to the horses, if they would live; or to the people who would be defiled by them, if they would die.

I let the reins drop and slid clumsily off my horse. The mare barely reacted, her head drooping and her sides heaving. I patted her side, an inadequate apology, and followed Parun down the stairs cut into the cliffside.

We were halfway down when I saw my first Cthonian. He was going up on a parallel set of stairs, moving with a lumbering animal-like lope that carried him past us almost before I could stare. His skin had an odd blue tint to it, his bald head a bit darker blue than the rest of his body. His ears were set deep in his head rather than sticking out, and his eyes, large and colorless, passed over us briefly.

Cthonians won't touch you, if you ask them not to. He wasn't even close enough to touch me. But I felt defiled, already. And there was worse to come.

When we reached the bottom of the cliff, and I stepped onto the white sand, I swayed. Partly because I was dizzy, and faintly nauseated; partly because I was scared; and mostly because Parun was close enough to reach out and steady me. Which he did.

Half-Cthonian. Now that I had seen a full Cthonian, it was harder than ever to believe.

"Siara," Parun said. "We have to go." He gestured at the closest ship. Its sails were snapping, its decks swarming with blue-skinned figures.

"I'm scared," I whispered, though I knew I shouldn't. Shouldn't say it, shouldn't lean toward him, shouldn't stop moving forward. I didn't care. I was doing all these things, and there was no *shouldn't* for me anymore.

Parun's eyes met mine. They were dark and deep, as full of sympathy as they had once been with hate. How could he be half-Cthonian? It fit not at all into the world I understood.

"I'm sorry," Parun said. "I really am. But the tide is going out. Every ship in harbor is leaving *now*. We have to get on the ship to the capital in the next few minutes, or it will be too late."

I didn't move. I didn't care. I did not want to get on a ship.

"If we don't go now," Parun said, "we'll have to stay here overnight."

My eyes popped open, and I started toward the ships, moving as fast as I could with the sand shifting beneath my feet. The ocean was coming straight at me, smooth long surges of black folding into violent sheets of white spray.

Don't think. Just walk.

I stepped onto the pier. The wooden slats moved beneath my feet, and I could see dark water moving sluggishly through the gaps. My stomach clenched, but I forced myself to keep going, almost at a run, until I was next to the ship, its black sides throwing a chill shadow over me. A long wide plank connected the dock to the deck of the ship, rising steeply upward over the brackish water.

Keijan's voice in my mind: *You only can't because you think you can't.*

The only way home was on that monstrosity. Hours, or days, with the roiling sea moving constantly beneath my feet. All I had to do was keep my mind blank long enough to step on board, and the ship would sail and it would be out of my hands. Already, the deck was sliding out from under the plank, widening the gap of water I would have to cross.

Minutes, Parun had said. That was all we had. Before I could scream and sob and change my mind, and it would be too late to matter.

Not that it mattered now. Not that I could change my mind, or make this decision to begin with, even if it felt like that was what I was doing.

"Wait!" Parun shouted, and I turned with a rush of relief.

But he wasn't behind me. I turned again, and there he was, on the pier parallel to mine. Standing next to a different ship, a smaller one.

"Wrong ship!" he yelled. "That one is sailing across the sea to the Cthonian homeland. *This* one is going to the capital. Come on, quick!"

Another man, too, was waving his arms at me from the side of the ship—a tall man with black hair, wearing robes in the imperial colors. I didn't recognize him, but clearly he was from the palace. Keijan had been right: we *did* have allies.

For the first time, I believed it would happen. I was going to rule. I had been hurtling toward this destiny all my life, without knowing it.

An Emperor has no Choices.

The decks of both ships were swarming with Cthonians, yelling at each other in a high-pitched, grunting language, all blue-tinted skin and oily scalps. A shudder ran through me, from my gut up through my heart.

And yet I didn't move.

An Emperor has no Choices.

I heard Keijan again, as if he was standing right next to me: *People can do the impossible.*

I stepped onto the plank. It swayed side-to-side, and I had to hold my arms out for balance.

"Siara!" Parun shouted. "What are you doing?"

I didn't look back. How could I answer him? I didn't know what I was doing.

It was, obviously, impossible that I would get on *this* ship. It was not a Choice I—or anyone—could make. Even if I'd had any Choices.

Which I didn't.

I *didn't.*

"That ship isn't sailing to the capital!" Parun ran down his own pier and across the sand. His voice grew fainter, almost drowned out by the sea. "It's sailing *away*!"

I took another step, and now it was just one leap to the deck. The plank was inches from slipping into the water.

It didn't matter, whether this was a Choice or not. Because if I did it—if I stepped off this plank, if I leapt onto that deck—it would change everything. I would no longer be in the world of the Bechirian priests. And how could they have predicted my Choices, in a future they couldn't even imagine?

But it was a world I couldn't imagine, either.

The water roiled beneath me, black and fathomless and terrifying. The sky stretched blue and gray into the unknown distance.

Parun was still shouting, now running down the pier toward me. The capital, with its dangers and opportunities, was a few days' sail away. I might die or I might rule, but either way, it would be in the palace where I had lived all my life. This ship, with its bow pointing into the unknown—where I wouldn't know who I was and neither would anyone else—this was not a Choice I could make. It was not a Choice anyone could make.

I knew what I was supposed to believe. That whatever I did next, it was not a Choice. That there were forces all around me, making me either step back or forward; that the decision had already been made, and all my thinking about it was an illusion.

I knew what I was supposed to believe, and I did not believe it.

I stepped onto the deck, and the plank fell into the water below me with a sharp, distant splash.

On the ship, the Cthonians were staring at me. I looked behind me, and saw that Parun had come to a stop, face white with disbelief. I tilted my head slightly, and saw the man in imperial robes watching me with the exact same expression.

Just because no one has, doesn't mean no one can.

I had done the unthinkable. Now it was thinkable, and they all knew it.

I wondered how many Choices they had, now.

I wondered how many I had.

And when I turned to face the Cthonians, and the vast sea unrolling before me, and the terror and uncertainty hovering around me, I found, to my surprise, that I was smiling.

THE END

Inspirations and Influences

LEAH CYPESS

TIMSHALA **WAS BUILT OUT OF THREE** entirely separate influences, that I hope I›ve melded together successfully into one coherent story.

The first inspiration is buried in the fog of time: the idea of a girl buried to die in her mother's tomb. I'm sure I came across this idea somewhere in my reading, but I honestly can't tell you where. I can tell you that I was in the basement of my parents' home, working out on an exercise bike, when the idea for that first scene came to me. I wrote it down immediately, planning to make a novel out of it; like many of my novel ideas, however, I ran out of steam after three chapters, and put it aside in case inspiration struck later.

Years later, I was reading the works of Rabbi Eliyahu Dessler, an 18th-century Jewish thinker. Rabbi Dessler, in discussing the issue of determinism and free will, posits the idea of a "point of choice"—that while every person has large areas of their life where nature and nurture have predetermined what they are going to do, there are also certain specific points where they actually have free choice. I found the idea compelling, especially since the problem of determinism and free will is one I've long been thinking about, and I immediately wanted to set up a fantasy world based on that idea. After taking various unsuccessful stabs at it, I realized that it was a good direction for that old "princess in a tomb story", and that clicked right away.

At around the same time, I read *The Pillow Book of Sei Shonagan* and became fascinated by the Heian period in Japanese history. I read a number on the subject, and a lot of elements of that period made it into the world of *Timshala*.

A Chat With Leah Cypess

LEAH CYPESS

Timshala **was built Timshala is about a young woman who "awakens" to a new life and therefore fits our Awakenings call for short stories beautifully. Can you tell us the ways that the story engages with the theme?**

While writing this story, I often though about the ending of one of my favorite movies, Castaway. Without giving away the movie for those who haven't seen it (go see it!), I was extremely impressed by the ending of the movie, and by the awakening it implies. Since watching it, I've aspired to write something in which a character undergoes something emotionally similar. I hope I've succeeded!

The story also, obviously, is about the distinction between choice and free will. A lot of the literature on that subject talks about the divide between what people are told is possible, and what they intrinsically believe to be possible. I wanted to explore that particular aspect of this unresolved problem, and to show a character who breaks out of what she is told is possible and comes to an "awakening"—one that changes everything not just for her but, possibly, for the entire world she knows.

On a similar note, you created a fairly developed secondary world Fantasy in *Timshala*. Are there any plans to extend it, write more stories in the same world?

Not at the moment, no. I created this world for the purpose of telling this exact story; and while I can see how the ending might call for a continuation, I also think a continuation might dilute the point of the ending.

Then again, I thought the same thing about my novel *Death Sworn*, and I was swayed to change my mind! So while I have no plans to extend it right now, I never say never.

In terms of inspirations and influences, what are the works and authors that have inspired you the most when writing *Timshala* (or your writing in general)?

I've been reading fantasy more or less since I learned to read, so it's difficult to pick out one work that has inspired me the most! Some of my long-time favorite fantasy authors are Megan Whalen Turner, Diana Wynne Jones, Sharon Shin, Juliet Marillier, David Eddings, and Dave Duncan; these are authors I've re-read so many times that I feel sure they influence what I write even when I'm not consciously thinking about them.

Ironically, the author who inspired my writing most is someone whose books I mostly haven't read: Diana Gabaldon. I read an interview with her where she mentioned that she writes her scenes out of order and then puts them together later. Ever since reading that, I have written all my novels and many of my short stories using that method.

Tell us about your experience writing short stories: what would you say are the advantages and potential pitfalls of writing short fiction versus a novel or novella?

For me, the distinction between novels and short stories is fairly distinct. Short stories are almost always based on an idea, and I then build a world and characters around that idea. Generally, once I think of the idea, it doesn't take more than a week or two for me to start the story, and not more than a month to finish the first draft. (There are exceptions, obviously!)

The start of a novel tends to be much more nebulous, and to build steam more slowly. Novels usually start with a character, rather than an idea, and I spend a month or more daydreaming about it and jotting down notes before I actually start writing it seriously. There are also generally several gaps during the process—times when I lose steam or get stuck, and don't make any progress for days or weeks. I've come to understand that these dead periods are not signs of a problem, but just a natural part of my process.

Novellas are new to me—this is the second one I've tried to write, and the first one I've succeeded in writing!—so I don't really know that much about them yet. But I'm having a lot of fun figuring them out.

Finally, a question we ask all of our interviewees: We Book Smugglers have faced condemnation because of the sheer volume of books that we carry back home on a daily basis. As such, we have on occasion resorted to "smuggling books" home to escape judgmental, scrutinizing eyes. Have you ever had to smuggle books?

I spent my entire elementary school career as a "book smuggler"; I used to smuggle books into the classroom, smuggle them into my lap, and read during class. I got caught a lot, and got into trouble, but I never really stopped....

About The Authors

MICHELE TRACY BERGER is a professor, a creative writer, and a pug-lover. Her fiction has appeared in *UnCommon Origins: A Collection of Gods, Monsters, Nature and Science* by Fighting Monkey Press, *You Don't Say: Stories in the Second Person* by Ink Monkey Press, *Flying South: A Literary Journal, 100wordstory, Thing Magazine,* and *The Red Clay Review.* She lives in Pittsboro, North Carolina with her partner Tim. Come visit her at The Practice of Creativity.

LEAH CYPESS is the author of four young adult fantasy novels published by HarperCollins, starting with *Mistwood* (2010), about an immortal shapeshifter trapped in the form of a human girl. She also writes short fiction, which has been published in *Asimov's Science Fiction, the Magazine of Fantasy & Science Fiction*, and *Strange Horizons*, among other places. Her short story "Nanny's Day" (*Asimov's* 2012) was nominated for a Nebula Award. Leah lives in Silver Spring, Maryland with her family.

SARA FOX is an information specialist and a ne'er-do-well often found wandering in airports both local and abroad. A fan of continuously recreating themselves, they've been a researcher, elementary through college teacher, and a techie. Their stories generally dabble around fantasy coming of age and emotive scifi with LGBT+ characters. To learn more please go to mxsfox.com.

Y.M. PANG's earliest memories consist of pacing around her grandfather's bedroom, telling him stories of magic, swords, and bears. Twenty years later, now living in Canada, she continues to tell fantasy stories, occasionally dipping her metaphorical quill into science fiction and poetry. Find out more about her writing at www.ympang.com or follow her on Twitter as @YMPangWriter.

REIKO SCOTT is a Japanese-American part-time writer and full-time medical student (so she's often reminded). She enjoys marrying the two through narrative medicine and tearing the two apart through speculative fiction. She's a graduate of the 2017 VONA/Voices workshop and calls Boston home.

ITORO UDOFIA is a writer, performing artist, cultural worker, and educator based in Oakland, CA. She loves to tell stories that showcase strong female protagonists defying social conventions. As a first generation Nigerian writer, writing in this way is a liberating and healing process. You can find her work in *Slice Magazine*, *Meridians: Feminism, Race, Transnationalism*, and the anthology *Two Countries: US Daughters and Sons of Immigrant Parents* published by Red Hen Press. She has received an Honorable mention from the Speculative Literature Foundation and recently, she won third place for Glimmer Train's Very Short Fiction Award for her story, *To the Children Growing Up in the Aftermath of their Parents War*. She is a SPACE on Ryder farm 2018 finalist and has received residencies and fellowships from the Vermont Studio Center, San Francisco Writers Grotto, Edward Albee Foundation, RADAR Productions, Summer Literary Seminars (SLS) and New York Foundation for the Arts.

36563326R00148

Made in the USA
Columbia, SC
26 November 2018